Cold Counsel

COLD COUNSEL

CHRIS SHARP

A TOM DOHERTY ASSOCIATES BOOK

NEW YORK

This is a work of fiction. All of the characters, organizations, and events portrayed in this novel are either products of the author's imagination or are used fictitiously.

COLD COUNSEL

Copyright © 2017 by Chris Sharp

Cover art by David Palumbo
Cover design by Christine Foltzer

Edited by Jennifer Gunnels

A Tor.com Book
Published by Tom Doherty Associates
175 Fifth Avenue
New York, NY 10010

www.tor.com

Tor® is a registered trademark of Macmillan Publishing Group, LLC.

ISBN 978-0-7653-9328-9 (ebook)
ISBN 978-0-7653-9329-6 (trade paperback)

First Edition: February 2017

For Lorna and Alex, and even Goblin

COLD COUNSEL

THERE WERE STRANGE PORTENTS the night he was born. He came at the heart of the longest storm the mountain had seen, tearing from his mother's belly as her wails were swallowed by the roar of the wind. They say that the babe climbed out red claws first, with arms too long and savage for a newborn, and a full beard already grown on the slab of his chin. He didn't cry, instead producing an odd burst of grunts before a spurt of diarrhea spilled out of him along with a wicked little chuckle that echoed about the cave. His mother bled out while he laughed in her arms, and even his father, chief of the clan, appeared shaken by the ferocity of his son's arrival. He named the boy Slud—an old trollish word for "bringer of troubles."

That same night, a hunting party of lowland goblins was found frozen stiff among the scraggly trees that climbed toward the high slopes. The goblins hadn't eaten for days, so desperate for food that they were foolish enough to trespass into the land controlled by the Blood Claw Clan. The trolls just carried their rigid little bodies higher and thawed them out for dinner. Still, the centers stayed frozen, and they had to crunch the organs like ice. More than one troll broke a tusk; and the stories tell that the cook-fires burned a sickly green and despite the freeze the meat was rancid.

The clan did not sleep well that night either, and by the following dusk, two of the oldest and wisest of the troll-hags were found dead in their earthen beds. None dared suggest it at the time, but all suspected the baby was somehow responsible. And the strange tales that surrounded him only grew from there.

In absence of his mother, a wet nurse was brought in, but she hurried out with a scream moments after her arrival and would not return to the duty again. She claimed to have found little Slud suckling from the full udders of a mountain goat. The sighting was not confirmed, though hooved tracks were found in the snow leading away from the mouth of the cave.

Another time, the lad's own uncle, Olek, swore he saw a golden eagle regurgitating meat into the babe's open maw. Olek skewered the eagle with a spear, and brought the feathery carcass back to his cave to hang, spread-winged, over the mantel of his cook fire for "good luck." Uncle Olek dropped dead from some noxious ailment of his bowels a week later, and still the storm blew on.

It would take a full month before the wind subsided and the snows ceased. By then, the whole mountain was buried. In some places, drifts covered entire stands of hundred-year-old pines. Only on the highest, steepest peak, where the Blood Claws had long made their home, could anyone venture outside. Slud was found perched on a rock ledge, having crawled out from the deep tunnels—surveying the white expanse that stretched below like a ruler over his kingdom. When the chief found him, and reached out to take the babe back to the warmth of the cave, Slud bit off his father's first finger at the knuckle and swallowed without chewing. His father was called Chief Nine-Claws after that.

By the time the snows melted and the day burned brightly again, something had come over Nine-Claws. Some speculated that it was due to the loss of his troll-hag; others claimed it came from being cooped up too long in the caves with his weird son—but the chief emerged from his den that spring with a bonfire in his belly and the want for blood on his tongue. For the first time since the lost age when giants roamed the land, an entire troll clan marched downslope to ravage and conquer. Within a year, the Blood Claws had established such dominance over the mountain that word of their terror had spread throughout the Goblin Horde and traveled all the way to the high courts of the elves.

Tales of giantlings on the march in the highlands did not sit well with the noble fae who remembered the wars of old. Still, they waited to act, preferring to let the most powerful clan of the lowland goblins do the dirty work. The Moon Blades outnumbered the Blood Claw war party by more than a hundred to one, but no one suspected that Nine-Claws might unite the other dwindling troll clans beneath his red-soaked banner. The Moon Blades broke against the guerilla tactics and sheer ferocity of what waited for them on the higher ground. The few goblins who returned from the battle, wide-eyed and muttering, only spread the legend of the troll army further. This time, the high elves did not ignore the threat.

They came twenty thousand strong: wizards, heavy infantry, expert bowmen, and a cavalry corps. The drums and horns of the elves carried across the land and shook the trees. They did not come to win a battle, but to wage a campaign for the extinction of what little remained of the troll race. Nine-Claws, and those who had rallied around him, fought fiercely and exacted a brutal toll, but they never stood a chance. The few that fled or didn't fight were hunted down and slaughtered in their bogs, dens, and caves, before the bodies were burned with elf fire. Neither babies nor the infirm were spared. Nine-Claws' severed, signature hand, and the monstrous, burning blade it had wielded, were the only things to escape the flame. They were taken back by the High King and put on display in the golden halls of the Sidhe.

Though it was not known at the time, two trolls eluded the elf hunting parties. An ancient troll-hag who lived alone in a forgotten vale within the Iron Wood had climbed the mountain that last night. She had carried many names over the ages, though none who still lived knew what to call her. She found Slud in the back of his cave with an odd smile on his face—as if he'd been waiting for her all along. Even as the elves followed at her heels, the gray, withered witch plucked the boy from his bed and carried him deep into the mountain through forgotten tunnels. The story of Slud was lost for a time, and the elves wouldn't know for many years that they had failed to complete their task . . .

But that would prove to be just the beginning of the legend of Slud Blood Claw.

ONE

Witch of the Iron Wood

HEAVY FOG CLUNG to wet earth beneath the trees. Thick-trunked conifers climbed high, and the dense canopy of needles and branches blocked the light even on the rare day when it broke through the clouds. It was a forest of gloom and chill, never fully dry, and the dappled light never held sway for long against the lurk of the shadows. Aside from the prevalent centipedes, spiders, and snakes, even the animals tended to give this section of the forest a wide berth. The ponderous creaking of the trees was at most times the only sound to be heard, punctuated occasionally with the squawk of a passing raven or the far-off howl of wolves.

Slud's feet sank into muck with every step, following the same worn trail from the woods, through the bog, to the river, and back every day for almost two decades. For more than half those years, fetching the water had taken him a full afternoon of heaving and cursing his way back up the hill to the hut. He'd grown large and strong since then—able now to carry the burden with relative ease.

He stopped at the root-strewn bank and swung the pine beam off his shoulder before lowering the oak barrel that dangled from a chain at the far end into the water. It filled, and he braced his legs to counter the heavy pull of the current. As always, he looked downstream and imagined where the river might take him were he to follow its path. As always, he was brought back to the moment when the fullness of the barrel threatened to carry him in.

His knees went to the mud, and the beam returned to his shoulder. With a grunt, he braced the wood against the thick pad of scar tissue in the crevice of his nape, and stood with only his long arms outstretched across the beam to counter the weight. A spill of water soaked the bank as the beam bent. He breathed in the pain, just as Aunt Agnes had taught—the discomfort gave him strength now.

His dark gray-green skin was a crowded tapestry of scars. There were burns and lashings from when he had failed in his lessons and countless "battle wounds" from the ceaseless weapons drills she had put him through, but many others were self-inflicted. His palms were dotted with raised circles from willful jabs with a sharp stick, and the fine white razor cuts down his arms were so numerous that they'd become a work of art.

The wet thud of his heavy footfalls sounded again through the woods, and for a moment even the creaking of the trees hushed before his approach. Sometimes, it seemed like the land itself was waiting for him to do something; the feeling that eyes were upon him never fully went away. He broke his focus from the exquisite pain to scan the fog, but of course no one was there. No one ever came to this forgotten crease of the mountain, and he knew that his aunt was back in the hut, preparing for his return.

Agnes had been growing angrier. Every day her temper seemed to flare a bit hotter, and her once ponderous movements now carried an erratic edge. That morning, she'd lashed out with a claw and raked his cheek when he'd accidentally dropped a bowl of swamp onions in the fire. Just to spite her, he'd plucked the smoldering bulbs from the coals and eaten them, one after the other, before belching up ash. Agnes had laughed then, but she'd carried a hint of menace throughout the day. It would soon be time for Slud to go, though he did not know where.

The ache in his shoulder and the burn in his thighs brought him back to the climb. Each step out of the bog was a test of exertion, and he was just reaching the steepest stretch of trail. His leg pounded into rock as he lifted himself past the tumble of a little stream. The barrel bounced cruelly behind him, and another spill leapt out to join the tiny waterfall. He inhaled deeply through his crooked nose and let the pain settle before huffing it back out between jutting tusks. He stepped again, and rose to the next shelf.

The bog viper that had coiled there unraveled in an instant. Its jaws unhinged and attached to the top of his foot before retracting and striking once more. Slud looked down at the startled beast as its long black body skittered back and hovered to deliver another dose. He breathed in the new sting and raised the damaged foot high. The snake got in one last bite to his heel before he crushed it into the earth with enough force to launch its skull out of its snout.

Yellow liquid dribbled from the four bloody holes in the top of Slud's foot. He gritted his teeth and exhaled slowly—stooping to peel his attacker from the rock. The foot was already starting to go numb, but he breathed in again, unhurried and unworried. With a grunt he rose tall once more, slung the viper across his unoccupied shoulder, and kept climbing.

AUNT AGNES PICKED Slud's dead skin from beneath her nails from when she'd clawed him that morning and dropped the scrapings into the iron pot that rested in the fire. The little gray flecks vanished into the muddy brew, and an unmelodious hum hung in her throat as she pondered what else to add. In an unlikely burst of movement, her bent and withered form crossed the room to dig through the cluttered shelves with a rough clanking of pottery and glass. Her hand emerged clutching a half-drunk bottle of spoiled pine-ale. She swiveled to dump the leftovers into the pot, and hummed again.

The hum stopped short. From outside, she heard the stomping of the troll lad. *Back so soon? He's grown strong.* She cocked her ear as he mounted the steps to the door with a hitch in his gait. *But is he ready?*

He swept back the drapery of old wolf furs that served as a door and ducked to carry the sloshing barrel over the threshold with a final grunt. Still clutching the water, he stood to the high ceiling as his spine gave a loud crack. His beard and hair were slick with sweat, but his breath remained steady. From beneath the heavy brow, he set his dark gaze upon Agnes with the same challenge that she'd seen in him as a babe. It was like the mountain itself was looking at her—untamed, uncaring, and immovable. All of her work and teaching had been in service of bringing that to the surface; molding him into the force he was born to be.

"Why do you limp? Is the water so heavy that bones break?" she asked, trying to sound stern, though her tired voice betrayed her. She was ashamed in that moment of the weakness that had gripped her form. "Give a splash to the pot, and stir."

Slud leaned toward the fire and poured some water into the pot with a loud hiss and a plume of steam. But rather than putting the barrel down in the corner as he'd been taught, he brought his maw to the rim and gulped loudly.

"I did not tell you to drink!" she snapped. "Do you wish the lash again?"

He ignored her for a last few gulps, and then dropped the barrel at his feet. "Slud's tongue was dry." His voice was a low grumble, like boulders grinding together.

It was only then that she noticed the mature bog viper that was strung over his shoulder, leaking blood across his back. She'd seen a bite from such a snake down a cave bear in minutes. "Are you bit?"

"Yeah, but Slud bit back."

She stepped closer and dropped her eyes to the fresh punctures in his foot. "Two bites?"

"Tree." He smiled. "Slud's heel's da last ting it saw er tasted."

"Sit down before you fall, boy," Aunt Agnes suggested with gentle hands coming to his aid. A swell of mother's love returned.

"Slud's good," he said, shaking her off. He dipped a finger into the boiling brew and stirred with a slow inhale through his nose, just like she'd shown him. The clawed digit came back out steaming with brown sludge. He licked it off with a frown. "Tastes like shit."

"Tell me what you feel of the venom?" she pressed, unable to mask her worry.

"Slud's foot tingled 'n' den stopped. Slud was t'irsty, 'n' den he drank. Now, Slud's hungry." He looked back at the gurgling pot. "But dis, he don't wanna eat."

Aunt Agnes clapped her gnarled hands together with glee.

"Unfazed by the strongest poison, yes, yes!" She appraised him with pride—he'd been molded well, twice the height of the tallest horse and made of dense muscle, thick bone, and sinew. Even among the trolls of the ancient world, she'd rarely seen his physical match. But it was what he contained within that made him truly special.

She grabbed the snake's tail and pulled. "Now we shall see how you fare against charms, yes? All your strength will be useless if a few whispers from the elves make you their puppet." She squeezed the viper's mangled head as its blood spilled into the brew before hanging it on the meat rack for later. *Just about done. Then we see how strong you really are.*

Agnes moved quickly again, crossing the room to retrieve the final ingredient she'd gathered on her far walk that morning. She was giddy for the fast-approaching chance to unveil her true form after it had been hidden away for so long. She'd forgotten how it felt. More clanking at another shelf, and she came away with an earthen jar covered in tight-wrapped leather. She gave it a shake and heard a displeased screech within as she returned fireside.

With a finger-blade, she sliced the leather covering and buried her hand inside the jar—coming back out with a terrified little pixie in her grip.

"Where'd ya get dat?" asked Slud, smacking his lip against a tusk.

"It's no matter, boy. Pay attention."

The pixie shouted an angry hex at Agnes, but she chuckled as she flicked it in the head and flipped it over to pluck the papery little dragonfly wings out of its back. She handed one to Slud. "Chew it up and spit into the pot." She jammed the other into her own mouth and started chewing as the pixie screamed in her hand.

Agnes had eaten pixies before, but the wings were far from the best part. She spit the mashed pulp into the brew and motioned for her adopted son to do the same. Afterward, his eyes lingered on the writhing little figure.

To test his speed, she flung the squirming morsel ragdolling toward him. His long arm shot out like the viper he'd just killed, and the claws of his thumb and forefinger pierced the pixie. He held it up and examined it closely as it cursed and shook. It looked like a tiny naked elf, dirty and skinny, with a crop of mosslike hair. He opened his mouth wide and tossed it between his tusks. A smile bloomed across his wide face as he chewed with a sharp pop and a crunch.

Agnes stirred the brew with a wooden ladle and raised a full steaming spoonful toward him. "Now this, yes?"

The smile faded, but he took the ladle as directed.

"Swallow it down. And then another scoop after." She clapped her hands with an eager grin and backed toward the cramped little room where she slept. Her nest of pine needles and sticks jutted from the opening. As always, no light escaped from within.

SLUD HAD NEVER been past the doorjamb. He wasn't sure if it was a lingering effect of the poison, but it seemed like Aunt Agnes was going weird on him again. He hadn't seen those rotten teeth break into a genuine smile in years. Seeing her withered old body bound around the room with such enthusiasm looked wrong. She clapped her hands again and martialed her best attempt at a laugh, but it came out sounding more like a hiss.

"Eat up now," she reminded him before slipping into the darkness of her hole.

Slud didn't like it. He was already snake-bit and exhausted, and had no patience for one of her tests right now, but he took a meaty slurp from the ladle anyway. The day's potion was thick with root and mushroom, and Slud hated the flavor of both. He ground it up in fist-sized molars and choked it down. She dosed him with mushrooms in every draft of tea and soup he ate, and the crazy it brought out in him had become as normal as sanity. The roots were much stronger. She usually only made him drink *that* tea once a year on his supposed "birthday," but he'd always been strapped down for those unpleasant trips. He took another slurp, finishing the ladle. As he dipped it back in the pot for more, a long, low wail sounded from within her room.

A violent rustling of the nest loosed a flutter of dried oak leaves. Slud took a third slurp of the crud and eyed the hot poker at his feet—if he had to fight, he would lead with that, and then go for the wood ax in the corner. More than once, she'd sprung at him with claws or a blade to teach him to always stay ready, and she'd proven time and again that she wasn't afraid to give him a good scar if he let down his guard. From her darkened hovel he heard the tinkling of little bells, cut by another keening moan, though this time the voice was not his aunt's, and it carried a lusty tone that raised the hackles on his neck.

The fourth slurp emptied the ladle again and he dropped it back in the pot, taking up the poker instead. He jabbed the red-hot tip into the first fang hole in the top of his foot and breathed it in nice and slow. The lance of agony cut through the poison and drugs in his system, and he felt his body come alive. He exhaled with the second jab, and his attention moved back to the murk beyond the doorway where a faint golden light had begun to gather.

He glanced down again to jab the third hole with another inhale, and this time, when he looked back to the door, a golden woman stepped to the light of the cook fire. Except in pictures drawn by her hand, Slud had never seen a woman outside of Agnes. The breath shot out of him in a gasp. She was naked and flawless—skin, hair, even her eyes shone gold. They bored into him with hunger and power.

"What're ya?" he muttered, stepping back and lifting the poker.

She smiled with plump golden lips and took a step closer. Slud wasn't sure if it was the roots kicking in, but when she moved, the firelight flickered across her skin and made it look like she was wreathed in flame. "I am Gullveig, the Golden Goddess. Kneel at my feet, and I will teach you the magick of the flesh."

Her words tickled across his mind and seemed to echo about the room. His knees started to buckle, but he jammed the hot poker into the fourth hole and found his footing again. For a moment, his head cleared, though his eyes couldn't help but travel down her body.

"Why resist that which you desire?" She slid toward him around the fire. "You have been strong for so long; surrender to your reward."

The room was awash in colors and light that Slud hadn't noticed before. Now the shadows were radiant, and even the gloom of Agnes's nest was no match for his true-seeing gaze. The walls, the ceiling, even the cramped air itself, were alive, breathing and expectant in that moment. The golden woman was the center of it all, the sun that the world revolved around. A spike of longing rose through Slud, and his knees started to shake as a cold sweat rolled down his brow.

"Give me a brood to sprout from my belly, and I shall remind this world of a forgotten age when giants ruled," Gullveig said. "Bow to me; drink of the Golden Goddess."

A tremble shot through Slud, threatening to pull him down. Instead, he set his wounded heel into the coals and cauterized the last bite in freeing pain. "Slud kneels fer none, witch! He'll show dis worl' what was lost hisself!" He swung the poker, and it connected with the side of her beautiful head.

"Yes!" she hissed as a spurt of black blood sprang from her temple. Slud lost control, hitting her again and again, driving her to the earthen floor with brutal abandon. "Yes," she choked out a last time as he rounded the pot and kicked her once perfect body into the fire.

Gullveig flailed and screamed, and the pot went over with a clatter. The golden woman was instantly engulfed in flame as if she'd been made from pine needles and tinder. Sparks flew dangerously about the hovel, and a heavy black smoke rose up toward the hole in the ceiling—too thick to pass as a choking wave spilled back down into the room. Slud coughed and covered his eyes as he stumbled back to the wall with enough force to shake the hut. Through the smoke he thought he saw a golden mist rise up from the coal bed and drift back toward Agnes's room. There were no other remnants of the witch, Gullveig, who'd been there only seconds before.

Though he could not trust his ears, again he heard keening from the nest—this time, agony had replaced lusty joy. The rustling of the sticks resumed, and again the shadows seemed to sink in around the room and come to rest. Slud rubbed his eyes and spied the barrel before him. He fought his way through the smoke and dunked his head in the cold water. The jolt snapped him back to the moment as he remembered the wood ax in the corner. Agnes's tests were rarely over when they seemed, and the heavier effects of the drugs in his system would soon set in.

As he looked up this time, sloppily flinging water, it was his aunt's familiar, withered form that came to the threshold. She gripped a wolf pelt around her wrinkled shoulders like she was ashamed to be seen, even frailer and more bent than she'd been before the coming of the Golden Goddess. She shivered violently, her voice almost too weak to hear.

"Good, my boy... You're ready." She shrank back toward the darkness of her room. "But now you need to run, and your Aunt Agnes needs to rest."

TWO

The Beast and the Flame

SLUD DIDN'T COME DOWN from the roots and mushrooms until well into the next morning's light. After wandering far, he slipped back into himself now covered in a thick layer of mud, blood, and leaves. It was the first time he'd been outside the ass-crack of a valley he called home, and he wasn't sure what to make of the crisp, moving air, or the birds of all sorts singing in the trees. A part of him wanted to sprint back to the miserable comforts of the hut, and another considered curling up by an oak tree and falling asleep for a week.

Instead, he lurched downhill through the alien forest, unsure of his course, with a head that felt like it was filled with sand. A bone-deep fatigue had set in with the dawn, and his badly blistered heel screamed now with every limping step—raw and inflamed after a full night of feral running.

He wasn't certain which parts of the night's odd sampling of images had been dreamt and which were real. The coppery taste in his mouth and the blood smears on his hands and chin added hard evidence that he hadn't imagined the part in the wee hours when he'd gotten hungry and run down that stag. And he could still picture the golden woman before him, an image that would be forever seared in his mind, though he couldn't fully grasp how she had come to be there, or what had occurred to drive her away.

He had the vague notion that she'd offered herself to him, but he couldn't reconcile the thought that he might have responded with violence rather than joyous acceptance. Perhaps Aunt Agnes's foul potions had finally turned him lunatic once and for all?

One thing was sure, he'd had enough. If he ever found his way home, he was going to eat all the food, pass out for a day, and then leave again for good, and there was nothing the old witch could do about it. For years she'd filled him with the tallest of tales—of the age when the giants warred with the gods. He was raised believing that the old myths were true. She spoke as if she'd seen those days herself, and then she'd spun his father's death and the last stand of his people on the mountain into the thread. She'd waxed on about Slud one day reclaiming kingship over the high peaks, but never would she let him venture out of the valley to test his strength or mastery of metal. Slud's entire life had been lived in isolation and ignorance. He didn't know about becoming some king, but he was hungry to climb the mountain and kill whoever stood in his way nonetheless.

Only after hours of stumbling through unfamiliar woods did he finally come to a stand of gnarled pines that he recognized. As a boy, he'd skewered a boar here with a sharp stick and a really good throw—back when the occasional game animal still ventured this far into the Iron Wood, before Agnes's dark conjuring had driven them all away. From here, Agnes's Hole, as he'd come to think of it, was only a moderate downslope walk, and already the mist and murk he was accustomed to gathered about the forest floor.

The howl of a wolf stopped him fast, and he cocked his

head to gauge its distance and direction. A wolf hadn't come this close to the house in a long while. Then another howl answered, and another. By the time the blare of a hunting horn joined them, Slud was running again.

————————

AUNT AGNES STEPPED to the rock ledge outside the hut just as the first goblin rider crested the ridge above her. The gray mountain wolf it rode was far larger, fiercer, and smarter than the average lowland wolf, with a thick mane and a long snout locked in a rictus grin. Agnes smiled at the mystery of life, always traveling in cycles. For a time, she who had been Gullveig had carried a different name after the warlike folk of Asgard had thrice burned her at the stake: Angerboda, Mother of Wolves. These same beasts, now used as steeds by the goblins, were the distant descendants of her long-dead son.

Two other riders carrying torches and spears sauntered into view. The goblins were clad in furs, and their wicked faces protruded from between the severed jaws of wolves that had not been broken into servitude. They were the far-traveled scouts of the Rock Wolf Clan, which had taken over much of the mountain once the Moon Blades and the Blood Claws had fallen. Until today, Agnes's magick had kept this dark pocket of the Iron Wood hidden from their search, but now that her mask had been lifted all was falling into place.

With a short string of whispers she could turn these wolves against their riders and watch as goblin throats were torn out, but Slud was finally ready, and Agnes had grown tired of this life. The leader slung his ram's-horn trumpet over his shoulder and dug his bone-spurs into the wolf's side. It jumped down from the ledge and stepped cautiously toward the house with a snarl.

"This be Rock Wolf land, witch." He unclasped his spear from the leather harness. "Yer name and business here?"

"I am Agnes, and it is you who tread on my land," she answered with a goading smirk. "Be off now, yes, or you and your clan will meet a most brutal end."

The goblins laughed and closed in.

"Funny," the leader said as he hurled his spear. It cleared the distance and buried itself in Agnes's stomach before poking out the other side.

She stumbled back but kept her footing.

"Think that's funny, witch? Ever felt a spear through yer belly before?"

Agnes gasped. It was not, in fact, an unfamiliar sensation, though no more pleasant this time around. Still, she managed to catch her breath and give a taunting nod. "Actually, yes to both—"

A second spear caught her in the shoulder before she could finish, and she felt her clavicle shatter as she dropped to her knees with an involuntary moan.

The impish cackles of the goblins echoed about the heavy air. "Not bad, not bad," observed the leader, before turning his yellow gaze on the third rider. "Come, Dingle, finish her good." The third rider was only half the size of his companions, but he wound up with all he had and released with a high-pitched grunt. His spear flew high and wide, lodging itself in the dried peat of the hovel wall. The other goblins erupted in a barrage of laughter.

"A filthy disgrace to the clan, Dingle! You'd better serve as wolf food," spat the leader before he dismounted and stepped toward the rock-hewn stairs. He flashed chipped, yellowed teeth as he came before Agnes and gripped the end of his spear. "Where's that funny now, witch?" He gave the spear a slow twist, and more of her black blood leaked to the stone. "One last joke, before you go?"

Agnes let out a string of wet coughs; she could feel her innards tear with each hack. But with the fresh shock of pain she found her voice again. "Burn me when you're through, or I'll come back to haunt you, yes?"

"Good idea." The leader ripped the spear out and jammed it back in through her chest. Agnes slumped over in a heap. "You heard her, boys! Light it up and throw her on top!"

The wolves yipped as the riders spurred them on. The torches moved from point to point around the hovel, finding the clumps of thatch and dried moss as the smoke started to billow. The goblin leader stepped over Agnes's impaled body and ripped away her wolf-pelt door. He peered inside and saw nothing of interest. "Shithole," he said, and tossed a bottle of oil into the still-smoldering cook fire. The house went up in an angry fireball, and the goblin leapt back down the steps with a singed back and a startled giggle.

In seconds, the house was burning in earnest as the roof caught and the fire reached toward the canopy. The popping of every jug and jar within sent a new burst of fuel to the blaze, and the climbing flames flickered with a green tinge. The heat of it drove the goblins and wolves back as Agnes's body started to smoke on the landing. But the goblin leader still wanted to retrieve his weapon. "Dingle, fetch our spears!"

The smallest goblin frowned, but he could not refuse. He grumbled his way off his wolf and up the stairs, finding that he had to crouch low and cover his eyes as he got closer. Dingle tried not to whimper as he reached his hand out toward the spear's shaft, feeling his knuckles cook and the hairs on his arm flake away.

"Push me into the flame, yes," Agnes whispered, sending the goblin stumbling back with a yelp.

"Sh-sh-she's alive!" he screamed, though his companions paid him no attention as usual. All had turned their gaze up-slope. The wolves cocked their heads and swiveled their ears forward. Then Dingle heard it too—something large crashing through the forest. "Wh-wh-what's that?"

"Shut yer hole, fool," snapped the leader as he drew his sword.

A foul smell blew into the clearing on the back of a breeze, and the wolves started to growl and tucked their tails between their legs.

"M-m-maybe we sh-sh-should get out of here?" Dingle suggested.

"Dingle's yella," said the other goblin, trying to mask his own nervous jitters.

The ground began to quiver with a series of recurring booms—like a boulder bouncing toward them, or maybe the rapid approach of an angry thunderstorm. Pine needles dropped from above in ever-greater numbers, and the leaves on the trees trembled.

"Maybe Dingle's right," suggested the leader.

They all went wide-eyed, and Dingle yelped as a massive, blood-soaked beast launched itself from the ridge and came down on the still-mounted goblin with a fist the size of an anvil. The goblin's skull split open like a pumpkin, and the punch drove him down to shatter the wolf's spine.

Without pause, the beast landed and spun with outstretched claws, catching a second wolf in the face with enough force to rip its head half off and send its body flying across the clearing to smack against a tree with a wet thud. The goblin leader tried to run, but the beast was too fast, kicking him in the back with a lift that sent him somersaulting through the air to land with a crash in the fire.

Dingle was weak, but quick, and by the time the beast had turned toward him, he'd already sprung onto his wolf's back and dug a spur deep into its side. The wolf launched itself away just as the wind from another claw whipped across Dingle's neck. Dingle did not stop his feverish ride until the wolf snapped a leg and collapsed in sight of the sprawling stronghold of the mighty Rock Wolf Clan half a day later.

SLUD KNEW THAT letting the last goblin go was a bad idea, but he had nothing to throw and was in no shape to run down a wolf. He turned back to the inferno that had been his home and stepped to Agnes's slumped, smoking body. The stairs burned the soles of his feet, and he could feel the hairs of his beard singeing as he stooped to pick her up, but her empty eyes flashed with life again. Her hand shot out to grab his wrist.

"No. Toss me to the flame, boy." Her voice was almost too feeble to hear beside the fire. "Time for old Agnes to burn away."

Slud nodded.

"Go to the river when it's done," she said. "There's a jar—hanging in the last tree. Drink it all. The final treatment."

"'N' den?" he asked, picking a strand of gray hair from her face.

Agnes's back was blackened from the heat, and the slick of

her blood began to bubble on the rock, but she smiled and reached up to touch Slud's face. "Climb, boy. They were Rock Wolf Clan. *They* control the mountain."

Slud stood with her in his crisping arms.

"Be strong, like I taught. Wits and weapons . . . I'll find you," she said, before turning her expectant gaze to the fire.

Slud had never seen so large a tower of flame before, and despite the torment both inside and out, he felt himself drawn closer, mesmerized by the beautiful dance. He tossed the only person he'd ever known into the blaze and forced himself not to follow, backing down the agonizing steps to safety. Agnes did not scream or make a sound as she curled into a ball and shrank away to nothing.

Slud watched the house burn for the rest of the morning, and finally found a deep sleep sometime after that. When he woke that evening, he had to brace against a tree as he fought to stand. He had raw burns across much of his body that made his skin feel too tight around his frame, adding to the previous night's abuse. He let go of the trunk to test his balance and immediately stumbled back to hug the rough bark. *Gotta move. More of dem wolf boys'll be comin'*. With a deep breath, he dug a claw into the meat of his arm and found his footing again.

The best he could do was to stagger along the path. When he went down, he tried to fall forward and roll for as long as his momentum would allow. He flopped over the waterfall ledge, and landed on his ass, which had until then been the only part of him not in pain. When he finally reached the river, the dark of night had settled, and a white haze encroached on the edges of his normally keen night vision.

He slumped against the last tree and glanced up to the tightly capped jar hanging from the lowest branch above him—hung so that only he could reach it without climbing. His blood was pounding in his temples. He doubted he had the strength to stand, and he surely wasn't prepared for another hard dose of mushrooms and madness.

Practical thought. Sure action. No reluctance or remorse. Agnes's repetitive nagging came back to him. He had no notion of how far the Rock Wolf Clan was from here, but he had to assume that word of his presence had been delivered. The only option was to cross the river and gain distance from the noses of the wolves that would come. He knew what he had to do. Instead, he closed his eyes and slept.

THREE

Crossing Over

DINGLE WAS MARCHED past the stockade wall of sharpened tree trunks with a hulking guard on each side of him. One of them stood three times his height and carried a great curving scimitar. The other resembled a fat angry toad and fondled a hatchet. The diminutive goblin scout had never been within the inner stockade of the clan, and was fast becoming convinced that he would soon feel the bite of one or both of those weapons.

He'd always been a bad scout and a craven warrior, more interested in the history of the clan than its future; more adept at writing his observations of the wide Rock Wolf territory than relaying it to his superiors on command. Given the choice, he would happily abandon speaking altogether for a thick stack of paper and something to write with. He'd always fantasized about becoming one of the hex doktors with their charms and symbols—they got to use paper, but Dingle lacked the aptitude for magick along with everything else.

The guards led him to the towering double doors of the great hall, and the squat escort banged on the heavy wood with the handle of his hatchet. Dingle could hear the crossbeam unhitch and slide from the other side before the doors creaked open to reveal the vast hall within. The tall guard nudged him forward with an ungentle knee to the back, and Dingle's little legs started working again. He realized where he was. He hadn't just been called to report what he'd seen to the Big Boss of the Rock Wolf scouts, as he'd expected, but to the Khan of the clan himself.

There was a wide fire pit in the center of the room, stacked with a pyramid of burning logs and emitting a heavy trail of smoke that climbed toward a hole cut in the roof high above. The two biggest wolves that Dingle had ever seen lifted their heads to watch his approach from the foot of an oversized throne carved into a huge boulder. Stone steps climbed to the towering seat where a broad goblin in a golden wolf pelt lounged with a jug of pine ale. Dingle could feel his bowels threatening to loosen as he walked with a hitch across the length of the hall.

The eyes of guards, warriors, and hex doktors all turned to regard him as he passed, but they turned away with disinterest just as quickly. Dingle had been the last-born runt of a rowdy brood of eight, and even his mother had shown little acknowledgment of his clinging presence. She'd called him Dingle because he was "utterly useless and always hangin' around." As he reached the far end of the hall, only the wolves still paid him any heed with an unsettling lick of their panting jaws.

Finally, a goblin not much bigger than himself emerged from behind the throne with an officious sneer and a ledger. He climbed to the first step above the wolves and cleared his throat. "Dingle: wolf rider scout, far territories."

Dingle was distracted for a moment by the crisp, clean pages of the ledger before he felt the fierce yellow eyes of the Khan upon him. He gulped and bowed, not knowing what else to do.

"Two scouts and two wolves dead, one wolf maimed. Tell us what you saw," said the impatient Herald.

Dingle struggled to find his words, but they wouldn't come.

The gruff voice of the Khan himself finally cut the awkward silence. "Do this runtling speak?"

"Mighty Arok Golden Wolf, Chief of the Rock Wolf Clan, King of the Mountain, and Khan of the Goblin Horde is waiting, imp!" shouted the Herald with a nasal whine.

Dingle looked up at the all-powerful Khan once more, but he couldn't help but notice that as tall as he was atop the massive throne, the beast from the Iron Wood had been taller still. "S-som-som-something big c-ca-came out of the ffforest." His heart was thundering in his chest, and he could feel the growing promise of violence about the room. He dropped his gaze and closed his eyes, picturing the beast again.

Its face and claws had been stained with blood. Its black beard and hair jutted out in crusty spikes, framing the snarling tusked mouth. For a second, Dingle had glimpsed the black of its eyes—brilliant and feral at the same time. Somehow, remembering it now gave him strength.

"A giant," he blurted. "M-m-maybe a troll?" Everyone was looking at him. "It-it came from the woods and killed the others in seconds." His squeaky, grating voice echoed back at him from the vaulted ceiling.

The Khan leaned forward to look down at him. "What?"

"A wwwitch," Dingle added. "There wwwas a witch at ffirst. We sp-sp-speared her, or the others did; I m-m-missed." The room rang with laughter, but Dingle sometimes had trouble stopping once he got started. "Agnes, she said. They speared her, and we burned the house, but she wouldn't die. She asked me to p-p-push her into the fffire, and then *it* came."

Chief Arokkhan took a hard pull of the jug and wiped his mouth on the back of his hand. "So, house, witch, fire, an' giant—right?"

Dingle could only avert his eyes and nod. "Y-y-yes, my K-K-Khan."

Arokkhan had an unpleasant reputation for literally biting the heads off enemies and failed underlings alike. Dingle had seen crudely cleaved heads on spikes beside the outer gates before. His mouth was very dry as he fought to swallow.

"Where's this house?" the Khan asked with a voice that betrayed nothing.

"Base of the m-m-mountain. Little v-valley in the Iron WW-Wood we hadn't seen before. Dark place."

"Find it again," said the Khan. It wasn't a question.

"Y-y-yes?" Dingle answered.

Arokkhan turned to his advisor. "Blades an' Fangs, tonight. Send Groole's twenty with... this." He regarded Dingle a last time and turned away in disgust. "If there ain't a house, a witch, a fire, an' a giant at the end—hang him by his wrists from a tree, an' lower him to the wolves real slow."

———

SLUD OPENED HIS eyes to the day when a splat of raven shit found his shoulder. He was still slumped against the tree, with a wet puddle of drool collecting on his already filthy shirt. He couldn't remember what color it had been when Agnes had first made it for him—now it was gray with liberal stains of dark red turning brown.

His neck protested and popped as he lifted his heavy head to examine the white and green splatter from the sky. The offending bird had flown on, but the jar still hung above him, swinging in a rare breeze for this deep crease of the valley. Somehow its presence reminded him of the disapproving scowl of his aunt, unimpressed with his stupidity.

Chagrined, he braced himself to stand, but his elbow knocked into something with a clatter. A large burlap sack fell over beside him. It had been covered with severed branches, so he'd failed to notice it the night before. Aunt Agnes had planned ahead.

The first things he found inside were the wood ax and his favorite cleaver-bladed sword. Below that were a coil of rope; oil, flint, and steel for a fire; a good knife; and a heavy package of cured meats—including the smoked bog-viper from the night before. Slud was starving, and he gnawed on the snake right then and there. Agnes had sliced it open and removed the guts and poison sacs, but left the scales on, just the way he liked it. He took another ragged bite of his chewy prize and pushed his back against the trunk until he was standing.

That was when he heard the first howl of the returning wolves. A blast of a hunting horn sounded, like the one from the day before, but then two others answered from different directions. *Move, fool boy!* It was like Agnes was still beside him, yelling in his ear. He reached up and snatched the jar from the tree. A note was attached with a string; a message in Agnes's scrawling hand:

DRINK NOW, THEN CROSS THE RIVER.

He ripped away the tight leather covering and downed the sludge in one gulp. It was the most noxious muck he'd ever tasted. The jar smashed on the ground as he buckled over with a hard gag. His eyes watered and his stomach did somersaults, but he forced himself upright and retrieved the ax from the sack. *No time to whine, lad!*

The first whack into the trunk of the tree buried the ax head completely. The second took a thick wedge of blond wood from the base. The yips of the wolves drew closer up the path, and Slud swung harder and faster, woodchips flying in every direction. With each strike, the blade bit deeper into the core of the trunk until the balance began tipping toward the river. He hacked once more for good measure as the tall pine tottered, groaned, and then went over.

Slud jumped to the side, snatched the burlap sack out of the way, and watched, mesmerized for a moment by the size and volume of the crash that followed. Jagged splinters of wood tore out of the base beside him as the tree bounced and then finally settled across the river with a violent shake of the earth. Slud was up and running across just as the wolves and riders came into view atop the cascading falls above.

DINGLE HADN'T BEEN sure that he'd be able to find the witch's house again; he'd realized with a growing sense of dread that he'd forgotten to pay attention to the journey in either direction the day before. When he finally saw the mangled bodies of his companions, he let out a loud yelp of joy that brought some hard stares from the pack of seasoned killers around him.

The house had been completely leveled by the fire, now little more than a smoldering pile of ash on blackened rock. There was no sign of the witch or giant anywhere, until the sharp whacks against a tree echoed from farther down the valley. Dingle followed the others along the well-worn path on his borrowed wolf with a surge of hope that he might live through another day.

Though he couldn't explain it, when he saw the beast again, sprinting across the newly felled tree in all of its hulking authority, he secretly hoped that the arrows and spears of his fellows would miss. The giant, or whatever it was, leapt to the other bank with the grace of a big cat, and immediately started hacking at the protruding branches with the biggest ax that Dingle had ever seen. It moved so assuredly that the projectiles of the goblins always seemed to target the place where it had just been. In mere moments, as the first wolf and rider mounted the fallen trunk and began to cross, the giant began to heave its bulk against the upper branches, and the huge tree, impossibly, started to move.

As the trunk lurched, the wolf lost its footing and fell into the fast-moving river with a yip and a splash. The other nineteen riders crowded the edge of the bank for a better shot, but none braved the crossing as the giant continued to push. In all his years, Dingle had never seen the proud warriors of the Rock Wolf Clan afraid before, but they could not hide their fear now as the giant ducked an arrow and snarled in their direction.

Dingle spurred his wolf down the rocky ledge as well, though not to be closer to the action. As his fellows continued to volley missiles and insults across the water, Dingle knelt beside the shattered base of the tree and plucked a little piece of fine paper from the roiled earth. He read the note, then slipped the prize into his pocket with care. If he wrote with very small letters, he would, at least for a little while, be able to scribe his thoughts in style rather than on the backside of stripped pieces of bark as was his custom. Then his beady little eyes swung back to the ceramic shards that the note had accompanied. Remnants of a thick sludge were visible on the inside of the shattered jar's base; it was mud brown with leaf pulp and fungus and heavily speckled with tiny bits of gold throughout.

The giant hacked at the bracing branches again as another wolf rider leapt to the tree to attempt a crossing, but Dingle kept his focus on the jar. He scraped his finger along the inside and gathered what remained. The muck smelled like rotting death with a lump of shit on top, but still, for some reason, he put it on his tongue and swallowed. A violent shudder shot through him and he immediately buckled over, heaving. His eyes felt like they might pop out of his head as he frantically grabbed at leaves, dirt, and anything else he could shovel into his mouth to erase the taste.

His gagging was so loud that some of the other goblins turned around to look, while the giant rammed the crown of the tree with his shoulder. It dislodged from the far bank and tumbled into the river, and in seconds the current dragged the trunk's cleaved base in after it. More goblins and wolves were caught unmindful of the danger, crushed by the shifting log or knocked from the shore into the water.

Dingle looked up with an odd warming sensation shooting through him—just as the giant made eye contact from the other side. It seemed to be looking right at him with those black, piercing eyes below a heavy shelf of a brow. After years of being ignored by all, it was as if a god had stopped to notice his presence. Dingle knew in that instant that he would follow it anywhere.

As the goblins of the Rock Wolf Clan screamed and flailed, the giant of the Iron Wood disappeared into the gloom of the trees.

THE STRANGE BREEZE continued throughout that day, carried down from the mountain. A delicate rain of dried pine needles fell over the Iron Wood. By the time the light waned, the first real wind in a decade was blowing across the forgotten valley, carrying ashes from Agnes's hut all the way to the river. The goblins and wolves had long since moved downstream toward the crossing, hoping to intercept the troll's path on the far side. None saw the shiny, black mound where the cook fire had been—uncovered by the wind, naked and quivering.

Two arms articulated from the mass and stretched out with hooked obsidian claws at the ends of long fingers. The skin, the color of a starless night, was smooth and taut over lean muscle. The head rose next, with long jet-black hair draped across the face as a stretched hook of a nose poked through and sniffed. *A group of mountain wolves and goblins, come and gone. Others, dead and rotting at hand.*

The nose angled higher and sniffed again, long and slow. *The troll was here as well. A ripe male . . . But he went down toward the river, and crossed.*

The sloped curve of the mound became a back, with the shoulder blades and ribs visible beneath the skin. A slow exhale blew the hair from her face as she rose. Long, lean legs emerged, and she stood to her new full height. She'd forgotten how good it felt to be young—how tall and powerful her body could be. She wanted to run, and fuck, and kill.

But then her stomach kicked, and she bent back to her former hunch and gritted teeth like needles. She'd also forgotten how hungry her younger self had been, and she opened her black-on-black eyes and swiveled her gaze to the corpses on her charred doorstep. The fur of the wolves would be a problem, but the tenderized goblin would do nicely. Before she knew it, she'd pounced down to the scorched earth at the base of the ruined stairs and taken a big bite out of the split-open head—equal parts bugs and brains. She found that she liked the crunchy bits mingled with the squish and took another bite.

She'd get her strength up first, and then she'd track down Slud like she'd planned. Aunt Agnes was dead, but Black Agnes was born from the flame.

FOUR

Neither-Nor

WHEN SLUD WAS SMALL, Aunt Agnes had told him a story of a bridge being built by the elves to span the river in the foothills at the base of the mountain. In that tale, the elves had finished the structure and bound it against the elements—just before a band of Nine-Claws' trolls set upon them and killed them to the last. The trolls tried to destroy the bridge, but their flames and axes failed, and they had none of their troll-hags with them to counter the elf charms. Ten thousand elves crossed that bridge soon after to flank the Blood Claw resistance and seal the doom of the troll race.

Everything Slud knew about the world came from that batty hag's stories. Sometimes he wondered if she'd just made the whole thing up because she was lonely and bored.

What fuckin' choice do Slud got now? If the bridge was real, the Rock Wolf riders would probably head there to cross. So he'd spent half the morning following the river downhill, and only after the riders had spurred ahead to cut him off had he drifted out of sight and doubled back. He'd been steadily picking up the pace ever since, leaving the howls of the wolves and the roar of the river behind.

Now, as Slud bounded up the increasingly steep and rocky terrain, he was surrounded by the noises of a healthy forest—which, after so long in the Iron Wood, seemed to rage with a mad cacophony of life. It was both exhilarating and unsettling.

He was amazed by how vibrant everything seemed. Squirrels skittered away as he approached, and a myriad of different birdcalls sounded above. Once he'd spied the retreating flutter of a troop of sprites through the branches, and, though his stomach rumbled at the sight, he tore another bite of the chewy snake and kept going.

Agnes's last potion had clearly been laced with a heavy dose of much needed stimulant. Six hours into the climb, Slud approached the first cliff face with his eyes on the top and energy to spare. Without pausing, he latched onto the rock, dug his toe claws into a foothold, and started up. The burlap bag slapped against his back as his other foot found a crack that ran up the wall, and he pushed himself higher. He'd completely forgotten about the shape his feet had been in when he'd woken that morning. At a glance, the red and blistering of the burns seemed to be completely gone, and even the fang holes of the viper had closed up nicely.

Dis potion's got real kick to it! If only it had come wit' a betta plan to boot. The mountain was vast, and Slud didn't know where he was headed aside from up.

He figured, however, that the wolves and most of the goblins wouldn't be able to scale the cliff, and their taking the long way around would buy him more time . . . That was about as far as his plan went. He couldn't stay ahead of a pack of mountain wolves for long; at a quick lope, such a wolf could go for days without stopping, and he doubted Agnes's brew would offer him the same longevity. Once he gained some distance, he'd need to mask his stink, but he hadn't seen anything so far that would hide his unique funk. These goblins would have some pretty good trackers as well, and Slud didn't step lightly across the earth. Taking the high ground, sticking to the rocks, and seeing what happened next was pretty much his best option. So he kept climbing.

NEITHER-NOR WAS HUNGRY and angry, as usual. The only thing he'd been able to catch in his snares was a skinny fox, which was hanging, throat-slit, over a pan as he stoked the campfire. The little red dog smelled like skunk, and he didn't imagine that boded well for the flavor of the meat. The hunting along this ridge of the mountain had been getting spotty as of late, and he wondered if whatever curse had claimed the Iron Wood on the far side of the river had begun to spread. Soon he'd have to move again, find another uninhabited cleft of the mountain beyond the prying noses of those infernal Rock Wolf scouts.

Neither-Nor had once belonged to a real clan—right-hand goblin to a Khan who was worthy of the Big Boss title of the Goblin Horde. He'd seen plenty of war, gutting more than his fair share of enemies, and feeling the bite of grievous wounds time and again in return. These Rock Wolves had never been tested, never had to defend their claim from thousands of chanting maniacs come to take it; or even a few hundred of the biggest, fiercest warriors that the land had ever known . . .

Sometimes, he still had nightmares from *that* battle—waking up in a cold sweat with his heart going at a sprint and the earth-shaking roar of the Blood Claws echoing in his pounding head.

He spit into the fire and slid a long, skinny blade from his boot. With a wince, he hiked up his pant leg to reveal the lines of runes that had been cut into his calf. As he waited for the coal bed to heat, he set to work, deepening those etched marks as the blood trickled again. It was his life's work, and he'd been going at it for a quarter century now, having covered every inch of skin across his entire body with the protective letters, save for a strip down his back and across his ass.

Before his clan had fallen, the Chief Hex Doktor of the Moon Blades had devised the body map of arcane sigils. It took him five years to complete Neither-Nor's chest, arms, legs, upper back, head, and neck. Neither-Nor had found creative ways to fill in most of the gaps in the decades since. In that time he'd taken six killing blows to test the design, and he'd always returned. As long as someone took out the arrow or blade, and put the pieces aright, the runes would shift and lock into place and his heart would kick again. The infernal markings themselves were the only wounds that never fully healed, always as raw as the day they'd first been carved. Now, the constant sting of the marks was the only thing that reminded him that he was still alive.

For all his protection and the rewards of his suffering, he awoke every morning feeling only the vulnerability of the last uncovered spots. He'd grown to hate the company of others, and he shunned the pursuit of kinship, which he'd once held so dear. He trusted no one to finish the work on his behalf; no amount of money could be exchanged to guarantee that one who saw the old map wouldn't just kill him mid-rune and take the precious paper for themselves . . . It was only a matter of time before someone buried a knife in his lower spine and ended him for good.

He stopped cutting and angled his pointy ear toward the

drop-off beyond the tree line. *Somethin' there?* Instead, the wind whipped past and the branches of the tree he sat beneath swayed with a sprinkle of leaves—yellow, red, and brown. The dead fox swung on the end of the rope, and the trickle of blood missed the pan. Neither-Nor tossed another couple of sticks on the fire and yanked the crusty hat from his head. Along with the scars, the red cap had become his signature over the years. He liked to keep it dyed a bright crimson, though at the moment the sickly brown color flaked off as he shook it out. He dabbed it against the fresh wounds on his calf, but the blood there was a paltry offering.

The goblin stood and moved to the swaying fox. Again, his long, pointy nose crinkled at the musk of it as he knelt beside the pan and dipped the cap in the pool within. It came out with the glistening color he liked, and with a last little shake, he slapped it back on his crown, sloppy drips and all.

Then he heard a scrape of the rocks again, and spun to see a monstrous hand reach over the ledge, just before an even more alarming head poked up from the lip with a grimace. Its black hair was matted and filthy, and the thick tusks that framed its face reflected the orange of the flame as if it were a demon crawling up from the pit. Its skin, gray-green and marred by hard use, was liberally spattered with dried blood, and it moved with a fluid grace that seemed at odds with the incredible bulk that continued to rise over the edge.

Just like in his recurring nightmares, Neither-Nor's heart leapt to a sprint as he dove for his fighting blades.

SLUD HEAVED HIMSELF over the edge, surprised to find the flickering light of a campfire. The vicious little goblin standing beside it sprang into an artful tumble that brought him up with a knife in each hand. He snarled with pointy teeth as what looked like fresh blood dripped across his face.

Slud furrowed his brow and scanned for wolves and companions, but saw neither. The bag came off his shoulder as he reached inside, nice and slow. He was hoping for the sword, but his hand came away with the ax, and he didn't want to take his eyes off the wiry little fucker before him.

"Oi, li'l fella, easy now," Slud cautioned as he raised the ax slowly. The goblin was covered with finely carved rune scars, and he handled the two knives like he was no stranger to their use. "If ya ain't Rock Wolf, dere's no need dyin' today."

The goblin's eyes were wide and filled with terror, but he spun the knives deftly and adjusted his stance for combat nonetheless. One of his blades was curved in the shape of a crescent moon and had been worn down after years of sharpening and use. Slud lowered his grip on the ax handle and shifted his shoulders ever so slightly. "Yer Moon Blade Clan, ain't ya? Ol' Aunt Agnes told Slud about ya fellas."

"Not possible," the goblin hissed. "Yer a ghost, come to finish me fer good."

This goblin was clearly insane. "No ghost, li'l fella. Slud's da name. Just passin' t'rough s'all."

"Yer here fer me map," said the goblin. "Well, ya can't have it, but ya can die tryin', troll wraith!"

The goblin lunged faster than Slud expected, but the distance between them was too wide. Slud cocked the ax and released. It was a good throw, and the ax spun once in the air before the heavy head whipped around to bury itself deep in the goblin's chest. The force of it took him off his feet and knocked him back beside the fire with a flop, and that was the end of it.

The troll chuckled as he advanced. Agnes had always said,

"You never know when you'll have to kill someone, so always be ready, yes." He stepped over the goblin corpse with a swift yank of the ax handle followed by a heavy spurt from the chest, but his eyes had already shifted to the dangling fox.

He took a long inhale of the rich, musky stink in the air. "Dat'll do nicely," he said, before reaching down to pluck one of the fallen goblin's blades from the earth. Slud had watched Agnes carve out the scent glands of a fox for one of her stews before, and though he did not carry fond memories of the smell that had filled the hovel that week, he couldn't pass up such an opportunity to throw the coming wolves off his trail.

The knife made quick work of the fox pelt; Slud had the little dog sliced and peeled in a couple moments. He looked down at its shaved hindquarters with a hard cough. This would be nasty, but as Agnes used to say, "The quickest path through pain is straight ahead." The knife tip went in at an angle, the way she'd shown him, so as not to rupture the first little sac before removal, but he lost focus when a rasping inhale sounded behind him.

The rune-covered goblin sat up with a dazed look, like the wind had been knocked out of him. Slud furrowed his brow and picked the ax back up. "Oi, li'l fella, dat's a fine trick."

The goblin's eyes focused again as his fingers curled around the handle of the moon blade. He turned toward Slud with a gradual dawning of recognition, followed by a fierce snarl—just before the troll buried the ax back in his chest.

FIVE

The Unforgotten

THE NIGHT WOODS had never been so bright and full of promise. Before, on his long rides away from the clan, every snap of a twig and skitter from the shadows had sent a jangle of unease up Dingle's crooked spine. He'd never been one to lead the way, and was not counted among the brave or self-reliant. But now, he was filled with a desire to see what mystery lay around each rock and tree, and moreover, a hunger to be the first to discover it. He couldn't explain it.

He'd been riding for two days straight without sleep. At first he'd held on to the shaggy fur around the wolf's neck for dear life, trying desperately to keep up with the Rock Wolf hunting party that had been instructed to kill him if he failed. He'd ridden to the witch's house, praying with every breath that he might find some way through this mess, just so that he could get back to his rotten little bed again and dream of a better life. Now, he wasn't sure he'd ever need sleep again, and the life he'd always imagined seemed to be waiting just ahead.

He'd forgotten all about how his thighs and back had felt like they were on fire that morning while he clung tight and low on the loping wolf's back and spurred ahead of the pack. His untrained eyes scanned the ground for the heavy prints of the giant's path, spotting broken branches and indented earth where he'd previously have proven useless. Some of the hunters around him had even commented on his surprising zeal for the mission—an observation that would hopefully keep him alive upon completion or failure.

Dingle kept mum. He figured that it had all started with that fingerful of the giant's potion—not just energy, but something more that spread through him and took root. The diminutive goblin fantasized that, whatever it was the two of them had drunk, the sharing of the draft linked him with the giant he hunted. As he raced up the slope through the darkened trees, he secretly wished that those around him would fall away, and that he alone would find their quarry and offer his allegiance. Clearly that was what the fates were instructing him to do.

Dingle's wolf stopped running, its nose snuffling along the ground. The others caught up with lolling tongues as the riders took a moment to adjust their equipment and crack their backs. A particularly burly goblin came to a halt at the head of the pack. He had chicken bones strung throughout his long orange hair and multiple rings through his nose, ears, and lips. Dingle thought his name was Groole, but he kept his focus on the ground, searching for signs of the giant's passing.

"Ya ride good, runt," said Groole. "Them tiny eyes spot real nice in the dark, don't they?"

Dingle ignored him as Groole's alpha wolf raised its huge head to sniff the air with alarm. It turned its gaze in the direction of the now distant river. The other wolves caught the scent and turned to face that way as well. Dingle's wolf flattened its ears and tucked its tail low as a snarl crept out of its throat. Another wolf took a step back with a quiet whimper. All eyes were locked on the darkness of the woods, but nothing moved there and no sound emerged from the still trees.

Groole stroked his wolf's neck. "Is the beast out there, boy?"

Swords and bows started to come out, but Dingle spied a muddy print at the top of a boulder ahead, and then a scrape in the bark high up on a tree where the giant must have passed.

"No, th-th-this way!" Dingle shouted as he turned his wolf back upslope and heeled it to action. Dingle had no time for distraction—he had to see the giant again. His wolf caught the scent and locked on to the trail once more, and with an abrupt bark of Groole's alpha, the rest of the pack followed the smallest goblin's lead.

FROM THE HIGH branches of a beech tree, black-on-black eyes watched the goblins retreat into the distance. The wolves had sensed Agnes's presence. They were right to be scared of her strange scent: like the dank, rich soil of a bog, overlaid with wild spices and anise. These wolves had never smelled a proper night-hag before, let alone the last vestige of she who had spawned the Demon Wolf himself—Fenrir Odin's Bane, Hound of Ragnarok.

Agnes had almost turned the wolves against the goblins, filled them with such hunger and ferocity that they would have eaten their riders, and then each other, until only the strongest and most insatiable of their ranks remained. Once, that had been how she'd chosen which wolves to breed, culling the pack so that only the largest beasts remained to run and fight beside the giants of the Jötunheim. But she needed the noses of these wolves to find the troll who would be king—now it was he alone who carried the promise to rekindle the ancient battle that she had sparked so many ages ago.

While the Rock Wolf riders had spent the day running

down and then back up the mountain to ford the river, Black Agnes had filled her empty stomach on meat, organs, and brain, and then asked the spirits of the air for a lift. They'd placed her gently among the upper branches of this tree where she'd taken a nap as she waited for the hunting pack to pass by.

She was the color of tar, her limbs like the gnarled branches of the trees she hid within. Even the keen eyes of the smallest goblin scout could not have picked her out from the night scene if it had locked its gaze right on her. Images of this same goblin came back to her from the life that had come before—the part of her that had been Gullveig, and would always be, never forgot. This goblin had been there at Aunt Agnes's demise. It had laughed with its fellows, and thrown spears at her withered form. Now, the tiny imp vibrated at a different frequency than the others, and Agnes recognized the dark magick at work in its little body. Him, she would eat in full, take back what was wrongfully stolen.

That had been a potion most precious, the Nectar of Amrite, a recipe passed down from the Golden Goddess herself. Gullveig had learned its mix from lovely Freyja, who had been a queen of the People and, for an age, the one who had united the tribes to keep the peace between the old gods and the new. It was a concoction steeped in whispers and shadow, a link between the worlds and a solution to the riddle of death. No goblin of the Rock Wolf Clan deserved to taste its mystery—only those who were destined to spin legend from life.

Black Agnes closed her eyes again—remembering Angerboda, her namesake, in her final days. She could still picture the vast field of Ragnarok from atop the high cliff of a mountain range that was no more. She could still feel the land shake as the giants stormed into battle, hear the piercing howl of

Fenrir as he broke from his chains and gave fear back to the night. She'd watched with pride as her daughter, Hel, called an army of the dead to rise from the earth; and the sting in her nostrils was still fresh from her middle child's poison breath, as Jörmungand, the Midgard Serpent, rose out of the oceans to swallow whole the world of the gods.

But those were old stories; it was time to carve new tales from the dwindling remnants of her people. Agnes's arms and fingers ticked, then creaked as they broke from the wooden mold they had assumed to become arms once more. The twisted claws of her feet came away from the trunk they had fused with, and a shudder of life licked through her form like an electric current. She would descend and follow the pack's trail. When she found the prodigy of death, she would teach him how to take back the dark places of the Dream, and use his killing gift to show the world that some nightmares should never be forgotten.

THE FIRST SENSATION always felt like an abrupt horse-kick to the chest. That was the heart remembering to beat. Then came the burning wave as Neither-Nor's lungs filled with air again in a desperate heave. His eyes registered light out of the darkness sometime around the second torturous inhale, once the air had reached his brain, but for the first few seconds he couldn't see anything but blurry colors—in this case, the searing orange glow of the campfire. The noxious skunk-waft of the damn fox found his nose next, and he was vaguely aware, once again, of his fingers groping for the knives that were no longer there.

The troll materialized out of the blur on the far side of the fire—scanning over the runic body map that Neither-Nor had hidden inside a secret pocket in his rucksack. The goblin instinctively snarled and tried to sit up, only to discover that now his arms and legs were bound tightly with rope. After a few guttural rasps he found his voice. "Get yer foul hands from me map, troll scum!"

The troll chuckled. He held up the crinkled page, and his unsettling gaze narrowed as he looked between the map and Neither-Nor's face. "Fine trick, indeed. Ya come up wit' dis yerself?"

"I'll gut ya, troll—watch ya bleed out on the rocks like I done yer kind before!"

"Easy now, li'l fella. Ya don't wanna hurt Slud's feelin's. He'll put de ax back in, 'n' den see how dose nifty runes work on fire." The troll motioned to the roasting fox on a spit above the flame. He'd added more wood and stoked the coal bed nice and hot. "More meat on ya den on de li'l red dog, 'n' Slud's gettin' real hungry."

Neither-Nor scanned the clearing for some means of escape, but all the knives and the huge ax were resting against a newly cleaved log that the troll was using as a seat on the opposite side of the fire. The knots that bound Neither-Nor were a little sloppy, and he was pretty sure that he could dislocate a shoulder and get his hands free if he had a couple moments to himself, but the troll didn't seem to miss much.

"Any bit o' ya not marked?" asked the troll with his deep, rumbling voice that seemed always on the cusp of wicked laughter.

Neither-Nor tried to betray nothing, but he tried too hard.

"Haven't finished her yet, ay? No worries, yer secret's safe wit' Slud." The troll winked before lowering the map. He picked up the goblin's moon blade instead. "Ya seem good 'n' handy wit' a knife, dough. N' ya recognize Slud fer what he is."

Despite his predicament, facing the living embodiment of his nightmares made Neither-Nor want to talk. "Killed trolls like ya at the battle of the Moon Blades and Blood Claws twenty years past. Yer s'posed to be dead."

"How 'bout dat . . . Agnes was right. But Slud heard it was de Moon Blades all died dat day, yet here's de two of us, talkin' 'n' breathin'." The troll ran the curve of the blade across the back of his arm and drew blood in a thin line. "What, ya turn tail 'n' run?"

Neither-Nor puffed himself up bigger. "No runnin' here, troll. Fought and died with me clan. Was the best goblin with a blade there was, and I took five of ya big fuckers with me 'fore I fell. What's yer excuse?"

"Slud was just a baby, ol' man. Him 'n' his li'l auntie slipped away 'n' been hidin' out since—preparin' fer dis day . . . Now, just Slud's left, 'n' de day's come." The troll stood with the map in one hand and the moon blade in the other. His deep, dark eyes suddenly became predatory.

"Preparin' fer what?" Neither-Nor hissed, trying to mask the jolt of fear that shot through him.

"Revenge," the troll answered with a humorless smile. "Slud's come to break de mountain, 'n' den de whole world af- ter." The troll stepped closer, and the overbearing reek of fox spray that wafted off him was enough to make the goblin shud- der. He rounded the fire with a poke of the browned, roasting meat, and came to a halt above Neither-Nor. The shadow he cast held an oppressive weight as he tested the heft of the com- paratively tiny curved blade in his hand. He dropped his piercing gaze to the helpless goblin once more.

"Ya kill me hog-tied and I promise to come back and haunt ya 'til the end of yer miserable days, scum!" Neither-Nor shouted.

"Kill ya? No, no, li'l man. Slud's got big plans fer ya," the troll said with a sharp smack of his lip against his tusk. "But Slud needs ya hungry 'n' angry, 'n' it's just 'bout time to eat . . . No hard feelin's, aye?" He raised the hooked blade above him as the goblin snarled and winced in anticipation of the blow, but Slud paused. "Oi, what's yer name, frien'?"

"Neither-Nor, ya big swine, and don't soon forget it."

"Slud don't forget." The troll smiled. "See ya soon." And he swung.

SIX

Fox Hunt

THE SKY ABOVE the Iron Wood had never fully shed its blanket of clouds in all the years that Slud had lived beneath it. He'd never seen stars the way they'd come out that night on the cliff that climbed toward the midway point on the mountain. More shining little dots than he could count in a lifetime dedicated to only that. But he had not spent the dark hours sitting idly and staring up as he would have liked, and he still hadn't slept a wink.

After he'd eaten the fox down to the bones, he'd spent some time smashing a boulder into fist-sized rocks with the butt-end of the increasingly handy ax. Now, two mounds of oblong projectiles were stacked at strategic points around the camp, and he'd tested the distance and aim of his throw from the rocky ledge down to the base of the climb with satisfactory results.

With the feisty goblin otherwise occupied with a blade through his heart, Slud had reclaimed the ropes that bound him, and put them to use instead setting big game snares farther out in the woods. He went with designs of his own, best for the sort of stopping power that could take out a bear or a moose without concern for maintaining the condition of the pelt.

Once that was done, he'd rolled Neither-Nor to his side,

ripped off his coat, and gone to work down his lower back with the body map in one hand and the tiny toothpick of a knife he'd found hidden in his boot in the other. It was delicate work, and Slud was not always one for nuance and patience, but Aunt Agnes had drilled a respect for precision into him over the years, and he gave it his best shot. After a while of cutting and recutting, he stepped back to compare his bloody letters to those on the page. Aside from a flub or two on the goblin's little ass cheeks, Slud was fairly impressed with his handiwork. *De li'l fucker will need it, fer what Slud's got planned.*

A thorough rubdown of the goblin with the second musk gland from the fox finished up the night's work. The other tiny blue sac was now braided into Slud's own beard hair, and as with anything unpleasant, he'd already grown used to the stink. After tamping out the fire and coating his skin and clothes with the black char from half-burned logs, he was ready for what came next.

As the stars were slowly overtaken by the light of dawn, the sky went from deep purple to pink and then blue. Slud breathed it in, long and slow, wishing he could stay for a while to enjoy these alien fineries of life. But when the first wolf howl carried up the slope, he ran his thumb down the blade of the ax and found his feet again. Just to be sure, he took that moment to drop his pants and piss in a long curving arc over the edge of the cliff.

THE WOLVES WERE frothing at the mouth, tongues hanging loose as they ran toward the cliff face. It was the first time since the hunt had begun that they'd caught a fresh whiff of their quarry, and after so long at the search, they weren't willing to lose it again. The riders were far less eager. Two had already fallen asleep while mounted and awoken only after their faces had connected with unforgiving earth. None had expected the giant to clear so great a distance before they caught up with it again. After the protracted night, the vibrant light of the new day seemed cruel.

Only Dingle remained alert and eager to forge ahead as his eyes climbed the steep rock face to the lip high above. He gave his wolf an appreciative scratch behind the ears and swung from its back to stand on his own two feet for the first time in many hours. For a moment, he felt like he might stumble to his knees, but he found his balance and managed to stay upright. For once, it was others, and not him, who groaned and fell to the ridicule of the pack.

Groole stepped from the alpha wolf, managing to maintain his balance and composure. As his underlings flopped to the ground and gulped feverishly at wine sacks, Groole strode forward to come even with Dingle. He followed the little scout's gaze up the cliff.

"What do ya see, runt?" he asked.

Dingle's eyes lowered to a fresh spattering of moisture around the base, just as a couple wolves came sniffing. "He wwwas here, not long ago." Dingle pointed straight up. "P-p-pissed from up there."

Groole furrowed his heavy brow, pierced with an array of various-sized loops, before turning back to face the group. "Flogga, Hat-Trick, an' Skinny Karl—climb up an' see what's what."

The hoarse voices of the three lounging goblins in question immediately rose up in joint protest, but Groole had been expecting that. He drew a curved blade and gripped the handle tightly. "Shut yer traps an' get climbing, lads, or all three o' ya bleed out where ya sit!"

They gradually stood, grumbling under their breaths the whole time. Groole's second in command slung a long coil of rope over Skinny Karl's shoulder; an iron spike and a hammer went to Hat-Trick.

"Get to the top quick an' secure the rope for the rest of us," Groole commanded with an encouraging shove to Flogga's back as he passed.

Dingle felt both giddy and a little lost. The nervous energy kept him pacing at the base of the cliff, and he found that if he focused on random things like the spattering of the giant's piss or the sky, the others would just leave him alone. What he really wanted to do was dig the little paper note out of his pocket and start recording his observations of the giant so far, but he didn't have a pencil, and he doubted the furlough on bullying would withstand the furious writing of tiny letters.

The trio of hapless goblins began the climb, and Dingle quickly saw why they had been selected for the task. They were three of the tallest goblins in the ranks, with long appendages and lean muscle as opposed to the bulky fighters who remained lounging below. Despite their fatigue and complaints, once they'd started up the cliff, they communicated well and made quick work of the ascent.

"Notch, Hot-Shot, bows ready an' stand watch," Groole yelled as the two longbowmen nodded and fanned out.

Dingle had to admit, this rough group of the Khan's elite were a disciplined unit when it came to business. It was a far cry from what he was used to among the long-range scouts. He'd even started to feel an odd sense of camaraderie with a few of them, though he couldn't fully shake the knowledge that they meant to kill him upon the slightest display of misinformation or failure. It had never occurred to him, until now, that they might actually be able to end the majestic giant that Dingle so longed to see again. Despite his better instincts, he began to ponder possibilities for sabotage as they drew closer to their goal.

Flogga was the first to throw a leg over the ledge and roll out of sight above. Skinny Karl and Hat-Trick followed soon after as those below quieted and watched with a keen eye. The silence stretched too long, and Groole started to shift and tense with a low hum in the back of his throat . . .

Finally, Flogga poked his head back over and cupped his hands around his mouth. "Campfire! Still smolderin'! Bunch of big stones piled up! It's gone now, but can't be far!" He disappeared back behind the edge, and there was silence again, until the sound of the hammer pounding the spike into rock echoed about the woods.

Skinny Karl appeared next, tossing the rope over the side to uncoil on its fall down to the earth. He pointed off to his right. "Even ground to de west! Smells bad! Wolves can get up and around!"

Groole nodded. "Right, lads, five more o' ya, on the rope quick! Black-Tooth?" A particularly ugly goblin with an array of rotten teeth locked in a perpetual grin stood. "Yer team goes up. Secure the site an' wait for us to come 'round." Black-Tooth nodded, and he and four others secured weapons, gripped the rope, and started climbing.

Dingle eased back from the rock and cupped a hand over his eyes to block the growing light in the sky—he couldn't be sure, but it looked like a trickle of red had spilled over the edge above. The others didn't notice, and a secret thrill went through his little body, like the feeling he got just before diving into a nice warm meat pie with no one around to take it from him. There were no sounds of scuffle, but no more sign of Flogga, Hat-Trick, and Skinny Karl either. With a muffled giggle, he stepped farther back and found a place where he could watch from behind the trunk of a tree.

As Black-Tooth neared the top, with three of his four mates climbing the rope at various points below, the sound of a hard whack against stone echoed from above. The high end of the rope slipped over the edge, and Black-Tooth and the others went with it—screaming and flailing their way back down to a hard landing. The fifth goblin, still at the base, didn't move in time as one of his fellows careened ass first into his open-mouthed stare and snapped his neck with a loud pop.

The giant stepped to the ledge with Flogga in one hand, dangling by the throat, and a big rock in the other. He was covered head to toe in black soot and looked like some sort of devil spewed up from the fire. The rock in his grip flew like a comet, connecting with the flank of one of the wolves with enough force to shatter a hip and some internal organs. The woods immediately filled with frantic yells, but Dingle couldn't peel his wide-eyed gaze from the giant, standing over them like a magnificent beacon of death.

Notch and Hot-Shot took aim and fired, but the giant casually swung Flogga to catch the arrows with his chest and thigh before he tossed the still-kicking goblin down into the scattering ranks. Dingle couldn't help it; he started clapping and jumping with glee. Eight of the clan's best and one of the wolves had been taken out in seconds. *So masterful! So efficient!*

His fawning celebration was cut short as more rocks started

flying, crushing another wolf's skull and sending the others scrambling. The branch above Dingle shattered with a rain of rock debris and splinters on his head. He leapt back to his wolf's shoulders and spurred it to a run, laughing as all the others screamed.

AUNT AGNES HAD forced Slud to play a board game called Tafl for as long as he could remember. He'd always hated playing it—moving the stupid little figures around a checkered square and having to plan all his moves in advance. Planning had never come naturally to Slud, and he'd relied on Agnes to tell him what to do for the duration of his life thus far. Now, he was beginning to understand her almost fanatic devotion to that damned game. She'd drilled a sense of competition into every interaction, teaching him the only real game there ever was—survive or die.

The first move of his contest with the Rock Wolf hunting party had gone as well as he could have hoped. Eight goblins and two wolves down. By his count at the river, there were thirteen more goblins, and seventeen or eighteen wolves, to go. With all those arrows, spears, and teeth, the numbers would be overwhelming, even for Slud. He tried to calculate how many more he needed to take out with his snares as he strode deeper into the woods toward his second position beside another stack of rocks.

The yipping of wolves was moving faster up the slope than he'd figured. They'd found a long-unused deer trail that Slud hadn't noticed the night before. With the loss of time, he'd have to improvise—another cornerstone of Agnes's tutelage.

On his last pass through the camp, he'd picked up the corpse of Neither-Nor, stuffed it in his sack, and slung it over his shoulder in case he didn't get the chance to swing back through. Slud hoped the scarred goblin was as good with those knives as he'd boasted, or else the third play of his game would go all to shit.

It wasn't long before the first rider came into view, moving through the trees at a cautious lope. Whoever was in charge of the hunting party was no fool; the wolves had fanned out with plenty of space between them. It slipped past the first trip-line without noticing, and Slud picked up a rock to gauge its weight. Another rider came up a few strides behind, and the back foot of that wolf clipped the line as it advanced.

The ironwood lever sprang free from its notch between two trees, and the log that was braced above swung down in a short arc. It slammed into the side of the wolf and shattered the goblin's leg, sending them both flying. It had been designed for two or three riders in a tight cluster, but Slud popped up from behind a boulder and threw his rock to even the score. It clipped the lead goblin in the breast, and Slud could hear the crack of its chest plate from across the woods. The wolf beneath took off in the opposite direction.

The goblin with the broken leg would never walk again, but he'd retained consciousness. Slud had been hoping to keep things quiet at first, but the pained wails echoed across the hilltop and the others approached with weapons drawn and eyes ready. The wolves hadn't expected the pervasive stink of fox, and they snuffled around in confusion, unable to get their bearings. Slud had smeared the musk glands against most every tree in a wide swath before turning them into jewelry. For the wolves, this section of woods had been turned into one big, muddy stew without a compass point.

Another snare was tripped, releasing a long greenwood branch covered in sharpened spikes to whip into the face of an unsuspecting goblin. He was done after a short gurgle, and Slud hurled another rock to bring down the startled wolf a second later. He reached for a third rock, but as he came up to find his next target, his gaze froze on the tiny goblin who had stared him down at the river. It was the same goblin who had escaped him the day before at the burning of Agnes's house. He was wrapped in a scraggly wolf pelt with tufts of missing fur, and lacked the weapons and adornment of the others. He sat atop a smaller, tired wolf, and stared at Slud with freakish intensity.

The runt pointed off to his side and pumped his little finger in a hurry, and Slud turned to see another goblin drawing down on him from behind a longbow. He spun away as the wind from the shot whipped past his cheek with a sharp bite at his earlobe. Slud released the rock too quickly in response, and it banged off a tree and ricocheted back. Another mounted bowman drew down beside his fellow, and this time, as Slud spun away, he felt the impact in the sack strapped across his back. He palmed two more rocks and took off as the barks of the wolves and shouts of the archers brought the rest of the hunting party at a sprint.

The final snare went off behind him with a yip and a yell, but he didn't look back to admire his handiwork—instead he fumbled in his pocket for the flint and steel that Agnes had packed. The goblins were coming fast, but he'd already poured out all of Agnes's home-brewed fire oil across the forest. He couldn't let that go to waste.

DINGLE WAS BESIDE HIMSELF. The giant had looked right at

him again, and Dingle had helped him get away from Notch and Hot-Shot, if only for a few more seconds. Now, the hulking beast was kneeling behind a tree directly ahead when he should have been running as fast as he could. The whole scene was chaotic and utterly perplexing, and Dingle wished he could record it all, entranced by every unpredictable move the giant made.

Groole and the rest of the pack were coming up fast now, but with the screaming and dying, and the pervasive skunk-reek that filled the woods, none were willing to push as hard as they might to reach the blackened brute who waited for them. Another arrow flew, sticking in the tree near his head, but the giant didn't budge, chipping away with a metallic echo and a little shower of sparks across the ground.

Wolves and goblins streamed by the spot where Dingle sat, but Dingle didn't budge either. A smile slowly bloomed across his face as he watched the spark catch flame amid a cluster of tinder and leaves. More arrows and spears took to the air, and another stuck in the sack across the giant's back with a peculiar bloodstain spreading there. The giant took no notice as he blew on the little flame and stoked it higher.

Groole bellowed a rallying cry as the pack swarmed. But the giant turned toward his attackers with a smile as he dropped the flame to the ground before him. The fires of hell sprang up in answer.

Dingle shrieked with delight as a green-tinged inferno erupted in a line across the ridge. The alpha wolf skidded to an abrupt halt, and Groole somersaulted over its shoulders. His boots brushed the edge of the fire and came away alight as the giant broke into a deep, rumbling laugh.

Dingle had never heard a laugh like it. It shook his bones

and made him feel small, as if the mountain itself was laughing at him. It echoed about the woods while the leaves above curled and turned to ash and the trunks of trees began to blacken and pop from the roaring flame. The heat of it drove the Rock Wolves back. Groole ripped the boots from his singed feet and hopped away with a look of dread worn openly on his face.

The hot wind made Dingle's eyes water, but still he watched, trying not to blink; he didn't want to miss a moment. The giant hurled a rock that pulverized the alpha wolf's head, and then another that clipped Hot-Shot in the shoulder with an audible snap, before he turned away and tore off through the forest. After a few enormous strides, the giant disappeared behind flame and shadow, and Dingle was left staring after him in awe. He slid off his wolf's back and dropped to his knees with a bowed head. None took notice of the littlest goblin amid the chaos, prostrate and muttering the same words over and over: "Let wretched Dingle be your servant, oh Lord of Death."

The green tinge flickered out of the flames, and the inferno settled back into normal fire. But with the wind and the dried leaves of autumn still clinging to the trees, the burn quickly began to spread across the canopy.

Groole knelt beside his dead wolf and lovingly patted the scruff of its neck as the rest of the pack cowered with ears pinned back and tails tucked between their legs. All of them had gone quiet. Even the wounded goblins with shattered shoulders and legs had been stunned to silence by what they'd seen.

But Dingle didn't want to wait or give up; he needed to follow the giant wherever he was going. He hopped back on his wolf and spurred it beside the smashed alpha. "It's g-g-getting away," he said to Groole. "I th-th-think it's wounded," he lied.

Groole did not look at him, but he nodded, and when he stood again, his tired, yellow eyes had woken with new fury. "Bring me a spare wolf, an' ready for fuckin' battle!"

Dingle leapt ahead again with gleeful abandon that read as courage. He urged his wolf upslope to get around the growing forest fire, and he did not wait for the others before taking off after his quarry on the other side.

Fueled by the scout's zealous display, Groole blew his battle horn and charged after him as soon as he'd mounted a fresh wolf. The others sprang at his heels a second later, and the chase was on anew.

Beyond the fire, the overpowering stink of the musk dissipated, and the wolves easily latched on to a single trail of funk that stretched off through the trees. Dingle let Groole and the others overtake him then—they would be his offering to the giant, proof of his devotion.

The wolves mounted a hill that topped off at a little clearing, ringed by steeper cliffs that climbed another twenty feet up in three directions. The scent trail ended here, but there was no sign of the giant as Dingle had hoped. Instead, a wiry little goblin, covered from head to toe in scarred letters, was propped against the far wall with a fighting blade in each hand. His chest was covered in blood, with a gaping hole in his shirt above his heart, and he was clearly dead. A blood-soaked cap slouched on the side of his bald head, and his fanged mouth had been locked ajar in rigor mortis.

The wolf riders all stopped and stared in confused silence. Then the dead goblin took a sharp inhale and blinked.

THE BLUR TOOK a moment to come into focus as electric

twinges rocketed throughout Neither-Nor's body. He would never get used to coming back to life, though this was the ninth time he'd experienced it, and the third in only the last twenty-four infernal hours. He expected to see the nightmare figure of the troll leering above him, to find his hands and feet bound, and to feel his newly restored heart starved for vengeance. He was only right about the last part.

More than ten mounted and armed goblins stared at him from the far side of the clearing, and he had his two favorite blades in his grip to greet them. The Rock Wolf Clan had taken or butchered every woman and child of the Moon Blades after their defeat against the troll army. Neither-Nor carried a little hate for everyone he met, but his fury knew no bounds for these goblins that rode upon wolves and called themselves masters of the mountain.

The murderous exploits of the rune-covered goblin still hiding in the hills of his fallen clan had made him the target of numerous hunting parties over the years. Every Rock Wolf in a command position knew his name and reputation. The kill-on-sight order and promise of reward had come down from Arokkhan himself.

The particularly large and heavily pierced goblin at the lead of the band went wide-eyed with recognition. "Neither-Nor." He smiled. "Today we kill us a legend, boys! Butcher him good!"

Neither-Nor leapt to his feet just as the arrows and spears flew. He sidestepped the first spear, dodged an arrow, and barely ducked another that ripped the cap from his head. Then he found his rhythm and sliced the next two spears from the air with his blades. "Come on, ya fucks!" He waved them on.

In they came, five of them, fanning out with enough space

to seal off any escape. Axes, swords, and a mace all came at him at once, but none expected Neither-Nor to drop to his knees between five snapping wolf jaws. As the wolves lunged, his blades danced between them, and with a final roll, he came to his feet again as four of the five riders tumbled off dying mounts.

He buried his straight blade in the throat of the closest goblin, and used the moon blade to open the chest of the next. The last wolf lunged, and he gave it a spin-kick to the snout before cleaving the skull of its rider. But then an arrow buried into his shoulder and knocked him stumbling back into the rock face. He snarled and attacked again, ignoring the wrenching pain as his blades ended the last two goblins who struggled to their feet. The final wolf, still feeling the ring of Neither-Nor's boot in its ears, took off toward the others.

Neither-Nor grabbed the arrow by its fletching and yanked it out just before another buried in his stomach and dropped him to his knees. A foolhardy goblin, looking to impress his boss after the quarry was already down, spurred his wolf in for the kill. Neither-Nor threw his straight blade spinning into the wolf's face, and the rider went screaming over its shoulders before skidding into a chop of the moon blade that pinned him through his back to the earth.

Already the wound in Neither-Nor's shoulder had mostly healed as the runes realigned to make his body whole again. His hand went to the arrow in his stomach, but a spear caught him in the other shoulder with enough force to spin him around to face the rock.

He ripped the arrow out and gasped with the pain of it, just as a thick curving blade jammed through his back. He looked down in disbelief at the pointy tip jutting out of the same hole that the troll had left in his shirt—it was notched, dull, and rusted in spots. *This* was the blade that had finally killed him for good. "Fuck it all."

Their big leader stepped over him with a victorious smirk. "Arok's gonna make Groole a Big Boss for this."

Neither-Nor tried to hit him with the moon blade, but that arm didn't work. He tried with the other, but the straight blade wasn't there. The goblin called Groole chuckled before head-butting Neither-Nor's nose with a sharp crack. He couldn't see past the white-hot pain, and he felt himself slipping back into the familiar darkness, but Groole slapped him back into the moment.

"Where's the giant?" Groole shook him by the spattered collar of his coat. "What's it want?"

Now it was Neither-Nor's turn to grin. "In yer nightmares, ya fuck . . . and he's comin' fer ya all." A trickle of blood spilled from his lips, and he slumped over dead.

SLUD WATCHED FROM above as the last of the Moon Blades keeled over amid a cluster of dead wolves and goblins. Slud was impressed. *Li'l fella did betta den Slud figgered.*

Only the weird goblin with the pinprick eyes had noticed him looming above, fixed on him with an open mouth and a half-wit expression on his tiny, pinched face. Again, he gave no warning to the last few warriors beside him. Slud gripped the sword in one hand and the ax in the other and bent his knees for the drop. It was time for him to end this game and move on to a higher-stakes board.

He came down sword first to cleave the Rock Wolf leader from collarbone to crotch, and spun into the others before they could react. By the time the two halves of Groole flopped to the ground, Slud had also made meat out of two more wolves and the last goblin bowman. The rest of the wolves broke and sprinted away through the woods.

Even the wolf beneath the final goblin spun and lurched after the others, despite its rider's fumbling attempt to hold it still. He tumbled from its back with a yelp and came up covered with leaves as Slud stepped toward him with the sword at the ready—noticing only then that the cut through Groole had left a crack in the metal half the length of the blade. The next chop would be its last. The troll was taken off guard when the tiny goblin inexplicably scurried toward him and dropped his head to the earth with barely coherent muttering. "Oh, ll-lord of d-d-death, let Dingle be your wwwitness, and scribe of your w-w-works."

Slud rested the broken sword on the back of the goblin's bent neck and looked out across the mountain. The air was heavy with smoke, and already he could see the orange flicker of fire approaching through the trees.

"W-w-what do you ask of mmme, my lord?" the goblin muttered.

Slud moved the blade below the goblin's chin and raised his head so he could look down into his crazy eyes. He saw blind faith and fealty staring back. Slud liked the idea of a follower who would do whatever he asked, and he wondered if others might also bow down before he was through. Perhaps he could use this goblin to his advantage? "Run back to yer clan. Tell 'em what ya saw here."

A hot wind blew across the slope to rustle the leaves above. Again, Slud felt the eyes of the mountain upon him, waiting to see what he'd do next. "A bad wind's blowin', 'n' a reckonin's comin' wit' it." Slud raised the flat of the blade slowly to bring the goblin up; the little fellow didn't even reach his knees. "Go back to yer Khan, tiny fella. Tell 'im Slud Blood Claw's comin.'"

———————

BLACK SMOKE FILLED the sky, blocking out the rolling clouds of a rose-hued dusk. The mountainside was burning. Agnes breathed in the mingling stink of char, fox, and rotting corpses, and bowed her head to the one who was responsible. The young troll still eluded her, having climbed on from the massacre of the hunting party that had been foolish enough to try to corner him here. One did not corner a force of nature.

But as Agnes had learned over the ages, such forces could be coaxed if one knew the right words. Her past incarnations had summoned rain and wind, called lightning, and induced the ground to shiver at her bidding, but this troll lad was her greatest feat since Angerboda's Children of Doom had tread across the Dream. Soon, the whole mountain would know the name Slud. Soon after, all would learn to fear it.

SEVEN

Black Cloud Rising

THE IMMENSE DOORS of the great hall swung open. The pair of wolves at the base of the throne raised their heads in unison. A wind had blown up from the lowlands, carrying the stink of wood smoke. Black clouds gathered in the sky above the mountain. The usual roar of the hall had dimmed to expectant whispers, and the clan's best hex doktors slunk off into a corner to cast bones and mutter to themselves.

Arokkhan wanted answers. He'd sent for the Big Boss of the scouts over an hour ago, and his two best killers finally escorted him in. He'd forgotten the scout's name again. He walked with a lazy left foot that scuffed behind with every step, and he had to be the shaggiest goblin that Arok had ever seen. Long mud-brown fur wisped behind him as he shuffled toward the throne; even his arms and legs were covered with it. Arok found it freakish and distracting, but the hairy bastard was good at both keeping watch and keeping out of the Khan's way—until today. As Arok eyed his approach with a practiced air of casual disdain, he contemplated which of the two escorts he might let open the scout to see if the hair grew on the inside as well.

The squat guard with the hatchets and the temper kicked the furball in the back to speed things up, and the dull murmur of the spectators went silent. That guard had been dubbed Short-Fuse. The tall, mute cannibal on the other side of the scout was called Long-Pig. The Khan had never seen two goblins with a greater fondness for violence, which was handy on days like this, as Arokkhan wasn't about to try to bite the head off this hairy monstrosity.

The hushed audience of bootlickers pressed close around the fire pit; even the hex doktors wanted to hear what the scout would say. Short-Fuse and Long-Pig moved to the sides and left the scout alone before the wolves. Arokkhan took a swig from the pine-ale jug and felt the familiar burn along the back of his throat. It was never too early in the day to begin dulling his way toward a long sleep. He was distracted for a moment by the wolf-jaw hood that framed his face—*Bet them teeth would look real nice dipped in gold.*

Everyone was looking at him expectantly, but when he lowered the jug and looked back they all averted their eyes. The Herald was still shuffling papers behind the throne, taking his sweet time, as always, to make an entrance. But the Khan had no patience for theatrics today. He cleared his throat, and it echoed back from the arched ceiling. Still, the Herald didn't come . . .

Only after the guards at the doors slid the lock back into place with a loud bang did the little fucker amble out with his pointy nose in the air. The Herald slid to his spot on the first step and held up his precious ledger. "Big Boss Harog of the far-rider scouts," he announced with a nasally whine.

Arok was starting to hate the screech of the Herald's voice, but he turned away from the pinched little weasel to face down this Harog instead. "So, why's my mountain burnin'?"

Harog wisely lowered his head before he spoke. "Forgive

the wait, my Khan. Wanted accounts from multiple riders before I came." His voice, by contrast, was deep and clear for a goblin. "Forest fire broke out on a ridge halfway up the western slope. It continues to rage with the hard wind, and it climbs quick."

Arok had to admit, *The hairy bastard speaks good.* "Do it come here?"

"Not today or tomorrow, my Khan. But if the wind continues on this path, it could reach us here the day after."

Arokkhan clenched his jaw, still feeling the strain from the last head he'd bitten off the week before. That one had been a miserable goblin tailor who'd brought him a new set of robes with sleeves too short. He'd mounted that head outside the tailor's shop in case the apprentice who took over the business shared his master's notion of quality workmanship. "Any stoppin' it—clearin' brush and timber; throwin' water and earth?"

Harog shook his head, and the fur that hung from his ears whipped back and forth. "Wind's too strong; sparks will carry across any gaps we make."

Arok didn't like what he was hearing, but he couldn't deny the authority in the hairy goblin's account either. The Khan couldn't remember much, but he was pretty sure his wife's brother had been the one to suggest Harog become the Big Boss of the scouts. He was starting to feel less inclined to kill someone for it.

Instead, his eyes peeled away from the freak to scan for the creepy doktors in the back, but the misguided intentions of the Herald broke his concentration again with a nasally shout.

"Arok Golden Wolf: Chief of the Rock Wolf Clan, King of the Mountain, and Khan of the Goblin Horde won't be told NO, you miserable buffoon!" A string of spit flew from the

Herald's mouth, and his face went red in an instant. "Give solutions or be replaced with one who can!"

Harog nodded. "I wonder, my Khan, if Bone Master might be able to turn the wind back? I'd take him there myself and guarantee his safety."

Now it looks like his idea! Arok contemplated leaping down to wrap his tusks and fangs around the head of the Herald, but his mouth ached just thinking about it. He looked past him and caught the fixed gaze of the Chief Hex Doktor at the back of the audience. One eye was black and one green; the black eye was twice the size of the other. Bone Master rarely spoke in the common goblin tongue, preferring to spout off in an old dialect that no one understood except his shifty apprentices.

He motioned for the withered goblin, who came with the clanking of a thousand little bones strapped across his body. The first apprentice followed at his heels, clad in a floor-length cloak covered entirely in black feathers. Others made a path for them and looked away; no one wanted to get too close or dare a direct glance, lest the evil eye fall upon them.

The doktors stopped before the wolves and bowed in unison.

"What do the bones say?" Arok asked.

The bent old goblin stayed bowed, his gaze locked on the floor. It was the apprentice who righted himself to answer with a voice broken by years of chanting and smoke. "Trouble's comin'. Might just be the fire, but me master feels somethin' more behind it."

"Can ya turn the wind or not?"

Bone Master looked up at this, and his oversized black eye found the Khan.

For a moment, it felt like someone was pissing on Arok's

grave, and an involuntary shudder crept across his shoulders. Bone Master gave a curt nod and thankfully averted his gaze again.

It took a slow inhale for Arokkhan to feel right. He blinked and took another hard pull from the jug. "Go with Har—Har— What's yer fuckin' name again?" he asked Harog.

The Herald answered with an unnecessary scream, "HAROG! Big Boss of the far-rider scouts!"

Arok was starting to get that head-biting feeling, but he kept his eyes on Harog. "Take these two to the edge of the fire, and keep 'em safe, or I'll toss yer goods to the rafters." The Khan glanced up, and Harog followed the gaze to the strings of dried intestines that had been previously flung over the beam that crossed the shadows above the throne.

Harog bowed with a muddy wave of fur crashing and retreating. "My Khan."

Short-Fuse cast Arok a hopeful look as he stepped back to the scout's side, but Arok shook his head. Harog began the slow shuffle back down the length of the hall as the hex doktors trailed after.

"Hargo!" Arok called out, silencing the gathering once more. Harog turned back and swallowed hard. "What news from Groole's pack and that stutterin' runt of yours about this *giant* in the Iron Wood?"

"Nothing yet, my Khan."

Arok frowned and waved them on. He needed to see someone bleed soon, or he'd pass out from the boredom and drink before his next meal. He turned to Long-Pig, still standing there with his sword in his hand like a disappointed statue. "Bring me whoever cooked them eggs earlier."

Arok hated a hard yolk. That morning he'd been served two.

Long-Pig didn't even acknowledge the Khan as he left, quiet and emotionless, as always, but Arok knew the killer would soon be happy.

————————

THE AIR BURNED Slud's nostrils and throat, every mouthful threatening to make him gag and sputter. He knew that if he stopped to cough in earnest the flames would overtake him in minutes. Long strands of spit clung to his beard and streaked his shoulders. Each thundering step was accompanied by a ragged grunt. The blue sky had been swallowed by thick rolls of black. A hot wind pushed him higher as if with some urgent destination in mind.

Slud hadn't slept since he'd downed that last potion the morning before, but Agnes's brew still kept his muscles going and the fatigue at bay. So he climbed on with the heavy bag slapping at his sweat-drenched back, the strap digging into his neck, no time to adjust for comfort. He'd discarded his broken sword and, in its place, picked up what he could scrounge from the Rock Wolves. The uncomfortable load had shifted again, poking into his kidney, and he threw an elbow in protest that landed with a meaty thud and little effect.

The flames would erase all evidence of the battle. If he reached a safe haven above, the board would reset for the next game. Slud doubted that the tiny goblin who had called himself Dingle had made it off that ridge alive. Without a wolf to carry him, those puny legs wouldn't have been able to clear the fire before it caught him—which was just as well, as the troll wasn't sure that announcing his approach would be the smartest tactic after all. The odds, one against thousands, were steep enough without him calling his moves in advance.

Still, he'd liked the way Dingle had stared at him. Something about the little fellow bowing at his feet felt right, natural even. He craved more of the servile attention. Burning to death seemed an unfitting end for his first follower. Or perhaps it was the most fitting end of all? Regardless, if Slud didn't move quickly, he'd be following the little goblin into the flames soon enough.

His legs pounded up a jagged cleft and brought him to an extended stretch of level ground before the next cliff face. There, through the trees, in the nook of the far climb, a small mountain lake waited, the reflective surface yet unmarred by the coming wind. He ran toward it full tilt as the backward-reaching pine needles of the closest tree started to bend and crackle from the heat.

Sprinting through the hushed trees, he could almost hear their slow, somber breath, the way Agnes had taught him. They knew it was their time to die; thousands of years of life were at an end, so much history soon to be forgotten. Slud had no time for their sorrow as his eyes settled on the glassy surface before him. He stopped at the water's edge—the lake looked like a hole in the earth dropping into smoke and oblivion. But then the wind found him again, relentless and uncaring, and the ripples turned the black cloud back to water.

Aunt Agnes had told him many stories over the years involving dangerous faeries who lurked below the surface of isolated mountain pools like this one: naiads, nixies, kelpies, and banshees, all waiting for hapless travelers who wandered too close. He pressed a soot-covered finger to his nostril and blew gobs of blackened snot into the water, first one, and then the other. His offerings floated for a moment before dropping stringy tendrils to the stones.

A last glance back found that the fire had leapt up on both sides of the little dell, as if working to block his escape and corral him here. He saw no point in arguing with the will of the mountain. In he went, the soles of his feet finding the smooth pebbly bed below the frigid water. In a few steps the bite had climbed to his knees, and the ache of it made him alert as his eyes scanned for movement. A few steps more submerged him to his waist, and he could feel his nethers trying to retreat into his body.

Behind him, trees popped and the roar of the inferno took over, but he kept going, the water climbing to his chest. His breath came and went in sharp bursts, and some of the contents of the bag started to float, but the hot wind pushed him on, brushing against his neck, both threatening and encouraging at once. Then he was swimming, unsure of what his destination could be. Slud was not a good swimmer, able to doggy-paddle himself upright and forward, but little else beyond that.

He was pleased to find the small rocky island that waited just below the surface at the lake's center, and he climbed up, scraping hands and knees with a fleeting sense of victory. He didn't shiver long as the flames spread, jumping from tree to tree in a ring around him and turning the dell, surrounded by tall cliffs, into an oven.

Slud eyed the far wall, almost twice the height of the sheer climb he'd made the previous evening. He doubted that he could make it before the rising heat became too much to bear. Was this what the mountain had planned for him? *Bakin' to death wit' a wet ass? Fuckin' grand.*

A silvery shimmer caught the corner of his eye, but when he

looked it was gone. He figured that going out with a belly full of fresh fish would be better than dying with an empty stomach but he didn't have a sharpened stick. He wasn't about to brave the shore again to get one as the now engulfed treetops started to drop burning branches and flaring pinecones on all sides.

It was like a scene from one of the demon realms that Agnes had said she'd glimpsed in a deep trance. He found it intoxicating, tranquil even—there were worse ways to go than at the heart of such a profound display of destructive beauty. The heat gathered quickly, the wind stoking the flames higher and sending sparks and ash whipping into little funnels. He began to feel flushed as a smile of acceptance settled across his face.

But he glimpsed the silvery movement again, and searched the water for its cause. The dance of the flames ringed the pond's surface, but the reflected picture of the smoke cloud shimmered apart in spots to show the deep rocky floor beyond it—like two worlds overlaid upon each other, both of them mercurial and distant. His mind began to drift once more, but with a gentle splash, something of substance broke the water's plane and his feverish daze with it.

At first, Slud didn't believe that the face before him was real—a delicately featured woman with large, dark wide-set eyes and a silver-green hew to her skin. Her hair was the color of freshwater weeds, and she bobbed effortlessly in place with the crown of her small breasts hovering suggestively just above the waterline. She wore no expression as she stared at him from a stone's lob out. He blinked and squinted, but she was still there, watching.

"Oi!" he shouted, his aunt's words of warning coming back to him. "What're ya?"

She immediately disappeared below, but he tracked her shimmering movement as she swam closer—coming to a submerged halt before him with slow undulations of her hands and feet. Though distorted by the water, she appeared more clearly to Slud now. She was long and bony, though oddly pleasing to the eye, with scales instead of skin and fine webbing between her fingers and toes. There was something alluring about her emotionless gaze; the hint of a smile tugged at the corner of her bluish lips.

She waved for him to join her in the water though Slud couldn't be sure if was an invitation or a command. The tingle of a charm gathered at the base of his skull, beckoning him to pitch forward and reach out to her, but he shook the impulse away. Still, the heat was building as a rain of ash started to fall around him. Each gray flake that landed burned his skin with a momentary sting. Every inhale made his chest heavier.

She opened her arms as if to welcome his embrace, just as Agnes's words echoed back once more. *The fae of the water will just as soon drag you down to your death as court your seed. They're some of the most wicked and treacherous of the Fair Folk.*

Even in the water, Slud was pretty sure he could overpower a skinny girl if she was looking to drown him. But if she was after the other, he sure as shit wasn't going to pass up such an opportunity again. He slipped his pack off his shoulder and fixed it atop the highest point of the island, before sliding into the pond. She reached out for him.

He felt the scaly grip of her cold fingers on his wrist, urging him away from the rock. She gave Slud a backward glance and nodded for him to follow as his eyes drifted down the distorted shimmer of her body. He stepped away from the ground and started kicking with his free hand and feet, pulling gently to raise her back to the surface. Then she yanked harder in the opposite direction. Slud's head went under before he could take a last breath. She was a lot stronger than she looked.

EIGHT

Witch Way the Wind Blows

A STRING OF HISSED WORDS carried on the wind. For astute ears that had been trained to listen to the hidden arts, the flow of arcane whispers could be heard from many miles away, though not even the goblin warlocks would recognize the dead language of their design.

Black Agnes stood at the edge of the cliff with her chin to the sky and her long arms held above her. The words she wove were of the old giant tongue, last uttered by the great wind-witches millennia before—a call to the elementals of the air, beseeching them to stoke the fire and drive it up and across the slope.

She'd cobbled together a makeshift frock and headscarf from the trappings of fallen goblins. At the base of the drop behind her, the broken bodies of the Rock Wolf hunting party had seasoned well, lending the reek of death to the squall she sent barreling up the mountain. As she spoke, she closed her heavy lids and listened for the thunder of Slud's steps.

He'd climbed far and fast, and Agnes had chanted hard to keep the wind apace with him. Now his steps had gone silent and the fire had overtaken his position, though she could still hear the muffled beating of his heart. *He's reached the lake. Now if he can keep from doing anything too impetuous.*

Agnes's chant trailed off and the wind went into a lull. Her throat had gone hoarse and she needed a drink to sooth the burn that had settled there. There was still so much left to do. She had to find a way to draw the Khan's army out, and she had to help Slud get into place for what would follow.

Her eyes snapped open as the sound of quick footsteps approached from above. She hunched further and shrank into herself, suddenly looking old and frail again—just as a young faun bolted out of the blackened forest with terror worn plainly on his bearded face.

His goat's legs stopped fast when he spotted her withered form at the edge of the cliff. His frantic eyes scanned for a way around that wasn't there before returning to her unreadable watch, hidden behind shadow, cloth, and hair. "Can't go that way," he said with a voice turned raspy by smoke. "It's all burning above."

Agnes flashed rows of needle-sharp teeth in a smile. "I do not mind the heat."

The faun eyed her warily. His ears twitched. "Is there a way down there?"

She glanced back to the drop and nodded. "A steep set of stairs in the rock . . . dangerous, but stairs nonetheless."

Without her influence, the wind shifted against her, and a snow of ash started to fall over the clearing. The faun caught a gray flake on the back of his hand and smeared it into a streak across his knuckles. He looked back to Agnes and took a few jittery steps. He wanted out of these cursed woods. "Something bad happened here. I'm going, and you should too."

Agnes pointed to the ledge beside her, and her smile grew. "Here it is, though I would not wish to go down; I had much trouble coming up."

The faun crept closer, trying to decide if he was more afraid of her or the fire. "I'll be fine. I trust my legs."

She turned her shiny black gaze on his furry haunches and couldn't help but lick her lips. "Those legs are nice, yes."

He stepped closer still, glancing between her and the place where the stairs were meant to be. She gestured down again. "Just there. It was a hard climb for this old body."

As he leaned past her, craning his neck to see, her claw lashed out and pushed. He went over face first and screaming. Then he landed badly and the screaming stopped. Agnes bent over the edge and admired the crooked splay of his appendages as the blood began to pool across the rocks below. Her stomach had started to feel tight again, but she looked back to the growing field of char and flame. Someone else was out there, another voice chanting into the wind.

She angled her head to listen. It came from higher up and across the mountain—a wavering scream in an old goblin dialect. *A Rock Wolf warlock seeks to turn the flame.*

Agnes looked back to the fresh blood below. First she would drink, then she would give this foolish goblin an ill wind he'd not soon forget.

———

THE MASTER SAT cross-legged on the ground, facing downslope with a bone rattle spinning in his hands. His voice alternated between a whisper and a shriek. Fixelcrick stood behind him, stroking the black feathers of his cloak as he watched and listened. The first apprentice did not yet have the knack for charming the wind, but if he was to one day take over as Chief Doktor, he'd have to learn. His innate skill lay in the alchemical arts, and in that he was unrivaled in the clan.

The cloak he wore had been fashioned over years. 184 grackles sacrificed thus far—fourteen layers of black and blue feathers, rubbed twice a week with cricket oil to keep them supple and shiny. He hunted the grackles by crossbow, bringing them down with bolts tipped in gold. The crickets he raised at home in vast numbers, and their constant chirping had driven some of the lesser acolytes mad.

He looked up at the swirling smoke cloud that blanketed the sky above, uncertain which way it would blow. The forest fire had crested the wide ridge that marked the mountain's halfway point. It had been moving too quickly to be governed by its own accord, but already Bone Master had turned back the buffeting wind and stopped the advance.

Harog and the other scouts were still jumpy. The spear boys had set up in a wide perimeter and their eyes scanned the wood for movement. If there was another doktor out there who dared to work against the Rock Wolf Clan, there was probably an army with him.

Perhaps the Iron Tusks? The Yellow Fangs? Fixelcrick couldn't guess which of the lowland clans was powerful or foolish enough to brave such an attack, but he knew it wouldn't be long before the Rock Wolves marched to war in answer. It had been over a decade since the Bone Shield Clan had made an attempt on the mountain, and now that name was dead among all the goblins of the horde.

Fixelcrick's master had been a Bone Shield once, the only of their ranks to survive. He had power to share and allegiance to nothing but the arts he trafficked in. It had been the most important lesson he'd taught the first apprentice—there were no clans, or families, or friends; only the Knack mattered.

The Big Boss of the scouts spurred his wolf beside Fixelcrick and leaned over to whisper so as not to disturb Bone Master's flow. "Is there a doktor out there? Working against us?"

Fixelcrick nodded.

"Got an idea who? Whole pack of the Khan's Blades and Fangs are still missing."

Fixelcrick didn't look at him. He didn't have any answers, and he had no patience for hearing information that he already knew. Instead, he arched his back and waved his arms in tight circles as the feathers came alive across his cloak. Harog stumbled back in surprise as the apprentice shot into the air and landed on a thick pine branch fifty feet up.

Fixelcrick smirked. He enjoyed surprising goblins with little shows of the power within his grasp, but the sudden strain in Bone Master's words brought him back to the battle for control of the air. The first apprentice peered out toward the dance of flames in the distance and opened his inner ear to the competing words woven into the breeze.

He heard the unfamiliar speech of the *other* like a chorus of hissed echoes about his mind. The language was harsher, more guttural and savage than the old goblin dialect of his master, and there was a vaguely feminine tone to the string of utterances. As Fixelcrick listened, a cold shiver worked its way down from his scalp. The wind began to shift again.

Bone Master shrieked with renewed vigor, spit flying from his mouth and the bone rattle furiously shaking a discordant beat. But the black cloud moved toward them across the mountain once more, rolling and angry. The heavy aroma of burning pine was mingled with a faint undercurrent of death. Even the wolves seemed to grow uneasy with the foul air in their snouts—they growled and tucked their tails, and some of the more craven of their number quietly whimpered.

"Any movement ahead?" shouted Harog from below, no longer concerned with the focus of the master.

Fixelcrick had begun to develop his own far-seeing eye, almost twice as big as the other and perpetually bloodshot and oozing. He turned it on the stretch of land between them and the fire. Nothing was moving except the swaying branches of the forest, but he sensed something drawing closer. The wind whipped against the treetops, and Fixelcrick had to brace against the rocking of his perch as he peered down to meet Harog's expectant gaze with a shake of his head.

The master's voice began to crack, and the fury of the bone rattle faltered, but the angry voice in the wind did not waver. Fixelcrick's far-seer spotted the dramatic lean of the trees ahead of him just before the first big gust bent the trunk he clung to with a loud *WHOOSH!* He dug his claws into the bark until he felt the sticky sap. Another gust bent the crown of the tree even farther, and he hugged the branch tightly, praying both he and it would hold.

The wolves barked frantically below, and the screams of Bone Master were now tinged with desperation and pain. Limbs and trunks snapped across the slope with sharp cracks followed by dull crashes. Fixelcrick dared to open his eye again amid the tumult. He thought he saw someone running toward them through the chaos, but he lost sight of them and almost came unglued as the trunk whipped upright once more. Back and forth he swung with gust after gust barreling through their position. He clung on desperately and muttered his own feeble prayers to the spirits in the air.

Finally, the attack ceased, and the tree settled with a thick rain of branches and needles. The apprentice's jaw ached from clenching. He was pretty sure he'd cracked a tooth, and he could tell that the lull wouldn't last for long. He rolled from the branch until he was dangling, and then dropped with a flutter and short glide. The feathered cloak plopped him back to his feet beside Harog's spooked wolf, and Fixelcrick unhooked the little crossbow from his belt and loaded a bolt. "Someone's comin.'"

Harog blew three quick bursts on his horn, and the spearmen converged around him. Neither goblins nor wolves made a sound as a small figure crested the rise at a quick lope. Fixelcrick pointed his crossbow, and the spears were readied to throw, but the little soot-covered figure kept on.

"Not until I say so," said Harog, though Fixelcrick could already see the whites of the beady little eyes that approached. It was a goblin, though possibly the smallest goblin that Fixelcrick had ever seen. He was very fast, and seemingly oblivious to the twenty goblins and wolves directly in his path.

"Dingle?" Harog shouted.

The blackened runt came to a halt a few paces away and promptly greeted them with a barrage of sneezes.

That was when Fixelcrick noticed that Bone Master had stopped chanting. The old goblin lay on his back with two streams of blood trickling from his nose and a spill of foam from the side of his mouth. The master was alive, his lips still trying to form words that carried no sound, but his far-seeing eye had burst over his cheek in a gelatinous dribble. Fixelcrick started toward him, but Dingle stepped closer with a wild look, and the first apprentice held on to the crossbow instead.

"Dingle, what happened to Groole?" Harog demanded.

The tiny goblin was panting heavily and he seemed to vibrate with a constant twitch throughout his body. "D-d-dead. Th-th-they're all dead."

"Who killed them?" asked Harog, lowering his spear.

Dingle's pinched face was covered in snot. He swallowed hard, and started to blink rapidly as his mouth got stuck in a rising hiss. "SSSSSLUD!" he shouted. "He ssspoke to me . . . He said his nnname was SLUD! The L-L-Lord of Death! K-k-king of the M-m-mountain! He's coming for the K-K-Khan!"

The wind was starting to pick up again, and the little goblin was inexplicably smiling and nodding as he yelled. Fixelcrick got the impression that it would be best to loose the arrows and spears after all.

"Dingle, what are you talking about?" asked Harog as the little fellow began to bounce in place with his red-rimmed eyes bulging.

"B-B-Blood Claw Clan has returned!" he cried. "T-T-TROLL!"

NINE

Call to Arms

SLUD WAS FACEDOWN in a shallow puddle that smelled of old fish. He couldn't see a thing. He knew that he was in a tight cave below the lake, but it was pitch black, and when he stood upright his head hit the rock ceiling. Instead, he hunched on the cold ground with the sound of water lapping at his feet and waited for the fire to subside or something to happen. There was no sound or sign of the weird water woman who'd pulled him here, but it seemed like she'd meant to help not harm. He couldn't be sure, but he guessed she might be a nixie. After the first frantic moment of thrashing against her surprisingly firm grip, he'd locked his breath as Aunt Agnes had taught him and gave into her.

He couldn't swim, but he knew how to sink. Sometimes Agnes had held little Slud's head in the water barrel as he thrashed and bucked against her rigid arm. Eventually he'd learned to channel the panic into something else. By the end, he could slip instantly into a trance state and survive on what little air was already inside him for more than half an hour. This time he hadn't even needed it, but his breath was already starting to pull shallowly in the little upside down bowl of a cave.

The utter darkness and the sound of his exhales echoing about the little chamber reminded him of the time that Agnes had made him build a coffin and dig a big hole. She'd fed him mushroom tea and left him down there with nothing but the silence and hallucinations for a full day before digging him back up to see what he'd learned. "Don't fuckin' trust no one dat tells ya to get in da box," he'd answered before his beating.

A hazy orange light gathered below to bring him back to his current predicament, illuminating the mouth of an underwater tunnel. It was the reflected light of the forest fire, and it brightened as the inferno reached full burn. His eyes needed only the faintest light to see, and he scanned his surroundings for the first time—no other way out, and no significant source of fresh air. But Slud did see the glitter of metal in the water at the base of the tunnel, and he leaned over for a better look just as the nixie swam into view carrying a fish. With a last graceful kick, she rose to the surface and poked her head up—no breath taken, no expression worn. She just stared as she had before without indication of her intentions.

"Oi, t'anks," said Slud with a nod. She didn't even blink, raising her arm to toss the still wriggling fish toward him. His claw snapped out and caught it, and the wriggling stopped. It was a good-looking sturgeon. "'Tanks again."

She eyed him for a long moment, almost as if trying to decide something, and then she dove back down. Slud took a bite of the fish and watched as she swam to the bottom and grabbed hold of something big that had been resting there. It was at least as tall as she was, and twice as wide at the base, but she hauled it up with a swift flurry of kicks and slid it with a scrape onto the bank beside him. It was crusted over with years of lichen and mineral deposits, and long pondweeds had taken root in places, but there was what looked like a large, two-headed battle-ax beneath.

Slud bit the fish again with a rush of juicy innards in his mouth before taking the handle of the old weapon. It was icy to the touch, and his hand instinctively sprang away. He dropped the fish and tried again, this time hefting the significant weight of the ax head and bringing the flat of it down against the rocks with a sharp *CLANG!* The cold of it sank into his palms and fingers as bits of the crust cracked away to reveal the gleam of the silver, almost white, blade beneath.

The nixie dropped out of view again to leave him with the curious offering as he continued to break away the weathered covering. After a flurry of scrapes and bangs, Slud held the bitterly chilled ax before him—still very sharp and etched with lines of crude runes along both blades and spiraling down the hilt. Axes had never been his favorite killing tool, but it seemed the mountain intended to force the issue. It was undoubtedly the finest item he had ever held, and he felt more like himself with it in his grip. How a giant-sized weapon had come to rest at the bottom of this cave was hard to figure, but Agnes had always said—*If life gives gifts, better to use 'em rather than squawk about reasons.*

The nixie broke the surface again and dropped something else big on the lip of stone with a hard *THUNK!* It was a wooden chest framed with thick iron joints around a keyhole. It wasn't as old as the ax, with none of the marks of age upon it, and she pushed it to the shore beside him before pulling herself from the water to sit with her legs still submerged on the far side. She eyed the ax and then Slud, ready to dive back to safety at the smallest provocation as Slud's returned gaze wandered down her form. Her body was framed in the orange glow just enough for him to imagine all that was still hidden in shadow.

She motioned to the chest with her chin, and Slud noticed the heavy key she'd placed on the rocks before it. The ax went beside the fish and he plucked up the key. The lock turned with a hard scrape; the lid opened with an echoing creak and a rush of earthen scent that reminded him of his lost home in the Iron Wood.

The contents were unexpectedly dry. A set of clothes, finer than he was used to, but made with the same unmistakable cross-stitching that had accompanied every piece of clothing he'd ever worn, atop a heavy coat that looked to have been made from the pelt of a cave-bear. Thick leather boots that smelled like wild hog were folded beneath, and at the bottom he found a note written in familiar script:

PUT THESE ON, TAKE AX, AND CLIMB.

Slud wondered how much of his path ahead had been or-chestrated by Aunt Agnes in advance, but as she had in-structed, he didn't bother wondering for long. He moved to close the chest, not wanting his new clothes to get wet on the way out if he could help it, but the nixie stood abruptly and ap-proached with an outstretched hand. She reached toward his soiled shirt and started pulling it up with the same unreadable expression as always. Slud followed her lead and peeled it over his head before tossing it with a splat against the wall.

If he'd been standing, she'd only come up to his hip, though she didn't seem to mind. Her hands were cold and a little slimy on his chest before moving down to the tie at his pants, but he didn't mind either. The orange glow in the water started to recede again, but Slud wouldn't need his eyes for what came next.

THE FAT GOBLIN that the Khan called Short-Fuse pulled the rope to hoist Dingle higher. The rope had been thrown over the rafter before the throne in the great hall, and Dingle dangled upside down by his ankles, swaying back and forth as the eyes of the wolves followed in tandem. Someone gave him a push, and he started to spin with the blood rushing to his head and a woozy churn in his gut. The realization that much of the audience had turned away or hurried out of the hall altogether did not bode well for his immediate future.

The tall goblin with dead eyes stepped forward and punched him in the chest with enough force to send him swinging in a wide arc before the Khan. A couple days ago, such a punch would have killed Dingle instantly, but now, even as his eyes watered and he struggled for breath, he could feel his bruised muscles and cracked bones start to tingle and warm agreeably.

"Lemme get this right," said the Khan. "Ya sayin' this . . . Slud, a *troll*, killed twenty of my best goblins an' wolves, by hisself?"

"Y-y-yes, K-K-Khan," said Dingle, with a string of spit clinging awkwardly to his lip as he spun. In the next rotation he noticed that Big Boss Harog and the hex doktor with the feathered coat stood nearby with their eyes locked at their feet. Half a turn later, he spotted the Herald on the first step, scribbling something in his ledger. Dingle's mind and tongue went in separate directions. "Well, not all by himmmself," he added before he was able to stop his mouth from moving. "A g-g-goblin called N-N-Neither-Nor killed some too."

The Khan shot up in his seat, and even the expressionless

goblin with the fists furrowed his brow. "What did ya say?" the Khan growled.

"G-G-Groole said his name was N-N-Neither-Nor . . . All c-c-covered with ssscars."

The Herald snapped the ledger shut and went red-faced. Short-Fuse's hold on the rope slackened a bit as Dingle dipped toward the bloodstained floor.

The Khan put down his pine-ale jug and stood. "What happened to Neither-Nor?"

Dingle's voice went up an octave. "G-G-Groole killed him . . . B-But Slud took the body."

The Khan started down the stairs. "So, Neither-Nor's back, an' he an' this oversized goblin think they can fuck with Arok Golden Wolf, son of Grummok Green Hammer."

He gave a nod to the tall goblin, and this time it was an uppercut into Dingle's side that might have ruptured organs. Dingle flew until the rope went taut, jerking him back into a frenzied jiggle before the Khan. He coughed up blood, but the warming sensation immediately spread across his torso. His prayers that he might pass out went unanswered.

The Khan stepped closer, working his lower jaw. "Now, why did this Slud let ya go, runt?"

Dingle knew he was about to die, but he pictured the massive looming face of the troll above him, the dance of the forest fire reflected in the dark pits of eyes framed by two yellowed tusks. It gave him strength. "He t-t-told me to tell you a reckonin's comin' with the wind. He wwwanted you to know, the Blood Claw Clan has returned!"

Dingle hadn't meant to shout that last part, stunned to hear the force and clarity of his own voice echoing back from the ceiling. A hushed silence fell over the hall. Even the Khan looked a little startled by the vehemence of his proclamation. Dingle shut his eyes as tightly as he could; he didn't want to see what was about to happen. He'd served the Lord of Death well and was ready to meet his horrible end having delivered the message entrusted to him.

Then the nasal screech of the Herald interrupted from nearby. "How dare you raise your wretched voice to Mighty Arok Golden Wolf, Chief of the Rock Wolf Clan, King of the Mountain, and Khan of the Goblin Horde!"

Dingle kept his eyes clenched, waiting for the scrape of teeth on his throat and the foul humidity of the Khan's mouth. Instead, he continued to hear the Herald's furious proclamation.

"Miserable lying swine! The trolls were killed off decades ago, and Neither-Nor wouldn't dare! You will die most grievously for your insolence, foul im—"

The Herald's screech turned into a muffled scream. There was a crunch followed by a revolting gurgle. The screaming stopped. Dingle opened his eyes and wished he hadn't. A shocking fountain of blood spilled out of the Khan's mouth as he held the Herald's head within and worked his teeth through the neck. The wolves sprang away just before Dingle was bathed in the warm spray. The Khan grunted as he sawed at the neck bone with his jagged molars.

Dingle threw up into his nose when the Khan ripped the head off with a final crack. The King of the Mountain spit it out to tumble across the floor as the Herald's twitching body flopped to the base of the stairs. Dingle averted his eyes, but the growing pool of red spread below him. The ledger had fallen unceremoniously in the middle of it, blood soaking through its precious pages.

The Khan was still standing before him, breathing like an

enraged bull as the last few spurts pumped out of the ragged neck at his feet. No one else made a sound.

Dingle sneezed a splatter of his own sick into the air. He was sure he'd die in seconds, but the Khan turned back to the throne and climbed up to his bottle.

He gulped loudly until the jug upended and then tossed it to shatter on the bloody stones. The audience remained frozen as he slumped into his seat with a weary sigh and pointed to Harog. "You there, hairy scout."

Harog looked like he might be sick as well. "My Khan?"

"Ya speak good, yer the new Herald . . . Hairy Herald I'll call ya. Take yer ledger an' fetch me another jug," he commanded.

Harog didn't know what to do, but doing nothing wasn't an option. He hobbled into the pool of blood to retrieve the book and then scuffed off behind the throne to look for more ale, leaving a red streak behind his furry, dragging foot.

The Khan pointed at the feather-robed apprentice. Fixel-crick gulped and bowed.

"Bone Master still breathes?" the Khan asked.

The apprentice nodded. "Yes, but his brain's broke."

The Khan yawned and rubbed his jaw, wanting nothing more than to go back to his room and sleep. "This other hex doktor, the one at the fire, was betta than yer master?"

The apprentice nodded again. "She'd the strongest knack fer movin' wind I've seen or heard of."

"She?" the Khan asked.

This time the apprentice's nod was more of a bow.

"So a witch, a giant, an' Neither-Nor . . . Blood Claw Clan, eh?" He turned to meet Short-Fuse's expectant gaze, and waved a dismissive hand toward Dingle. The dangling goblin fell headfirst to the wet stone with a yelp.

"I want me five thousand best Blades an' Fangs ridin' by end of day. Short-Fuse and Long-Pig, take them out yerself. Bring me heads of a witch, a giant, that fuckin' scarred goblin, an' anyone else who's with them, or you'll be danglin' next." The Khan spat toward the place where Dingle slumped. "But first, hang this one from a cage in Clan Center, an' let the crows pick him clean."

SLUD CLIMBED OUT of the blackened bowl of forest that surrounded the pond. The huge ax was strapped to his back between his new bearskin coat and the charred bag he'd left on the island while he'd gone below with the nixie. He glanced back down to the water, half hoping to see her unreadable gaze watching his progression, wondering if he'd made as much of an impression on her as she had on him. She was nowhere to be seen.

The valley smoldered, still and quiet save for the crackling of coals that had been trees. The wind had stopped, and the fire had moved on across the slope. Slud could see the towering flames from afar as they leapt from tree to tree along the ridge. He hoisted himself over the high cliff ledge and tossed Agnes's burnt old sack to the earth, before removing the frigid ax from his shoulder and testing its swing. At first touch, the icy sting of it was almost too much to bear, but he breathed it in and the chill settled into his hands and moved deeper into his body. The cold pain made him feel alert and lethal.

He sent a horizontal chop into a nearby tree and was startled to see the blade pass all the way through the trunk and crack out the other side with an explosion of jagged splinters.

Slud had to jump aside as the top came down with a loud crash. He chuckled and gave a nod in the general direction of his lost home before turning back to the bag.

Half the contents had marinated in lake water and the other half had baked to a crisp. He dumped it all out at his feet and sorted through it with a boot: the last few bites of soggy snake, the remnants of Agnes's spiced meats, the now obsolete wood ax, his flint and steel, a couple jugs of Rock Wolf pine-ale, and the seared, pincushion body of Neither-Nor. An array of blades and arrows still stuck through him. The goblin's head had clearly been above water; it was now browned and leathery below the red cap, which had been reduced to a crusty crumple. Slud removed the rune map scroll from where he'd buried it in the goblin's pack, but the combination of water and fire had left it brittle and washed out beyond use. It came apart in his hands, and bits drifted over the ledge in the breeze. *Damn.*

Slud was tired of carrying the scrawny corpse, and he was going to stop now one way or another. He yanked out Groole's curved sword first, then the arrow and spearhead, before tugging out the goblin's own fighting blades, which Slud had buried in his chest for safekeeping. He tossed the pile of blades out of arm's reach and stepped back with the battle-ax at the ready. Nothing happened.

———

IN ALL HIS suffering and dying, Neither-Nor had never been horribly burned before. Though he couldn't move or make a sound, the first thing he was aware of was screaming pain across much of his body. He felt like he'd been flayed, or perhaps coated with a swarm of angry wasps as jolts of white-hot agony jabbed into his mind. After what might have been minutes or days, the debilitating assault ebbed, and his skin was left feeling like it crawled with a whole colony of riled ants.

Finally his body shuddered to life and he produced a long, low wheeze. He peeled his eyes open to the blur of another campfire, and he wondered if he'd ever left his spot above the Iron Wood. Then he remembered the Rock Wolf hunting party, and the image of the big goblin's blade jamming through his back and out his chest. *Ain't possible. I was dead fer good.*

"Oi, welcome back, frien'," came the rumbling voice of the infernal troll. "Took ya long enough, dis time."

The troll who called himself Slud was standing beside a little fire, covered now in heavy furs and carrying the meanest-looking ax that Neither-Nor had ever seen. Maybe he really was some creature spat up from his nightmares, but Neither-Nor was too tired to fight anymore. "How?"

"Slud took yer map 'n' worked on yer back las' time ya was out . . . If yer done wit' all de leapin' 'n' snarlin', ya can come over and get yer belly right." Slud motioned to long strips of cured meat drying out on the rocks beside the flame. "But if yer lookin' fer more, dis time Slud'll chop ya ta bits 'n' use ya fer kindlin'."

Neither-Nor met the troll's dark gaze, then eyed the runes etched along the twin blades of the ax, and nodded. He stood with a wince and moved to the fire, noticing his moon blade and gut sticker in a pile nearby. He was thrilled to see them, but he tried to play it off like he didn't care. The two blades were filthy with day-old blood and in need of a good whetstone, but they hadn't been lost as he'd feared. They'd been forged by his grandfather over a century ago, both cast from the metal of an elven sword found on a forgotten battlefield. He'd never met another blade that held its edge so well; hundreds of lives had been taken by each. They were all that remained of the once-proud Moon Blade Clan.

But the troll was watching, and Neither-Nor doubted he'd ever been so hungry in all his lives. He dropped to his knees beside the meat and started devouring it in frantic gulps as Slud reclined against a recently felled tree on the opposite side of the fire.

"Why?" Neither-Nor managed to ask between bites.

The firelight reflected in the blacks of the troll's eyes. "Seems Neider-Nor 'n' Slud want de same t'ing. Why not work it togedda?"

"Yeah, what's that?" asked the goblin mid-chew.

"Rock Wolf Clan's gotta go," the troll answered.

Neither-Nor choked on his last bite, coughing a ragged clump of meat into his hand. He put it back in his mouth and kept chewing, waiting to see if Slud laughed. He didn't. "More'n ten thousand goblins behind that stockade wall. Prob'ly five thousand fighters and half as many mountain wolves with 'em." He took another bite. "What're you and me s'posed to do 'gainst that?"

"So ya know where 'tis den." Slud flashed a wicked smile. "Slud knew dere was a reason ta keep ya 'round."

TEN

Walk with Thunder

THE SPIRITS OF THE AIR had been left to their own devices, but the flames continued a slowed advance along the ridge. The ground was still hot below Agnes's feet. A crust of char covered the earth in the fire's wake, and the dense, towering woods had been turned to a spotty field of blackened spikes. The air was heavy with smoke, and with every breath, Agnes sucked more of it into her lungs, inhaling the essence of the trees she'd destroyed. All of the forest's anger and sadness was hers to taste, but the smoke was murder on her voice—reduced now to a husky whisper.

The faun's blood had soothed her throat for a spell, more heady and delectable than she'd expected, but the effect hadn't lasted long. After she'd silenced the goblin warlock and announced her presence to the Rock Wolves she'd gone back down the cliff for more. She'd tried to fill one of the discarded drink sacks for the road, but most of the precious blood had already leaked out to congeal on the rocks. She took a short swig of what was left, mixed with crab-apple cider, and stopped climbing to eye the lake through the burnt landscape. A thin layer of ash coated the water.

The nixie had done her part as promised. She was an old spirit in her own right who remembered when the walls of ancient Rome had gone up—Nicaeva, she'd named herself, and like ancient Angerboda, she'd carried her hatred of the old gods with her across the ages. In her younger days, Aunt Agnes had helped the water nymph track down one of the splintered remnants of the god called Dionysus who'd wronged her so long ago. Together the witches had dragged him below the water and dined on his flesh. Now, that favor had been repaid in Slud's safe passage, though Agnes suspected that the watery temptress had taken something extra for herself in the bargain. The nixie's chaste youth in the service of Artemis, Goddess of the Hunt, had long since been abandoned.

Agnes kept moving after the fire. She could sense the place where the goblin warlock had made his stand nearby, still able to hear the echo of his last psychic scream imprinted on the land. She'd used her aerial servants as her conduit, blowing through the feeble partitions in his mind and flooding him with millennia of memories and grief—enough to drive him mad in an instant if he'd marshalled the will to survive at all.

Perhaps that would be sufficient to draw the Khan out of his fortress and bring him to the field where Slud could get at him. But Agnes had heard that Arok, supposed King of the Mountain, had become paranoid and lazy, rarely leaving his great hall behind the inner stockade of the clan compound. She'd need to do more to give the troll lad his chance, but the elementals of the air had grown weary of her command, and her cracked voice had lost the timbre to properly form the intricacies of the old giant tongue.

Instead, she scooped two smoldering coals from the ground and blew fresh life into them. The coals flared orange, and the heat bit into her palms as she whispered to the spirits of the flame locked within. "Come forth. I release you from the embers."

The orange glow of burning trees framed the slope against the darkening sky. Agnes's legs worked faster to bring her across the ruined land. The day was retreating quickly, and a cold snap descended from the snow-capped crown of the mountain. It always loomed above, the mountain, reminding all who trod upon it that they were small, insignificant. At this elevation, the weather could turn in an instant, with plummeting temperatures and heavy bands of snow from previously clear skies, but the air around Agnes grew hotter as she climbed. Her hands began to vibrate, and flames sprang up between her hooked fingers. She crested the hill where the warlock had fallen and breathed in the resonance of his suffering with a shudder. The flames in her grip swelled, and the coals in her palms cracked open. Two tiny salamanders crawled out.

Agnes smiled and held them up for a closer look as the flames in her hands were consumed by the little creatures. They started to grow, feasting on the heat. They were charcoal black with smooth, shiny bodies, but as they moved to survey their surroundings, bright orange cracks showed the flow of molten lava within. In seconds, they'd already grown to fill the length of her palm, and she stooped to gently place them on the scorched forest bed. The salamanders continued to swell as the smoldering remains of fallen branches flared around them. They took a few darting steps through the ash field and lashed glowing tongues into the air.

Agnes pointed in the direction of the Rock Wolf stronghold, still half a night's walk across the ridge. "Go, follow the flames, feed on virgin forest. Soon an army will come to challenge your hunger." The salamanders scurried off toward the fire line, gathering speed and size as they went. Agnes had seen these same minor elementals grow to the size of large horses and burn hot enough to melt stone. The Rock Wolves would have to answer.

As if in protest of her actions, a wolf howl rose up from a higher slope, then another, and more followed. These were not the pinched wails of the traitorous mutts who'd bowed down to the goblins; they were the proud and sorrowful calls of the free wolves of the Pack. Their dwindling numbers had fought and died at the hands of the Rock Wolf goblins for decades, driven ever higher, though still they would not relinquish their home on the mountain. Agnes cocked her head to listen, easily finding the thunderous footfalls of her protégé moving toward the howls on the ridge.

Then a piercing howl sounded above the rest, and all the others were instantly silenced. Agnes closed her eyes and smiled. She knew this wolf. The hands of her former self had helped to birth him years past—the only pup to survive that litter, with black fur and golden eyes that looked back with recognition. His call rose and fell gradually, filled with a lifetime of rage and regret. In it, she felt the stirring of memory, the last haunting cry of Fenrir, Angerboda's son, before he'd charged to battle and devoured the one-eyed god who would slay him in turn. This alpha was the direct descendant of that Demon Wolf of yore, the last in Fenrir's line.

It seemed that the mountain intended for her two erstwhile children to meet. She doubted it would go well for both sides.

———

NEITHER-NOR STOPPED abruptly after the last wolf howl.

"Fuck." He scanned the trees and turned back to Slud with a scowl and a whisper. "You've no idea where ya brought us, do ya, troll?"

Slud made the goblin walk in front, and he still hadn't given him his weapons—figuring that the wily killer would likely stab him in the back if he was armed and had an opportunity, and that he was less likely to run away without the blades. "Goin' to de Rock Wolf walls. Sounds like we found some 'head o' time. We kill 'n' keep goin'." He unslung his ax and let the cold settle into his hands.

"Those ain't Rock Wolves, ya fool!" The goblin hunched low, and his eyes darted about the trees. "This territory belongs to the free wolves of the Pack. Goblins don't come here . . . Gimme me blades or lemme go over the edge. Can't come back from inside a wolf belly."

Slud glanced over the cliff where the forest fire flared big and bright once more, casting an orange flicker across the night slope. "Slud don't run from a few dogs." He tossed the bag of weapons and sundries to Neither-Nor's feet, and the goblin scrambled to reclaim his knives with a hint of glee overlaying the worry.

With the moon blade and gut sticker in his hands, Neither-Nor turned back to the woods where dark shapes loped silently through the trees. He rolled his neck and hocked a loogie as eyes glinted from the shadows. "These ain't normal wolves."

Slud counted over fifteen pairs of watching eyes before a curt growl sounded from upslope. The circling beasts advanced on all sides, stepping into the firelight in practiced unison, with lolling tongues and restrained snarls all around. They were the biggest wolves that Slud had ever seen, each of them almost as long as a cave bear, with shaggy manes at their shoulders and broad jaws that seemed to smile. "Oi, big lot."

Neither-Nor took a second look at the waiting ledge as the blades started to dance in his grip. He was pretty sure that if he jumped he could come back to life from the landing before the wolves could get down to him.

Slud adjusted his grip on the ax. The wood and metal felt like it was vibrating with excitement—it wanted to hit something, and these wolves would do nicely. But the upslope shadows spat out a massive shape, and two piercing golden eyes cut through the dark. It was a black wolf even bigger than the others, and its gaze seemed to glow as it laughed with a staccato snarl. Slud took a step back and cocked the ax to swing.

"Goblin scum," said the wolf in a low growl. His huge head dropped below the peaks of his shoulder blades as his intelligent eyes moved between them. His pelt was marred by countless battle scars, and the other wolves moved away from his approach. "You walk so loudly we could hear your tread from the other side of the mountain."

In the stories, Agnes had told Slud of animals that talked, but he'd never met one before. Some of his favorite tales had been about the Demon Wolf, Fenrir, who was as cunning as he was savage. He'd asked Agnes to tell him the stories of the Binding of Fenrir, and Fenrir Odin's Bane, more than a hundred times each, but that wolf had died ages past.

"Luther," said Neither-Nor with a little bow, though his blades were ready to dance. "Didn't mean no trespass. Neither-Nor was dead in a sack, and this one don't know better."

Luther's eyes held the goblin's as he sniffed. "Neither-Nor . . . We've heard of you." The other wolves pressed in with a series of yips between them, corralling the intruders closer to the drop. Luther's golden eyes moved up to Slud, and he sniffed again. "But you're no goblin."

"Nope." Slud shifted to the side and widened his grip on the handle.

"We thought your kind all dead," said the wolf, stepping closer.

"Not Slud." The cold had traveled up his arms to his chest. His breathing was steady and slow. He bounced the ax head to test the weight.

Luther eyed the ax with a hint of recognition, then returned his gaze to Slud. The wolf stopped advancing and sat on his haunches, tall enough to face Slud's chest and tower over Neither-Nor. "What of the old witch from the Iron Wood?"

"Aunt Agnes? Dead 'n' burnt, like da rest."

Luther cocked his head and an ear swiveled toward the fire that raged below. "You saw her burn?"

"Slud tossed 'er to de flames hisself."

The black wolf laughed again, hushed and without humor, and the rest of the pack yipped and snarled along with him. Slud wasn't sure what the joke was, and he was fairly certain the other wolves didn't either, but soon Luther's attempt at mirth devolved into a low growl, and the rest of the pack fell silent.

Neither-Nor had been steadily inching closer to the drop-off, but he stopped fast as Luther's gaze found him again. "Where you going, goblin?"

Slud also looked over his shoulder at his traveling companion—he bounced the ax and smacked his lips against a tusk before answering for him. "Neider-Nor's takin' Slud to de Rock Wolf camp." He turned back to Luther and stepped closer—just within ax reach. The other wolves bristled but

Slud ignored them. "Gonna kill de Khan 'n' every fuckin' goblin or wolf dat gets in de way," he answered. "Sounds to Slud like dat's not yer lot, but we'll let de ax decide, if ya prefer?"

Luther flashed his teeth in something between a snarl and a grin. Slud grinned back. The wolf's snout lowered, and his ears flattened against his head as the surrounding wolves rose in a chorus of growls. Neither-Nor glanced between the closest threats as they readied to lunge. His blades prepared to answer as he took a backward step toward the drop. But the alpha wolf produced a curt snarl and the other wolves froze in confusion. They looked to their leader for more, but the black wolf still hadn't taken his eyes from Slud. Reluctantly, some of them began to turn away, retreating back up the mountain.

The giant gray wolf closest to Luther let out a questioning whimper, and the alpha lunged with a ferocious snapping of his jaws into her haunches. She instantly took off, yipping into the shadows with her tail tucked low. The other stragglers bolted, disappearing into the dark as quickly as they'd come. Luther was the only wolf that remained. Slud and Neither-Nor still didn't lower their weapons.

The black wolf turned back to Slud. "Kill the Khan, what then? You become king of goblins?"

"Slud don't know de future, just know what he gotta do."

"Go, then. Kill them all, and the wolves of the Pack will come to eat the corpses. You are free to pass through our territory this once."

"Ain't yer territory, wolf." Slud looked up at the tallest peak where Agnes said his people had once lived. "All kings—trolls, goblins, or wolves—dat mountain'll be here long after we bleed out on 'er slopes." He swung the ax shaft to his shoulder with one hand, and the curved, two-headed blade at his ear rang with unspent energy. "Sooner or later, we all gotta choose—run, bow down, or die."

Luther dipped his head in what was almost a bow. "Tell Agnes the debt is paid when you see her."

"Slud ain't plannin' to die so soon," he countered.

The wolf's smile was unsettling, even to Slud. "Death cares not for your plans, troll. You above all must know that." Luther turned and loped away, vanishing into the shadows in a few long strides. Slud lowered the disappointed ax and looked back at Neither-Nor, still wavering on the edge of the cliff.

The goblin dropped his knives at his sides. "Who the fuck're ya?"

Slud shrugged and kept walking. "Don't know yet, but aimin' to find out."

ELEVEN

Watchers on High

THE ENDLESS HAMMERING of drums in the clearing below made Dingle's cage vibrate. Every twinge and sway sent another shock of pain through him, but he still hadn't managed to pass out. Short-Fuse and Long-Pig had beaten him stupid before they'd locked him in and hoisted him up—dangling now a hundred feet above the cobbles from the lowest branch of the Clan tree at the heart of the compound. Other unfortunates were rotting in the cages around him, each offering a window into his short, horrendous future.

The goblin-shaped cages were lined with inward-facing spikes. Designed to keep Dingle's arms, body, and head pinned in place, with needlelike points poking at his skin in a hundred spots. If he moved at all they would draw blood, but the spikes weren't long enough to kill if he moved a lot. He was locked in a seated position with enough support to keep him alive while the elements tenderized his flesh. The birds circled, their dark eyes always watching. His naked feet hung below for the biting flies.

The cages had been built with an average-sized goblin in mind. Luckily for Dingle he was far from it, unlike his closest neighbor who'd been an overweight brute with obvious ogre blood in his family line. That cage was overflowing with red, pecked-up meat. It looked like a giant sausage had burst out of its sack, covered now in a rustling blanket of black feathers. The crows had taken up residence atop the cage, and had already eaten the goblin's face and fingers. The swarms of grackles dove and swooped about his legs, pecking the flies from the rotten flesh.

The big corpse would satisfy the crows for a while, but the flies and some of the other birds preferred fresh blood and warm meat. With the press of spikes at the back of his head, Dingle raised his gaze to find the particularly large raven that had taken up roost among the higher branches. That bird had been watching him with those pitiless eyes behind its broad dagger of a beak all afternoon. He knew it wouldn't be long before it came pecking.

So far, Dingle wasn't bleeding too badly—mostly just from the fists and kicks of the goblin guards prior to his hanging. The alarming sway of the cage had gone with the wind, but the flies that gathered instead were relentless. Every bite on his ankles was like the prick of a salted pin, and when he kicked out or banged his legs together, the spikes drew more trickles down his back to further tempt the raven.

The cage spun slowly with the latest useless flail of his leg, and he got a good view of another dangling neighbor—reduced now to tattered rags over bones with a last few strands of old flesh and hair clinging to the skull. Dingle spun on and came face-to-face with another goblin staring bug-eyed back at him. This unfortunate soul was somehow still alive, but he had already descended into full-blown madness with only one extra day of suffering.

Dingle had met this goblin on occasion when he'd gone to Clan Center to buy his eggs in the past. He'd carried the widest variety of eggs in all sizes and colors and had labeled himself the finest egg connoisseur in the whole clan. Though Dingle could rarely afford his offerings and found the chubby merchant officious in his dealings, he wouldn't wish this fate on anyone. He couldn't imagine what offense the egg seller might have committed to cross the Khan and wind up here.

Someone had chopped off his fingers, toes, and manhood before he'd been locked up and hung. The spikes had pierced his belly and jowly head with a constant drip of red, and Dingle had been forced to listen as the big raven had eaten his ears, nose, lips, and eyelids—hence the bug-eyed stare. Once the frantic screaming had turned to an even more disturbing laughter, the raven, and even the flies, had inexplicably left him alone to bleed and mumble.

"They're coming, they're coming, to get your tongue strumming. It stings when the wings come to make your mouth sings," he sang with his gaze locked on Dingle. "The raven comes first, his pecks are the worst. The crows come next and make you most vexed. But the maggots come last, and they don't eat you fast." He laughed as he spun out of Dingle's view.

The little goblin tried to block out this nightmarish reality he'd been elevated into, wondering how it was possible that he'd been able to ignore all of this horror for years as he'd gone about his business unaware and uncaring below. He looked down past his knees to the world he'd come from, but the movement drew blood on his forehead. Still, he could tell that hundreds, maybe even thousands had gathered in Clan Center, and the rhythmic pounding of the drums swelled again as another core of wolf riders and their accompanying drum team joined in.

All of this was for Slud, all because Dingle had delivered

his message to the Khan. All designed to display the strength of the Rock Wolf Clan, though Dingle knew now that it only showed their weakness. He tried to spit down upon them, but his lip was fat from the beating. The foamy tendril he'd been able to muster dangled uselessly before dropping onto his own thigh.

The flutter of wings sounded behind him, and the cage jostled as something heavy landed on the bars above his head. He glimpsed the movement of black feathers, but he couldn't raise his chin to face the raven's emotionless gaze one last time. He contemplated shouting, but clenched his eyes tightly instead, waiting for the first stab of its beak. The cage wobbled, and the spikes jammed into his earlobe, but no peck came . . .

His eyes snapped open as the sound of a bowstring released above him. He saw a golden bolt skewer a grackle as it swooped between the legs hanging from the overstuffed cage. The black bird snatched a fly from the dead goblin's ankle just as the bolt caught it through the back, but its fishtailing plummet was stopped short by a shimmering thread that trailed back to the cage behind the bolt's fletching. Dingle glimpsed a goblin's hands pulling up the golden thread—long, sharply trimmed claws and spiraling tattoos of jagged letters that wound about the wiry wrists and knuckles.

The pierced grackle was still jerking as it was raised toward Dingle. Its trembling wing slipped between bars and clipped him in the nose as it passed, triggering an abrupt sneeze. Spikes jammed into his skull above his brow before a handful of others dug in to the back of his head with the recoil. The wash of fresh pain made his vision go white for a moment before the warm buzz settled over him again. When sight returned he saw the hands carefully remove the bolt from the bird before stuffing the kill in a leather satchel beneath a black-feathered robe. For an instant he saw a thin quiver with two more golden bolts. Then a small crossbow came into view, clipped by its handle to a braided wolf-hair belt, before the robe closed over it with a wall of black feathers. The goblin deftly slid down the bars before Dingle's view.

It was the hex doktor that Dingle had seen beside Big Boss Harog on the burning mountainside. The apprentice turned his engorged eye on Dingle, and an unpleasant shudder passed through the scout with sharp pricks at numerous spots along his back and shoulders. Dingle was too far gone to think it particularly odd that this goblin would willingly perch outside of his cage more than a hundred feet above camp. He tried to say something, anything, but his mouth couldn't yet form words in the wake of the evil eye.

"Still alive," the apprentice observed. "Ya heal quick, don't ya? Beatin' like that would kill most."

Dingle averted his gaze from the enlarged black eye that bored into him. Instead, he found the continued gaze of the raven on the branch above. It cocked its head and opened its beak as if it was about to say something. "D-d-do you th-th-think you could shoot a b-b-bolt at that bird?"

The apprentice adjusted his hold on the bars and glanced over his shoulder at the raven. Its head ticked to the other side, but it still hadn't closed its beak. "No shootin' that bird. Bad luck's all that'll get ya." He waved a hand toward it. "YA! Be gone with ya, devil! Go back to yer master!"

The raven took a hop toward them along the branch and let out a loud squawk that echoed about the canopy. It closed its beak and lowered its head like it was going to attack, but then straightened again and turned away, as if hearing something off in the night. Dingle was shocked when it unfurled its giant wingspan, at least three times as wide as Dingle was tall. He instinctively tried to back away, piercing his skull and shoulder blades again as the bird dove from the perch, but the flutter of feathers carried it sailing overhead. With an audible flap it lifted away through the trees, and rattled off another piercing squawk before it disappeared completely into the gathering evening shade.

"Goodbye, raven king, come again to hear me sing!" called the insane egg seller from his nearby cage.

Dingle looked back to the apprentice. "Th-th-thanks." But the apprentice was reaching through the bars of the cage with a little blade at the end of an outstretched finger. He sliced across Dingle's chest without warning.

Dingle yelped, jerking into a back full of the spikes. His vision went white again before the warm tingle spread across his torso on both sides. When he could see, the apprentice was filling a small glass vial with the blood that spilled from the fresh cut, his big eye locked on the wound with penetrating focus.

The vial and finger blade slipped back into the satchel below the feathers, and the apprentice adjusted his hold on the cage once more. "Ya spoke of a witch in the Iron Wood when ya first saw this Slud . . . Did ya take anythin' from her house? Did she give ya somethin' to eat or drink?"

The apprentice spoke with an intensity that made Dingle nervous, but he doubted his lot in life could get much worse than his present predicament. He remembered the awful taste of the gold-flecked potion he'd sampled—the potion that had been made by the witch for Slud. Dingle nodded, with a spike jabbing him in the bridge of his nose.

The apprentice's hand slipped into his robe once more, and this time it came out with a little key. He reached between the bars toward Dingle's neck and slipped it in the inner lock that held the spike mold around his head. With a turn the spikes blissfully clanged away from his skull and throat. His neck popped as he rolled it with a gratified sigh.

"Can help ya, goblin. I'm Chief Doktor now . . . Just start at the beginnin'. Ya tell Fixelcrick everythin'."

WITH ANOTHER slow flap of his wings, the raven crossed over the spiked-log wall of the outer stockade and left the sprawling Rock Wolf stronghold behind. The Raven Lord navigated through the maze of dark trees by instinct; his eyes were always scanning below. They didn't need the light from the torches or forest fire to take in every detail of the land and life that he passed over. A flurry of short flaps brought the giant black bird swooping up through the higher branches. As he slipped above the canopy, the world opened around him.

The night sky was clear heading away from the mountain. Stars clustered in a thick shining band that cut the horizon, but behind his tail feathers the mountain was socked in with rolling clouds above the tall peak. The temperature had plummeted. The air smelled like snow. A storm was coming, and it made the ancient bird uneasy.

Muninn was his name, and he did not forget. He'd sat at the shoulder of Wotan the Wise, and whispered counsel in his ear at the dawn of the age of man. He'd stood proudly, across from his brother, Huginn, and the symbol of the twin ravens had spurred the hearts of the followers and sent fear to the heads of the faithless. He'd flown above the field at Ragnarok as the giants stormed down from the Jötunheim and the Demon Wolf pierced the dark with his infernal howl.

Something in the air this night made him remember those dark days. Perhaps it was the stink of death in the wind or maybe the beat of the war drums, but when the black wolf howled again from a higher ridge, Muninn heard the echo of monstrous Fenrir in the call. By the end of the reign of the gods, his master was called the Allfather, Odin One-Eye. Muninn remembered the sight of the Demon Wolf's jaws around the old man's waist, breaking his back with a ferocious shake just as Odin released his spear with a killing blow in return.

Muninn did not like this black wolf that reminded him of the other; he did not like remembering those old days at all. But his new master, who he and Huginn had followed now for only four centuries, sent him to watch over the activities on the mountain more and more, and the old memories returned amid the cold air beneath the towering peak.

Soon, Muninn would return to eat more of the caged goblins and bask in their suffering. Soon, the army of the Rock Wolf would march out to crush the last remnant of the Demon Wolf's line. Muninn would watch the black mutt bleed out on his precious mountain, and he would peck the golden eyes from its head and remember the old prayers for Odin's blessing as he tilted the prize down his gullet.

A single crisp, clear note of a flute sounded again, carried through the night from far across the land. Soon, Muninn would return to the high country to watch and remember, but now, his master, the High King of the Fae, called the raven brothers home.

THE IMMENSE GATES of the outer stockade wall creaked open, and a raucous cheer joined the incessant pounding of the drums. A swarm of goblins riding broken wolves spilled forth, filling the night with a chorus of yips, hollers, and howls. Snow had begun to fall across the high reaches, and the tops of the trees were already white and sagging. It was beautiful, but the wind had started to gather again, this time from above rather than below, and now with a frigid bite in each gust.

Luther had climbed quickly from the odd meeting with the troll as the rest of the Pack struggled to keep up. A few clung at his heels, trying to impress, but he only had a mind for the events that unfolded across the mountain.

He'd led them to the upper slope where the trees thinned and the vantage opened, but his keen eyes had lost count of the enemy behind branches and distance. He turned away from the emerging army to watch the spear of flame that advanced along the lower ridge to meet them. Even from afar, it looked like the fire had a will of its own, darting strangely from tree to tree and consuming the towering pines with ravenous appetite.

Luther swiveled his ear, and for a moment he heard a harsh whisper clinging to the air. The Wolf King didn't like it. A low growl hung perpetually in his gut; he needed to kill something and eat its flesh to relieve the tension. Luther was always hungry. After years of forcing it, he'd finally acquired a taste for goblin meat, something the other wolves of the Pack had yet to join him in. For Luther, all that stringy tendon and muscle had become better than deer. He was half tempted to run down there and dig into the first goblin he found, but the thousands behind it, and the traitorous mutt beneath each one, stayed the impulse.

Sometimes Luther longed to let the savage craving in his belly be his guide, but he was afraid to give in to it fully, unsure if he'd ever be able to stop once it was released. The rest of the Pack was counting on him; there were only twenty-seven free wolves left. His failure as their king was almost complete.

Hundreds of his kind had been captured and locked behind those walls, abused into servitude or broken into thrall by the goblin warlocks. Hundreds more had been born and raised in goblin kennels, trained to cannibalize the weak wolves in their own litters and feed on the old and injured after that. They'd become twisted, craven things, and Luther hated them even more than the goblins who had made them that way. He'd killed almost as many of his own kind as he had the real enemy, but he'd never seen so many of them march at once.

Dark magick was at work this night. The suicidal troll and renegade goblin had something to do with it all, but Luther didn't yet see what. Whatever was happening, it was not the free wolves' fight. This was not a battle that the Pack could win.

The whispers in the wind found his ear again, closer than they'd been before, words he did not recognize. The Pack was jumpy, and the omega female started to growl and bristle with her gaze locked on the tree line below. She was the daughter of the former alpha pair, before Luther had come to challenge and lead. They had fought back against his claim and lost, but rather than bow down before his ferocity, they'd joined the sworn enemy of the wolf in their defeat. Now they sat at the feet of the Khan himself, alpha pair of the broken wolves. Their pup had been left to fend for herself.

The omega female ate last and had not yet been permitted

to mate. Her once beautiful gray pelt had been marked by numerous bites and scratches from Luther and others over the years, but she still carried the keenest senses of them all, and she never wavered in battle despite her stooped and cowering stature at home.

Luther followed her gaze to see a night-hag climb up from the trees with a sharpened pine stick jabbing the snow-covered ground with every step. The hag's obsidian skin stood out against the white backdrop, and she continued a string of hushed words that echoed back from above as another icy gust lashed branch and fur. The other wolves noticed the approach and joined the omega's defensive stance with a barrage of snarls. All but Luther.

He'd never seen this hag, bent and bony beneath her ragged covering of leathers and furs, but he'd only seen such magick once before when he'd been a pup himself. Something of this witch reminded him of that one, and a sense of foreboding crept over him as she stepped closer. It seemed the dark fates that swirled about the mountain did not intend to let him escape so easily. The wind quieted as her whispered words ceased, and Luther finally caught her familiar scent—wet, roiled earth mixed with spices, blood, and wood smoke.

Her sharp-angled face split into a wicked smile with long, pointy teeth as she bowed before him. "Good evening, Wolf King," she said as the Pack circled and bared their fangs in return. "You may not recognize Agnes, but we've met before, yes? It was old Agnes who pulled the little black pup from yer mum's belly. Agnes who saved you from a goblin war party many moons ago."

He'd only been a few years old when he'd first met her. She'd been hunched and withered then, though she'd appeared out of the night without fear just as a large Rock Wolf hunting party attacked. The goblins and their twisted wolves had come from behind, intent on killing the young and old at the rear as the Pack moved across the slopes in search of a new den. The spirits of the air had carried the old witch as she descended from above and spoke harsh words that turned the broken wolves against their riders.

After the goblins had been torn apart or run screaming, the possessed beasts of the clan turned on each other, ripping out throats and bellies until none survived. Luther had never felt so hungry or alive as he had watching the carnage of that moment. Afterward, the witch spoke to him, and he realized that he understood her language, and could even form words of his own in response. She'd told him that he was not like other wolves, the last descendant of a great line of kings. His name would be Luther Ever Hungry, son of Magyard the Mad, son of Hrumox Doom Hound, son of Skoll Sun-Eater, son of Fenrir Odin's Bane—all marked by the blood of the demon coursing through them.

"I remember," Luther growled as the rest of the Pack waited for his order to attack.

She eyed them without fear. "The Rock Wolves march; it is time for the enemies of the clan to strike." Her wicked smile did not fade.

"The Pack cannot fight an army. We defend our territory—attack fast and retreat before the enemy can regroup. Keep moving or die."

"Chasing your tail like a common dog," she hissed. "You sully the noble blood of your fathers."

Luther's ears swiveled forward, and he stood taller. "We are only nineteen hunters left; fewer than that wait for us back in the den. Last spring, only four small pups were born. Some of them will not last the winter."

"Your seed is weak," she said with a dark chuckle. "I can make you a potion to give you powerful sons, if you wish."

The dormant growl that had been lingering in his gut climbed out, and the fur on his mane bristled. "Do not taunt me, witch."

At once, Agnes rose up from her hunch to twice her previous height. Long, black, curving claws emerged from her sleeves, and the pine staff fell away at her side. "*Hic-thnah drächt thu ghul,*" she said.

It felt like the lash of a whip across Luther's mind, and the other wolves immediately fell prostrate and whimpering. Luther snarled through the pain and held his ground—noticing that only the omega female also remained standing and defiant. The troll-hag gave her a look and chuckled again, flexing her claws before turning back to Luther.

"I do not ask, Wolf King . . . Perhaps I make you eat your friends until your stomach bursts, yes? Shall we test how much it takes to fill that ravenous hunger you carry?" But the pain in Luther's mind receded, and the pitiful whimpering of his fellows ceased. When she spoke again, the words were softer, though the threat behind them had not diminished. "Forces move against the clan soon, and you will move with them one way or another."

Luther shook off her lingering presence in his mind with a snarl. "You mean your pet troll? Doesn't even know you live, yet he follows your bidding."

The hag smiled with something resembling pride. "He was sent to me by the mountain itself. It is not my bidding he follows."

"He's been sent to his death," Luther countered.

Agnes shrugged. "That is up to him, I merely point the direction and help to clear the way." She turned back to the omega female who continued her vigilant stance. "Make this one your bitch, Wolf King, and a pup will follow to deserve that blood you carry." She raised her arms at her sides, and the bitter wind gusted again. "When the snow's piled high, and the fire's cleaved their number in two—you will strike or I will return to take back the gift I've given you."

With that, the wind took hold of her, lifting her from the slope to disappear into the snow-filled sky.

TWELVE

Drink Before the War

A SYMPHONY of high-pitched chirps rose and fell behind Fix-elcrick in a steady wave. The male crickets made the sound by rubbing their wings together. Most of the time it was just a mad cacophony of competitive noise, but every so often the various calls aligned to form a sort of undulating music. It happened rarely, but when it did it was usually followed with a breakthrough in Fixelcrick's studies.

It had started snowing on his return from the hanging cages, but the perpetually large fire in the hearth kept the room hot. He'd always been better at manipulating fire than air. The warmth made the male crickets horny and loud as they claimed little territories throughout the pen and tried to attract mates. Almost a thousand of them covered the moss-, stick-, and stone-clad terrain he'd built. Even more remained beneath, in the dense maze of dens they'd dug in the hard-packed earth. Some had long since leapt over the thatch wall, making homes amid the books and bed sheets. Fixelcrick had learned to live with them, but the other two apprentices assigned to the space had fled for other housing. Now that he was the de facto chief of the hex doktors, he wouldn't have to worry about roommates again.

He assessed his prized possession; the feathered coat hung

on a gold hook in front of him. *Outer left wing could use a fuller reach.* He peeled his eyes from his life's work and dropped the dead grackle into the gold basin on the table. He used golden tweezers to pluck the longest feather he could find, and he leaned over the thatch wall to snatch a couple of noisy bull crickets midchirp. Fixelcrick rubbed the shiny back of the first against the spine of the feather—up and down its length repeatedly before he tossed the bug in his mouth with a crunch. The cricket oil kept the feathers shiny and free of parasites, and to stay pure he'd been on a strict diet of nothing but crickets and water for months. The second cricket he brushed against the black vanes of the feather until it took on a bluish sheen in the firelight. He examined his work, turning it this way and that. Satisfied, he tossed that cricket back to the pen to sing and breed another day.

He was fastidious about every addition he made to the coat; his masterwork was almost complete. The gold needle and thread waited on the table beside the basin, but as always he needed a little blood for the quill end of the feather before he stitched it in place. Usually he pricked a finger with a needle for that purpose, but on a hunch he went back to his satchel and took out the little cork-stopped vial he'd used to collect a sample of the doomed goblin scout's blood. He held the glass tube before the fire and gave it a shake; it looked like regular blood.

Bone Master twitched on the bed in the corner as the old goblin's endless muttering took on a more fervent tone. The withered old fellow's remaining eye stared through the ceiling like it wasn't there. Before that morning, the master had shown the greatest knack for the arts that Fixelcrick had ever known, but the witch who had done this to him wielded the wind like the warlocks of legend. She had to be the same witch that the little goblin, Dingle, had seen at the burned house—the same one who had concocted the potion that Dingle had tasted.

Fixelcrick had watched as the cut he'd made across Dingle's chest had resealed in minutes. He'd never seen anything like it before. He removed the stopper from the vial and dipped the sharp point of the feather in to dye the tip red. The gold thread slid through the needle with practiced precision, and Fixelcrick pierced the quill just above the blood line and dragged the thread through. He moved to the coat with a bowed head as he tied an intricate knot, and knelt beside the draped layers with a low note vibrating in his diaphragm.

His nimble hands brought the feather to its place along the outer row and began to stitch it into the patchwork lining. He worked quickly, binding it with thread and intent to the feathers in the row beside it. With the last knot he leaned over and kissed the new addition, just as he had all the others before it.

Usually, he'd put the coat on to activate it and assess his work, but this time the feathers began to ruffle and twitch of their own accord. A jagged-toothed grin cracked across his face as the long flaps of the coat flared like a couple of wings readying for takeoff. He couldn't wait. He grabbed it from the hanger and slid his arms through the draped sleeves, immediately feeling the energy swell around him. The coat was alive; it wanted to fly. Fixelcrick didn't need to call the spirits of the air to master the wind. With his far-seeing eye, he peered out the small window they used for sunlight rituals and picked out the little caged goblin high up in the shadows of the Clan tree.

Of course, that was when one of the Khan's idiot lackeys banged on the door with something metallic and heavy. Fixelcrick had little patience for clan duties on a normal day; interruption now was inexcusable. His grin turned to a sneer as he marched to the wooden door and flung it open. "Fuck you want?"

The runner averted his eyes to avoid the piercing stare of the far-seer, and the spindly goblin spoke with emotionless clarity. "Arokkhan says Chief Doktor's gotta report to Short-Fuse at the front." He turned and ran away before Fixelcrick could respond.

Fixelcrick snarled at his back, wishing a pox on him and his family, before slamming the door and latching it again. He glanced over to Bone Master, still muttering and trembling, and then to the vial of blood waiting in the gold basin beside the grackle. In a flurry of activity he dove into his desk, tearing through drawers of paper, charms, jars, and bobbles. In the third drawer he found the little wooden box he was looking for.

He hurried to the basin and opened the box to reveal a delicate syringe of gold and glass within. There wasn't much of Dingle's blood left, but the syringe sucked up what remained. The Master's voice rose up in an indecipherable string. "*Hicthnah shuk-tuk decrahn hĕcht,*" he blurted, just before the fire flared oddly and the crickets went silent.

Fixelcrick froze. He didn't know the words, but he could tell they held the Knack. The air itself seemed charged with potential as he eyed the old goblin, waiting for something more. But the prone figure remained prone, and the fire receded as the muttering returned to hushed whispers. The crickets began to chirp again, but no longer did their individual songs rise and fall in unison.

The master's words had sounded like those whispered from afar by the witch in the wind. Everything led back to her. Fixelcrick could inject Bone Master; maybe he could revive him so that he would have to answer the Khan's demands and leave the first apprentice to his important work. Instead, he jabbed the needle into the heart of the dead grackle and pushed the plunger.

Nothing happened for a long moment ... then a wing twitched. The bird's beak opened, and its drooping neck ticked upright. Fixelcrick's big eye widened further as the grackle began to screech and flutter frantically. Its yellow eyes darted about the room in terror. The grackle knocked the basin over and fell to the floor, its wings and legs flailing as it skittered across the dirt. Fixelcrick danced away with a shriek of his own, and grabbed a bucket from beside the fire. The handle was hot enough to burn his fingers, but he held on anyway as he brought it up and smashed it down on the screaming bird again and again. Finally, with the third dull thud, the reanimated beast stopped moving, and he dropped the makeshift weapon at his side with a hard swallow.

He stared at the twice-dead thing, waiting for it to move again. When it didn't, his eyes moved across the floor to the syringe lying in the dirt beneath the table. He needed more of Dingle's blood. *Fuck me master. I'll show the Khan what a real warlock can do!*

SLUD BRUSHED SNOW from his bearskin coat and peered out from between the sagging limbs of a towering white pine. The flakes were coming down wet and heavy, and the long-reaching branches were bent all the way to the ground, providing some protection from the wind and the eyes of the enemy.

Neither-Nor couldn't sit still, busying himself with cutting away some of the smaller branches and shoring up the tight perimeter. He tried to block out the fact that thousands of his sworn enemies were marching by only a few hundred paces away.

Slud watched as the last of the riders ambled out of the clan compound followed by a ragtag collection of goblins banging on drums without the faintest notion of rhythm. The tall gate began to swing shut again behind them, and Slud was half tempted to break cover, slide down the last little drop to the lower ridge, and make a run for it. Instead, Neither-Nor whacked him across the back with a severed branch, and he turned around to eye the ornery little bastard.

"So sorry, ya majesty," the goblin muttered. "Don't wish to interrupt yer important stare down of that army ya wanna pick a fight with." He jammed the branch into the snow to block a hole in the cover. "No doubt they're quakin' in their saddles just feelin' those hard eyes upon 'em."

Slud chuckled on his way to the trunk and flopped down to the cold earth beside it. "Quit fidgetin' 'n' take a seat, goblin. Rock Wolf ain't gonna see us here, 'n' de cold ain't gonna back off cause ya stuck a few twigs in de way."

"Good thing ya found us a spot where we can't have a fire then, ain't it, ya big genius?" the goblin countered. "Half the fuckin' forest's burnin', but we're sittin' damp-assed in the cold a stone's throw from a few thousand killers."

Slud didn't bother with a response, instead digging through his sack to retrieve the two jugs of pine ale he'd taken from Groole's dead crew. He tossed one to the goblin and bit the cork off the other. He spat it away and took the first stinging swig of the spicy brew. He actually missed the foul taste and unpredictable effects of Agnes's mushroom additives, but the harsh booze sent the warming sensation through him that he was looking for.

Neither-Nor frowned before biting the cork from the other jug and taking a seat against the tree beside Slud. "So this is the big plan, eh? Walk up to the front door and get drunk. Fuckin' brilliant." The goblin shut his mouth with a few hard gulps and a soft shiver.

Slud still wanted to hit something with his new ax, but he was starting to appreciate Neither-Nor's unflaggingly negative demeanor. He'd never actually spent this much time with anyone besides Agnes before. The huge double-bladed head was ringing expectantly on the ground at his side, but he took another gulp of the harsh brew and wiped the drip with the back of his cold hand. The ax would have to wait just a little while longer.

The ale had rancid clumps of fermented pine needles in it and burned going down. Slud had always preferred the sweat and scorch of a good fire, but with a little booze the cold didn't bother him much either. Agnes had made him spend a few nights naked and alone in the Iron Wood every winter since he was five. Each time, she'd dose him with another of her potions first, modifying the concoction as he'd grown accustomed to the torture. The last few years she'd started getting creative before sending him into the cold, just to add a challenge. Once she'd cut him across his back with a jagged knife, and another time she'd starved him for a week leading up to the test. Last winter she'd blown a powder made from dried flowers into his eyes before kicking him down the snowy steps. He couldn't see anything for a full day and night as a freak blizzard pounded their little valley, as if called down by Agnes herself.

"So, ya was at de battle 'tween de Moon Blades 'n' Blood Claws, eh?" Slud asked.

The scarred goblin gave him a hateful glance between gulps. "Yeah, I was there . . . Trolls like to raise up for an overhead smash with yer stupid, two-handed weapons. I slide in low and open up yer bellies with me moon blade 'fore ya can swing. Spilled five sets o' steamin' guts at me feet 'fore yer big fuckin' king cut me in two." He raised the jug in a toast. "Last thing I remember 'fore a Moon Blade doktor found me and put me two halves back together."

The drums and howls sounded muffled and distant beyond the branches and snow. "Big troll dat killed ya—he got nine claws on 'im?" Slud asked.

"How the fuck'd I know? Wasn't countin' the nasty fucker's fingers." Neither-Nor spat, and a clump of snow fell from a branch beside him.

"He cut ya down wit' a big-ass sword look like it's on fire?"

Neither-Nor lowered the jug and fingered the hilt of his curved knife with his far hand. "Yeah. That's right . . . What d'ya know about it?"

Slud chuckled, deep and mean. "Was Slud's pop killed ya dat time."

Neither-Nor grabbed the blade and brought it up fast, but Slud just took another swig and looked down at him. "Bad angle, 'n' Slud's neck's tough . . . Betta be sure ya get t'rough it wit' de first swing, frien'."

Neither-Nor dropped the blade and snarled. "We ain't fuckin' friends. I showed ya where the Rock Wolf lives like ya asked, now lemme go. Time to put yer infernal breed back in me nightmares where ya belong."

"Nah, drink up, goblin. Slud likes yer company, 'n' we ain't done just yet." Slud took a drink himself. "Ya got lucky wit' dat stab in de back from de big goblin yesterday. See, Slud left a spot empty o' yer letters just over ya spine, here." He leaned away from the tree and jabbed a thumb into the small of his own back above the belt to show where. "Fret not, Slud's got yur map hid away safe if ya do just one more li'l t'ing to help him on his way."

The blood drained from Neither-Nor's face. He looked like he might scream. "Gimme the map, ya fuckin' lyin' swine!" He stood, still not reaching up to Slud's chest even though the troll was seated. His hand groped at his back, feeling for the scars of the runes cut there, searching for the hole. "I only came with ya cause ya said ya did me whole!"

"Quiet, li'l fella." Slud brought a finger to his tusked maw and motioned toward the hidden army that continued to march beyond the branch wall. "Dem bad wolves got good hearin'."

"I swear to whatever gods might listen, I'm gonna see ya dead before this is through, troll!" Neither-Nor whisper-shouted.

"Might be," Slud answered. "But when Slud was watchin' de march, ain't no Khan walked out of dem doors wit' dat army."

"So fuckin' what?" Neither-Nor sat back down in a huff and chugged his ale.

"So, dat leaves de Khan sittin' in his big hall wit' all his blades out stuck in de snow, pissin' at fires 'n' lookin' fer us," Slud said with a wicked smile creeping across his face.

"Yeah, so?"

"So, dis ax'll chop t'rough dat wall in seconds. Slud'll cut down de Khan 'fore his big fuckin' clan even knows what 'ap-pened."

"That's it, eh? All figured out, easy as pie," Neither-Nor said. "Then ya don't need me fer nothin.'"

"Oh, dere's plenty o' guards still mannin' dose towers 'n' watchin' dat hall. No doubt, dey got horns 'n' bells fer callin' home de troops right quick. Slud saw ya 'gainst dat huntin' party. Ya kill good, goblin. Yer fast 'n' quiet, 'n' dat's what Slud needs to grease de way. Yer blades, 'n' dis ax, we'll take dat t'rone 'fore anyone's de wiser." Slud raised his jug in the direction of the clan, and tilted back the swill with a gulp. He felt nice and warm. "Ya do dat, 'n' de map's yers. Hell, Slud'll finish ya up proper hisself. Take wha'ever ya want when it's t'rough, or ya can stay on, be head goblin just like ya used to."

Neither-Nor had a glassy look as he chugged the last few gulps of his own jug. He tossed the empty bottle in the snow, a little disappointed that it didn't break. "Yer fuckin' mad as a foamin' weasel, ain't ya?"

Slud thought about it for a moment and shrugged. "Yeah, may very well be."

THIRTEEN

Elements of Surprise

SHORT-FUSE HATED wolves. When he and Long-Pig had first come to the mountain looking for employment with the ruling clan of the horde, they hadn't taken into account the origins of the clan name. Rock wolves, to his thinking, were filthy, mean-spirited dogs undeserving of the food and space wasted on them, let alone a place of reverence—blazoned on every banner and seated at the foot of the Khan's throne. For the fat goblin and his tall, mute friend, riding on the bony, stinking backs of these wretched beasts was akin to torture.

Morning's light had finally come. Short-Fuse had spent the night freezing, wet, and miserable. His ass felt like it had been hit repeatedly with a club. The wolf beneath him struggled with every step, sinking up to the top of its legs in the heavy snow. Short-Fuse's boots left a trail on both sides, and his toes had gone numb. Some of the goblins around him spoke to their mounts by name, but the toad-faced goblin didn't care if his wolf was a he or a she—only an it. He jammed the heel of his boot into its side again, daring it to snarl or look back. "Get a fuckin' move on, mutt."

After hours of such abuse, his boot had ripped away all the fur in that spot, leaving a surprisingly pale patch of bald skin. His latest heel-strike had drawn blood, but not enough for his liking. Short-Fuse fingered the handle of one of his hatchets and imagined swinging it into the wolf's skull: the dull thunk of the blade through bone, and that first spurt of blood. Then the way its legs would give out as his weight drove its snout down into the snow. The thought of all that white powder soaking red sent a twinge to his balls. Aside from a little torture and a couple beatings, he hadn't gotten to dole out any really good violence for a couple days. It made him antsy.

He wanted to see this "troll" for himself. *Prob'ly jus' a big goblin in need of a bad death.* He'd see how big it was once he'd hurled a couple hatchets into its chest. And if Neither-Nor had really returned, Short-Fuse would relish watching Long-Pig eat the scarred goblin's flesh.

He'd seen his cold-minded compatriot down an entire corpse over the course of a day. Once, a few years back, when they'd worked for the Yellow Fang Clan, the two of them had murdered a real shitsack of a goblin merchant with powerful friends, and Long-Pig had disposed of that body even faster. Afterward, the silent killer had ground the merchant's bones into dust and added it to his gruel the next morning. Even the legendary Neither-Nor wouldn't come back from that.

Short-Fuse blew his nose into his hand and wiped it on the wolf's fur as he scanned the woods ahead. They'd been told to expect the full attack of an entire clan, but so far there'd been nothing else moving on the mountain except the wind and cold. He wasn't even sure where they were going, just moving forward until someone attacked—more like a big herd of idiot sheep than a pack of wolves.

The goblins at the edges of the loose formation had been jumping at shadows all night. They all knew the story of how the elves had tried to erase the Blood Claw name from history twenty years past. The old tales of vicious giants and the terrifying magick of the troll-hags came back now, hovering uneasily in their thoughts as the trees creaked and the wind howled around them. With all their wealth and long unchallenged power, the Rock Wolf Clan had gotten soft and lazy. Only a few of the wide-ranging hunting packs had seen any real combat in years. Short-Fuse doubted there was a goblin among the thousands of warriors behind him who could take him in a fight—except Long-Pig, of course.

Some of them were big enough and certainly looked the part, with their shiny weapons and tough costumes, but when it came down to it, they'd all rather be drinking by a good fire than spilling guts in the cold. Short-Fuse agreed with the drinking and cold parts, but he'd never be able to give up gutspilling. Violence was the only thing that had ever truly made sense to him.

How the hell had someone put him and Long-Pig in charge of an army? They despised armies. Rules and marching had never been their thing. Usually, if someone tried to tell them what to do, they'd kill them before the day was done. But this time around, he and Long-Pig had put up with the Khan's degenerating behavior for almost a year. No one else had ever willingly provided such time and space to really experiment with killing. The Khan had an inspired flair for doling out pain, and he liked it slow and messy, which worked just fine for them. Now they lived in the warmth and comfort of the Big Boss's great hall, killing by day and drinking to oblivion every night. It was the best their lives had ever been and they didn't want to lose it, but this army shit was beginning to test their patience.

Short-Fuse had seen the Khan's fickle whim turn on his

closest advisors and trusted friends more than once. If this cold march was a test, Short-Fuse was pretty sure that he was failing. He'd gotten too used to the indoor life, more than happy to forgo the hardships of the elements. Long-Pig never complained, but Short-Fuse had already stopped the advance three times that night to piss, stretch, and try to pick a fight. The fat goblin looked over his shoulder at the few thousand would-be killers riding behind him, then back to his only friend. They'd given Long-Pig the biggest wolf the breeders could find, but it still looked absurd beneath his gangly form. The goblin's dark, dead eyes looked over at Short-Fuse's scowl, and he gave a tiny nod. That was the most emotion Short-Fuse had seen from him in weeks.

Long-Pig set his dead eyes ahead once more, and stopped his wolf abruptly with a hard tug on its neck fur. He jerked his square chin, and Short-Fuse followed to see the advance scout slogging his way back through the snow toward them. The heat from the forest fire turned the snow into dense mist that clawed through the woods at the scout's back. It almost looked like it was reaching out to swallow him up as his wolf fought to outpace its grip. The blaze made the mist glow orange behind him. Somehow, the fire had been unfazed by the foot of snow that had fallen that night.

Short-Fuse put his hand up to stop the advance again, and immediately stumbled off his mount with a groan. His thighs burned, and it felt like there was a rock lodged in the small of his back. Many others also dismounted with a wave of grumbles—half of which might very well have been directed at him. Most of them knew not to test his reputation, but hopefully someone would say something this time.

The scout's wolf struggled up an incline to the front of the march. Goblins down the line pointed toward Short-Fuse, and the scout changed directions. His wolf's heavy panting sent bursts of steam into the air as he approached. "What'd ya see?" Short-Fuse asked.

The scout shivered and his eyes were wide, but he still dipped his head in a bow before he spoke. "There's things in the fire, moving from tree to tree. I dint get too close."

Short-Fuse gave Long-Pig a glance and got nothing back. "What ya mean, *things*?"

"They're fast, an' black, don't touch the ground neither; just jumpin'." He made a leaping motion with his hand between two trees.

Short-Fuse considered killing the scout, but he couldn't see how to explain it. Instead, he turned to the goblin on his other side. This one was broad-shouldered and had clearly seen some combat. He had a battered war hammer strapped to his back and a large iron ring through his nose. The army seemed to do whatever he said, but he never seemed to have much to say. Short-Fuse was pretty sure he was the clan War Boss, but he hadn't bothered getting his name yet. "You, where's the hex doktor?"

The War Boss shrugged. "Told someone to send someone to get 'im hours ago."

"Yeah?"

The War Boss shrugged again. "Usually Harog deals wit' all dat."

"Where the fuck's Harog?" Short-Fuse asked.

The War Boss furrowed his heavy brow, notched with a thick line of scar. "Heard Khan made 'im Herald now."

Short-Fuse felt his face getting red. He was keenly aware of the weight and feel of the two hatchets holstered at his sides.

"Well, what ya normally do wit' a fire, and things jumpin' in trees?"

War Boss was trying not to shrug, but then he shrugged anyway. "Don't know 'bout dat. Don't sound right."

Short-Fuse was quickly becoming apoplectic. After marching through a blizzard all night to get here, no one actually had a clue what to do once they'd arrived. He looked to Long-Pig for something, anything, but his friend kept his gaze locked on the orange fog.

The fat goblin turned back to the stupid expression that waited on the face of the War Boss. "Then get down there and look yerself."

The War Boss looked for a moment like he was going to say something. Short-Fuse rolled his feet, trying to regain feeling; his fingers tapped the handle of one of the hatchets. The War Boss thought better of it, and turned to the goblin beside him. "Send a pack o' twenty down. Groole's group."

The other goblin shook his head. "Groole's group's dead, rememba?"

"Right . . . Filch's crew den?" the War Boss suggested.

The far goblin turned around on his wolf to shout. "Gemme Filch's pack up front, now!"

More shouting traveled through the ranks, and slowly the group parted to allow a ragtag collection of twenty mounted goblins to the front. Filch had his long brown hair tied up in a ridiculous topknot, and the tiny mosquito bites of his eyes were so far apart on his face that he looked like some kind of moron. "Yeah?" he said to the War Boss as the goblins around him grumbled and wiped their runny noses.

"Scout says somethin's in de trees." The War Boss shrugged. "Get down to de fire an' see what's what. Give 'em spears an' arrows, an' a horn blow when it's done." He pointed lazily toward the orange glow.

Short-Fuse didn't like the look of this Filch, and Filch didn't look too happy with the War Boss. Filch frowned as he turned back to the nineteen expectant goblins around him and unhooked a spear from the side of his wolf. "Bows an' spears, lads. Go slow an' look to the trees."

Short-Fuse yawned as the twenty exhausted wolves carried the cut-rate goblins into the mist. He snatched his last winesack from the back of his wolf and took a few hard gulps. As the advance pack was absorbed by the gloom, he half hoped he'd never have to see them again. It was too cold and uncomfortable to even feel the effects of the wine anymore, but he was already eyeing some of the surrounding goblins' sacks for the return journey. *Privilege of bein' in charge.*

The breeze shifted, carrying the stink of wood smoke and brimstone. He wrinkled his nose. His wolf started to growl. A wave of palpable unease spread through the ranks, but Short-Fuse didn't give it a moment's thought—until Long-Pig drew his big curving scimitar. "What's the problem, Pig? Somethin' in them trees?" he whispered.

The answer came with muffled yells and the sound of bowstrings releasing ahead, quickly followed by the screams of goblins and the high-pitched yelps of wolves. The orange glow flared brighter in a few indistinct spots, and the screaming stopped. One growing flare emerged from the mist amid a pitiful string of whimpers. It was a wolf engulfed in flames, trying to outpace the agony that silenced it a few frantic strides later. It slumped to the snow, but somehow the flames kept burning around the charring, hairless corpse.

Another hazy tree went up in the mist, its black, clawing

lines instantly cloaked in fire as if the wood was soaked in oil; then another, and the one beside that, coming closer. Short-Fuse dropped the wine-sack and gripped the handles of his hatchets as the goblins around him also unsheathed blades and drew bows. Long-Pig calmly dismounted from his wolf and took the scimitar in both hands.

Short-Fuse followed Pig's gaze to the large black creature that vaulted through the mist to the next tree before it burst into flames like the others. The thing looked like some sort of giant lizard, with creases in its obsidian hide that glowed like cinders. Its tongue burned white-hot as it licked the air, and a fresh spiral of smoke swallowed it again. Short-Fuse took a couple steps back, bumping into the snout of the wolf behind him.

"Ge' ready to fire, boys!" the War Boss shouted.

But then another of the burning things shot from the mist and landed in the instantly boiling snow farther down the line. Even from five paces out, the closest riders began to smoke and shriek. Bows and spears flew haphazardly before the War Boss got a chance to yell, "Fire!" With a darting step, the lizard charged, and the riders that stood before it were engulfed in flame.

Panic spread throughout the ranks, and Short-Fuse picked up the pace as he backed away through the ebbing throng of fighters without a moment's concern for tactics or morale. Long-Pig was moving back with him, seeing the same futility in standing his ground when there were other goblins to burn.

The tree just ahead of the line went up like a flaming geyser, and more goblin voices rose in terrified wails. This was no attacking clan; this was devil's work. Short-Fuse turned to run but stumbled back as a flutter of black feathers dropped from the sky, and the warlock apprentice came to his feet before him. The feathered goblin's evil eye looked wider than ever as he stepped toward the fire lizards with a burning branch in one hand and a blood-filled syringe in the other.

FIXELCRICK HAD NEVER been so afraid in his life. His hands shook as he forced his legs to step closer. He needed to show the Khan that he was ready to be Chief Doktor, to show the witch that he was worthy of her teaching; this was the only way. He took a deep breath and jammed the needle of the syringe straight through his breastplate and into his heart. Before he could second-guess it, he squeezed the plunger and felt a hot tingle course through his body—then the pain hit.

He had to cough, but found that he couldn't. It was like an electric current rocketing through his veins and sparking every nerve ending. He'd dissected a few bodies throughout his studies and knew the ways his blood flowed within, but never had he been so instantly aware of every faculty and function of his inner design.

All at once, his heart jolted into a hard sprint, and he felt like he was drifting upward to the point of disassociation with his body. But his thoughts remained clear and focused as his arm raised the burning branch over his head and he slipped into the old goblin tongue with an ear for pronunciation he'd never possessed before.

SHORT-FUSE TRIPPED on a wolf leg and wound up in the snow. Without thinking, he swung one of his hatchets and chopped the offending leg in two. The wolf and rider tumbled in a mess of blood and flailing, but Short-Fuse stayed down beside them as a scorching wind washed over their position. Riders scrambled back on both sides as more screaming voices rose at the front.

Only the feathered goblin advanced into the heat, stepping over Short-Fuse with a syringe buried in his chest, the burning twig held high, and strings of spit and gibberish flowing from his mouth. The air around the hex doktor crackled, and Short-Fuse could feel his hair stand on end as he passed. The downed goblin beside him was hollering angrily as he tried to free his leg from under the wolf. Short-Fuse silenced his yammering with a short swing of the other hatchet. He could smell cooked meat and burnt hair, and he felt his own cheek beginning to crisp.

He'd lost Long-Pig in the commotion of legs and arms, but the young warlock stepped toward the fire lizard undaunted. He'd always thought that the black-feathered apprentice was almost as creepy as the Bone Master he served. The apprentice locked his evil eye on the closest lizard and inexplicably lowered the burning branch to the snow.

———

FROM ON HIGH, Agnes could see over the outer stockade of the clan compound, and she did not like what she saw. She'd had the spirits of the air drop her among the highest branches of one of the thousand-year-old pines at the base of the ridge. One of her hooked hands gripped the trunk as she leaned out for a better vantage. She hadn't expected to see so many wolves and warriors left within the compound. Bowmen walked the walls and manned every tower, a hundred warriors waited just within the front door, and two packs of heavily armed riders sat at either side of the inner gate to the Khan's hall.

The troll's tracks passed the base of the tree far below with the comparatively tiny prints of his goblin companion alongside. She'd heard of the scarred goblin's exploits in her previous life: Neither-Nor, the troll slayer, fastest blade on the mountain. With him, maybe Slud could stand a chance at taking out the Khan. Perhaps the goblin killer had been sent by the mountain itself to aid their cause.

Still, the hubris of the young troll to think that the two of them could take on the entire remaining clan was confounding. *Perhaps he is not ready after all?*

She watched as the two renegade fighters emerged from the wood far below to survey the fortress before them. She could not guess what the troll had planned next, but even from the distance she could feel the bravado wafting off him—as if he somehow believed he possessed the upper hand. All she could do now was add more chaos to the fray and see how resourceful her pupil could be. A hard wind would soften the goblin nerves before she turned the cowed wolves upon their masters in the streets.

But a murmuring in the air drew her attention away. Agnes swung around to peer toward the smoke and clamor in the far distance. Something there worked against her fire minions; someone dared challenge her mastery of the arts. She shut her eyes to listen and heard the old goblin language spoken in the wind. *Another clan warlock thinks he's got talent.*

She would show them that no one of this age could defy her pull on the elements.

FOURTEEN

Blood Pressure

THE INFERNAL TRAIL of the demon lizards cut deeper into the Rock Wolf ranks; fire splitting the army in two, just as the night-hag had foretold. The Wolf King watched them dart forward through the crowd as nearby bodies charred and burst with their insides boiling over in an instant. Goblins and wolves scrambled away in a frantic press of meat. The few arrows and spears that launched true burned away before reaching the black lava hides, but most of the goblin missiles flew wild and struck other screaming Rock Wolves. The chaos of it was too much for Luther to resist.

He rocked back on his hind legs and raised his snout to the sky. All of his hatred and hunger filled the howl that pierced the valley, and the hearts of those below that still held firm broke at the sound. Thousands of eyes and ears swiveled toward him, searching for the yellow gaze of Luther Ever Hungry in the dark shadows beneath the trees.

The rest of the Pack came at the back of the army while their heads were turned. The deep snow muffled their approach, but did not slow the free wolves of the mountain. Amid a sudden barrage of snarls, seventeen throats were torn out before the Rock Wolves knew what was happening.

As the screams sounded and a horn blew in the rear, the

panicked eyes shifted again. That was when Luther and the omega female sprang over the lip of the upper ridge and sprinted through the woods toward the confused flank. The gray bitch surged ahead and tore out a big goblin's throat while she raked her claw across the eyes of its traitor wolf. In her eagerness to impress, she cracked another goblin neck with a snarl and a shake before Luther arrived.

Mid-leap, his snapping jaws took off the head of the toughest-looking goblin he could find, and it only took a moment for him to swallow the prize before striking out again at the horrified spectators. He tore off a goblin's arm and tossed it to the snow before crushing the skull of a traitor wolf with his next bite. The wide-eyed goblins hollered and stumbled back as if he burned with the same heat as the demon lizards, and he took the moment to select another big goblin for his departing leap. This one he took with a sideways bite across its broad chest. The iron tang of its blood filled his mouth as he felt its ribs break beneath his pressure. The gray bitch also took a screaming goblin with her, dragging it by its legs back into the mist as a couple arrows tried to follow.

The Wolf King's ear swiveled as the other group attacked a second spot farther along the line. This time, the shrieks of goblins and mad yelping of traitor wolves was joined by the sharp yip of one of his own. He knew that he should attack again before the goblins could regroup, but instead he savagely tore into the stomach of his catch until he'd found its entrails. The foulness of the smell and the sharp bite of the flavors had become comforting. The omega followed his lead, biting into her goblin's loin as its desperate yells became shrill screams. Her snout wrinkled at the taste, but she ripped and chewed anyway until the screaming stopped.

Perhaps the troll-hag is right about her. But the duplicitous witch who called herself Agnes could not be trusted. She had yet to appear at the battle as she'd promised, and he could never forget the way she'd made the broken wolves turn on their masters and each other long ago—he could not let this fate befall his pack.

Luther plunged his snout under the rib cage and chewed a path to the still-quivering heart. His teeth gripped the hard ball of muscle and pulled. He swallowed the heart and licked the blood from his nose as his eyes met the gaze of the gray bitch. She held her head high, panting as goblin blood dripped from her lolling tongue. Luther was not one for affection or sentiment, but he stepped forward and licked the mess from her muzzle. Their heads touched, and he gave her a nip at the scruff of her mane. She was the omega no longer.

Together, the new alpha pair circled back toward the army. Witch or no, it was too late to turn back now. They would attack again.

THERE WAS SHOUTING to Fixelcrick's right, and more from somewhere behind, but he did not look away from the salamander directly before him as the fire in his grip fizzled out in the snow at his feet. Bone Master had taught him the old words for binding flame, and the former apprentice had always had a mind for memorization. The heat of the fire elementals was linked now to the heat of the branch in his grip. As the twig's light was snuffed out in a last wisp of smoke, so, too, was the source of these creatures' link to this plane.

The closest salamander let out a sickening croak and lashed

its head back and forth before belching up a molten spew onto one of the charred bodies beneath it. Steam billowed from glowing crevices between its scales as it shrank in on itself, losing mass as it lost heat. Fixelcrick knew the other of its kind was equally suffering, but he kept his newfound focus on the one before him, knowing that they were linked by his binding, and that if he let down his guard for even an instant, this one would feed on his warmth and leave behind nothing but ash. It vomited again, this time in a projectile spray that splattered the face and chest of the clan War Boss a few strides away. The big goblin didn't even make a sound before the lava dropped him with a molten crevice where his chin and upper torso had been.

Fixelcrick stepped closer, the intoxicating power flowing through him, fully at his command for the first time in his life. All of his studies and monastic discipline had been leading to this moment. He repeated the words of binding again, his pronunciation more exact than he'd ever known his tongue capable of producing. He began to shout with confidence as the salamanders backed away and shrank further with every verse. "*Nixt flacht, al zu-gahul! Migsen-glut sevdacht! Ginevdna gedkravtcha höx!*"

The two salamanders backed into each other with their fire-red eyes locked on Fixelcrick's advance. Their tails lashed erratically, and they belched little pools of lava every few jerky steps. The steam that whistled out of their nostrils and poured from their open mouths stank of brimstone.

Fixelcrick remembered, only then, to yank out the syringe that was sticking from his chest. He tossed it aside and took Bone Master's rattle from his cloak instead. It was a tiny, double-headed drum on a stick with strands of silver hair and little bones tied at the ends. He held the stick between his palms and started spinning back and forth—at first too fast, but then he eased into a steady rhythm. He'd been told that the hair had belonged to a great elf witch, and that the bones had come from her inner ears, plucked from the corpse after she fell in battle a hundred years before. Fixelcrick had always doubted the truth of that story, but when the rattle spun, the salamanders hissed and began to shudder as if a chill had come over them.

They'd been bigger than one of the fighting wolves when Fixelcrick had first landed amid the goblin ranks, but now they were only the size of small dogs and withering more by the moment. He stepped over the last of the blackened goblin corpses and spun the rattle harder as the salamanders retreated through the scorched swath of forest. He was their master now.

He drove them down the slope of the hill, back through the ruined woods where they could claim no fuel for their inner furnace. One tried to break from the backward march, but Fixelcrick's will and the beat of the little drum kept it at bay, corralling it further as it hissed and withered. With a last stuttering step, they shriveled down to the size of his crickets, and after a final molten belch, they burst into little tufts of ash in unison. Still, Fixelcrick stepped over their remains and continued to spin the drum—too focused on the flow of power to notice the raucous cheer that had risen among the army at his back.

The energy that coursed through him had nowhere to go, cycling without purpose, sapping his own strength. The bone rattle in his hands came to a gradual halt, though the pounding of his heart continued the rhythm. He was lightheaded, and his hands shook as he turned back to face the cheering army above. Spears and blades were held high, and more and more voices joined the ovation until the sound filled the woods. Fixelcrick's vision was still blurry at the edges, dreamlike, and framed by the burning of trees at the top of the rise. The advance of the forest fire had stopped. He'd saved the clan.

The Khan's pet killers who led the army emerged from the broken front line and set their unnerving attention on his position. The tall one with the big sword and dead eyes was unreadable as always, but the fat one with the hatchets gave him an appreciative shake of his wide chins.

Fixelcrick had done it. The Khan would hear of this and be sure to make him Chief Doktor now. It was the most coveted position among all the warlocks of all the clans . . . But where was the Witch of the Iron Wood? It was her potion that had made this possible through Dingle's blood, so much power even when diluted time and again. The witch possessed knowledge that Fixelcrick could barely imagine, things Bone Master had never known. The Nectar of Amrite was the pinnacle of alchemical pursuits. Compared to the possibility she offered, the Rock Wolves meant nothing to him.

As if in answer, a fresh wind blew along the ridge, this time coming from the direction of the clan compound.

BLACK AGNES SHOULD have been focused on Slud's assault on the walls. Now was when he'd need her guidance more than ever. But the banishment of her summoning could not go unanswered, and the meager remnants of the free wolves would not be enough to slow the return of the Rock Wolf army for long. From the high perch in the tree, her hooked claws were raised to the sky, and the spirits of the air had answered.

The rhythm of the goblin's spirit drum had tapered off, but Agnes could still hear the pumping of the warlock's blood from miles off. Even more goading was the cheering of the army, still believing they were the masters of the mountain. She would make an example of this strong-hearted goblin, and then see how loud the cheers got with the jaws of their wolves wrapped around their throats.

FIXELCRICK LIKED THE attention, but the cheers faltered as the whistle of the wind grew louder than their voices. The adoring faces that had looked to him as their savior all turned away as the tops of the trees started to dance. Wolves whimpered with tails tucked low, and a disquieted murmur traveled through the ranks.

Fixelcrick waved his arms in little circles and the wings of his robes caught the current of the air. He landed with an awkward stumble among the charred bodies at the front of the army, but the eyes of the goblins held on the circling mist that crept across both sides of the ridge like two giant serpents. This was the witch's response; she was coming. Fixelcrick had hoped to get her attention, but he had no idea what to do now that he had.

Goblins yelled from the far side of the loose formation; others shot arrows into the circling mist. Many of the shell-shocked survivors of the front line were still hunched and muttering beside the smoldering remnants of their friends.

"Wha' the fuck's all this then?" asked the fat goblin in charge, with his bloody hatchets held at the ready.

"Witch," said Fixelcrick. He opened his robes and grabbed

one of the golden bolts from his quiver. He closed his eyes and tried to settle his breathing, but his blood was still flowing so fast through his veins that he huffed like he'd run the whole way there. In his mind, he pictured the protective ward that Bone Master had taught him, and he immediately started to scratch a circle around himself in the blackened earth.

"Wha' the fuck's that fer?" asked Short-Fuse with a little spin of a hatchet.

Fixelcrick ignored him, kneeling with the bolt to carefully scratch the accompanying sigils in their exact spots as the wind grew stronger still. A fell voice clung to the air, just like when Bone Master had been broken. He abandoned perfection and started scribbling the markings as quickly as he could get them down.

"Oi, make me one o' them, too!" Short-Fuse raised a hatchet over Fixelcrick's head, but before he could swing or Fixelcrick could answer, an invisible claw of wind lifted the warlock from the earth and launched him through the air to slam into the scorched remains of a tree.

He was pinned twenty feet up with his legs dangling, and somehow, in that moment, he could only think of the damage the still hot wood might be doing to the beautiful feathers at his back. But the witch's screeching voice entered his head, and all other concerns fled him.

Words he did not know yet somehow understood echoed within his mind. *Drive them. Bind them. Cast them aside. The will of the giants will not be defied. All of my memory, all of my pain, the choice is yours, dead or insane?* His eyes rolled back, and he shook with seizure. Blood poured from his nose, and a memory not his own washed over him—as if he were there, living it in the moment . . .

He was on fire in a massive hall of burnished wood and gold, cast into the great hearth in the center of the room among logs and flames that rose toward the vaulted ceiling. A host of tall figures circled, shining and powerful, crowding around to watch with disdain. These were the foreign gods who had come from the south to challenge his native people for control. The powerful spirit that looked like an old man with a long white beard was their leader. He stepped forward to jam a broad-headed spear into Fixelcrick's stomach. The shock of pain almost killed him then and there, but he looked down to see the long, naked, golden body of a woman where his feathered robes should have been, and he was so curious that he forgot to die.

The old man twisted the shaft as Fixelcrick gasped, unable to draw breath while the flames climbed around him. Then his shining form crumpled to the coals when a massive weight came down on the back of his head. From behind the veil of fire and pain, he could see the hulking form of a red-bearded brute step beside the old man with a bloody hammer in his grip and a grin on his smug face. Others laughed and spat flaring spirits to the flames.

But even then, Fixelcrick spoke up from among the logs and embers, using the woman's defiant voice in place of his own. "Thrice I have come, and thrice you have struck me down! I am Gullveig, the Golden Goddess, and you will know my vengeance!"

Fixelcrick snapped back into himself, but the searing agony of fire and steel lingered as he writhed against the tree. He tried to move his arms, to catch the wind and fly back to the ground, but he could not rebuff the spectral grip. He managed only to hook a finger around the flap of his cloak, fighting to work his hand toward the satchel beneath, but the foreign memories took him away from his body again . . .

Surrounded by high, snow-clad mountains, he crouched behind

a rocky ledge, looking down past a winding staircase that traversed the cliffs. A valley opened below: a glacial blue lake with a barren slab of an island in its center. There, a giant black wolf was tied.

The beast was as long as the oldest pines were tall, and as fierce as any creature that had ever lived. Fixelcrick's heart shriveled at the sight of him, consumed with a terror he'd never experienced before. He was forced to watch rather than run as the same host that had stabbed him and jeered in the great hall gathered around the edges of the island. Most of them were also frozen by the monstrous visage, standing with their heels in the water for fear of getting too close to the snarling jaws. But one, with huge shoulders draped in mail and furs, closed his eyes and held his fist out toward the wolf as if in offering.

The old man who had stuck Fixelcrick with a spear stepped away from the wolf's tethered ankle as others bound the far end of the thin cord tightly to a protruding rock.

Fixelcrick stood with a rush of alien anger mingling with his fear. He knew he should stay concealed, but knew also that the wolf had been tricked by these wicked folk. He waved his hand, hoping to catch the wolf's attention, but it wasn't his hand. Instead he saw the long arm of a woman: pale gray skin mottled with age, and hooked claws at the ends of her knotted fingers. He sensed great power coursing through the bent body he inhabited, but despite that, he could do nothing to help the wolf. He knew, in that moment, that the monster was his own son, and that he loved him as assuredly as he'd loved anything in his long life.

With a nod from their king, the wolf jerked his leg against the tether and found no give. Shattered remnants of thick chains lay scattered about the island, but this thin ribbon held fast against every lunge and kick he made. The host laughed at the wolf's consternation, and realizing only then that he'd been deceived, the beast bit off the offered hand and swallowed it whole. The broad-shouldered sacrifice leapt away screaming as the host only laughed harder, baiting the helpless wolf that could no longer reach them.

The wolf lunged at the old man and his kin, but they stood proud with hands on their hips just beyond his reach. Some of those who had moments before been petrified by his presence threw stones, while others circled menacingly with a huge sword clutched in their grip. The massive, red-bearded brute had crept behind the wolf and now came upon him with his hammer raised high. Fixelcrick wanted to cry out in warning, but he held his tongue, helpless, while the rage and sorrow grew within.

The hammer fell against the wolf's head and was raised again and again. Two others grabbed the stunned beast by his jaws and yanked his mouth wide while a third jammed the sword inside. The hilt wedged beneath the wolf's great lolling tongue, and the blade pierced the roof of his mouth as he roared out in pain.

Fenrir, Fixelcrick's oldest and greatest son, was left lashing and snarling at the center of the forsaken island as blood and drool spilled from his mouth in a growing river. Fixelcrick shut his eyes, trying to block out the image of the gods taunting his progeny, but their cruel laughter and the wolf's agonized growls carried across the valley and shook the mountainside.

His own words rose up, using the cracked voice of the witch from the Iron Wood. "I am Angerboda, Mother of Wolves! Heed my words. One day I will watch my children devour you all!"

Fixelcrick was quivering violently. He could taste blood in his mouth as red foam dribbled onto his precious coat. The fear and grief clung to him like the massive rock tied at the wolf's ankle, tugging him down, threatening to drag him back into the cascade of alien memories.

His hand fumbled desperately past the feathers to plunge

into the satchel at his hip until they wrapped around a second cold cylinder of metal and glass. His heartbeat had slowed to a faint thump as he fought to bring his salvation up to his chest, but then he slipped away once more . . .

He was perched at the crown of a towering pine, looking down into the dell of the clan compound with the first light of day upon it. Snow covered the ground, unmarred by the passage of tracks save for two sets that cut across the long shadows of the upper ridge. The clan was quiet, though plumes of goblin breath rose from the towers and heavily armed groups clustered behind every gate.

He leaned around the tree further, his hand gripping the trunk with hooked talons at the end of his long fingers. Now his arms were young and strong, with obsidian skin stretched taut over lean muscle. This was not some vision of the ancient past. This was to-day—moments ago.

He looked back to the tree line, waiting for something with hungry expectation . . . Finally, a figure emerged from behind the largest tree and swung a massive battle-ax to his shoulder. It was the troll, and Fixelcrick knew this was Slud of the Blood Claw Clan, last of his kind.

Fixelcrick had no idea what the lad might do next. It had been centuries since he'd been truly surprised, but this troll, his adopted son, never ceased to confound him. Slud was perhaps even more brazen in his actions than the Demon Wolf had been. All of Fixelcrick's plans, all of the training and toil for twenty years, all of it likely wasted on the next few minutes—

Fixelcrick jammed the second plunger into his heart and broke out of the vision with a desperate shout: "NO!" The word reverberated within his head and across the woods, and he immediately fell from the invisible hold. His chin smacked into his knee in the landing with a burst of white across his vision. He slumped to the side with a pitiful groan. His face pressed to the hot earth as the kick and tingle of Dingle's blood swept through him again.

He was himself once more, but only because of the thinned trace of *her* potion. His heart raced as he lurched to his feet and found the piggy eyes of the goblin called Short-Fuse staring back.

The wind had stopped blowing, and the mist no longer swirled with menace. He knew this was not the attack—this was only a diversion. Fixelcrick stumbled up to Short-Fuse, his far-seeing eye looking through him, beyond, still seeing the clan compound from on high, unaware and unready for whatever was coming. He tried to shake off the lingering effects of the assault, but his psyche had been stretched thin, ready to snap at the smallest provocation.

"It's a trap, a trick to draw us away from the compound. Clan's under attack. The troll, Neither-Nor, they're there." Fixelcrick wasn't sure his words made sense; he still heard the ancient tongue of the giants echoing in his head.

But Short-Fuse's eyes widened and settled on the black feathered robes. He raised one of the hatchets ever so slightly. "Coat lets ya fly?"

Fixelcrick wiped his nose and smeared blood across his cheek. He nodded.

Short-Fuse reached over and pulled the syringe from Fixelcrick's chest. "And would it work fer anybody?"

This time Fixelcrick didn't respond as the scary, mute goblin with the big sword stepped behind him.

FIFTEEN

Chop, Chop

THEY COULD HAVE snuck back into the trees and made off without anyone taking notice, or at least waited until night to try to sneak in through the shadows. Instead, the lunatic troll rolled his neck and took off the absurd bearskin coat. He spat into his hands and took up the ax again with a last look at the compound wall a couple hundred paces away.

"Don't fuckin' do what I think yer doin'," said Neither-Nor.

But Slud grinned as he cocked the ax and swung into the base of the monstrous tree with a loud *thwack* that echoed across the ridge.

Neither-Nor was still a little drunk, but he sobered instantly. It was the damndest thing the goblin had ever seen. "Ya crazy fuckin' bastard! Ya just killed us!"

Slud ripped the ax out of the tree and swung again with an even louder *thwack*. The broad blade disappeared completely into the wood. This time, when he ripped it back out, a thick wedge of wet tree came with it—big enough to have felled any normal-sized trunk already.

Neither-Nor looked up; this tree was far from normal, wider than the best house he'd ever lived in and stretching higher than most birds cared to fly. The scarred goblin had never seen its better save for the giant pine that the Rock Wolf compound had been built around. Slud seemed to be aiming this tree at that one.

The heads of guards started to pop up above the sharpened logs of the stockade. After the third echoing *thwack,* a horn blew from somewhere behind the wall.

"Dey'll be comin'," said Slud between strikes. "Yer blockin' arrows fer de bot' of us 'n' killin' wha'ever gets close." He struck again with another resonant *thwack.*

"Fuck." Neither-Nor turned back to the wall and gave his knives a spin. Another horn blew, and the sound of harsh yelling carried from within.

Slud kept working at a steady pace, unhurried but relentless. Already four heavy wedges had been ripped from the trunk, then five, but there was an ominous thump followed by a resounding creak at the front gate to coincide with his next strike.

Neither-Nor could see a siege crossbow being set up on the closest tower. Other goblins with longbows were lining up along the wall. "Fuck."

The first arrow flew from the wall a moment later. It fell thirty paces short of their position—just a test shot to gauge the distance as the creaking of the front gate continued.

"What's the plan once that tree comes down?" Neither-Nor asked. The troll didn't answer, lost in the rhythm of the ax while the pile of cleaved wood grew at his feet.

Riders on wolves began to appear from around the corner tower—first just a couple, milling about in the snow with their eyes on the action, but soon a full pack of twenty had come into view amid a flurry of snarls and shouts.

"Fuck." Neither-Nor was beginning to think he should forget his map and make a run for it, though he doubted he could climb back up to Luther's ridge before the Rock Wolves caught him. Another couple arrows whistled out of the sky, each disappearing into the snow up to the fletching. The closest was only ten paces away.

The riders made their way along the wall for a pending charge as more shouts brought all the bows above them cocked toward the sky. The bows released at once, and a swarm of arrows launched in a high arc.

Neither-Nor tracked the approach—at least half lacked the power to reach them, and half of the rest were aimed poorly, but five or so were dropping fast. He ducked one as he skipped back toward the troll with a last-second leap. He clipped two arrows from the air as three more sank into the snow nearby.

Neither-Nor ducked again, just before Slud's ax swung back an inch above his red cap. The troll didn't notice or slow the chopping, having already hacked out a gap in the tree big enough for Neither-Nor to stand in.

The goblin scampered away with a sneer before returning his eyes to the wall. "Yer fuckin' welcome," he muttered, just as the giant crossbow released and an eight-foot javelin hurtled their way. This one flew with little arc, and Neither-Nor didn't have time to react before it sailed over his head and buried itself in the trunk of the tree just a few feet to the side of the troll.

Slud glanced over his shoulder with a frown, but didn't miss a beat as another wide chunk of blond wood ripped out with the ax. "Do betta."

Neither-Nor cracked a shoulder and gave the moon blade a spin as the next volley launched from the long bows. This time, only three of them found the range. Neither-Nor ducked the first and cut the second from the air, but the third was meant for Slud's head. The goblin leapt back and tossed the moon blade spinning straight up. The hilt clipped the arrow midair and knocked it off course to clatter uselessly against the tree. Neither-Nor caught the knife and grinned.

The grin failed when the siege crossbow fired again. His instincts took over as he dropped into a crouch and leapt as high as he could with the moon blade swinging in an upward arc. The blade caught the thick shaft at the peak of his swing, and the momentum of the missile ripped the knife from his hand. Both spun away, buzzing Slud's head again before they landed quietly in the snow. The troll glanced over his shoulder at the tower and smacked his lip against a tusk—and kept chopping. Neither-Nor sprinted over to retrieve his knife, but again there was no acknowledgment from the troll.

"Oi, lemme see dat arrow," said Slud. He left the ax buried in the tree and spun toward Neither-Nor with an outstretched hand. Neither-Nor raised an eyebrow but tossed the javelin. Slud caught it with his dark gaze settling back on the tower. A third volley of arrows climbed into the air, and this time Neither-Nor wasn't close enough to defend the troll. An arrow came for the goblin, but he sidestepped it as another three sped toward the bigger target.

The troll just stood there as two missed him by inches. The third, he swatted out of the air with the back of his hand. He gauged the weight and balance of the javelin before bringing it up to his chin. He cocked his arm back and hurled with a deep grunt. It flew high and long, but the damned troll had already turned around to keep chopping before the shot landed.

Neither-Nor watched with his mouth agape as the javelin came down atop the tower to impale the trigger-man at the crossbow. It was the most remarkable throw he'd ever seen. The longbow team at the wall stopped firing. Even the twenty-pack of the Khan's wolf riders had gone silent at the sight of it.

But with another yell, the bows rose up and fired again, just before the riders spurred the wolves forward with a chorus of shouts and snarls.

"Hold 'em off," said Slud between chops.

"Ah, fuck it all," said Neither-Nor before he started to dance again.

———

AGNES REGAINED CONSCIOUSNESS hanging upside down fifty feet above the ground with a branch sticking through her thigh. A repetitive chopping echoed across the ridge, and she could hear the howling of wolves, though she couldn't see much past the freezing blood in her eyes. She hadn't expected the wave of air and energy to rebound back at her, knocking her from her perch to tumble down through the dense branches. Her hand went to her scalp and came away dark red. There was a long gash beneath her hair, and the muscles in her leg tore further with every movement she made. She snarled with the pain and hoisted herself back up to the larger limb that held her.

A hundred years earlier, an elven war party had caught her scent and ridden her down while she was wandering to gather roots and herbs in the hills at the base of the mountain. They ran her through with a lance and shot her full of arrows before nailing her to an oak tree and leaving her to feed the crows. Once their proud horses were out of sight over the hills, she'd called lightning down to the tree and burned it and herself to the ground. Aunt Agnes had been born out of that fire, but she remembered, as did Black Agnes now, what it felt like to be hung out to die. This was nothing.

But she liked this new body and wasn't pleased to see it damaged already. A goblin warlock shouldn't have been able to resist her attack. None still alive, save for maybe a few of the high elves, should have had the power to counter her pull on the flow. This goblin carried the divine trace in its blood, but it was not the same tiny imp she'd seen hunting Slud on the lower slopes.

Agnes sat up on the broad limb and twisted her leg around the blood-tipped branch with a hiss. She removed a serrated knife from the belt she'd lifted from one of the dead goblins and slipped it under her leg to saw through the base of the stake. Now that she was upright, the blood started to run across her face from her scalp. Her black hair was soaked with it, and she was beginning to feel the cold.

The steady chopping had not wavered below, but the frenetic sounds of combat replaced the twangs of bows. She wiped the blood from her eyes and squinted down at the commotion. The scarred goblin was surrounded by a pack of wolf riders, skipping between them as the troll kept hacking at a massive tree like he was the only one there.

She'd meant to turn the wolves on their riders and let Slud go in amid the chaos, but between the loud chopping and her current predicament her plans had soured. Now she needed all of the Knack at her disposal for healing. The troll and his lively little friend would have to make their own way. *Slud alone must prove he's worthy of the mountain's blessing.*

Agnes gritted her teeth and sawed until her leg came loose. Before she could think it over, she raised her thigh, grabbed the bottom of the branch, and yanked it out. As much pain as she'd swallowed in her lifetimes, she never really got used to it, just less afraid of its return.

Blades clanged together below and a couple goblins gave their death grunts before a wolf yelped its last yelp. She watched the goblin spring up from a roll with a jab and a slice that offered two more red sprays to the snow. Slud kept hacking at the ancient tree, wielding the giant's ax as if born to do so. Her vision began to swim as she scooted toward the trunk and turned all of her energy inward.

Her claws reached back to grip the bark until sap ran down her nails, and her head tilted against the rough surface as her heartbeat began to slow. While the fight continued below, and the rallying horns of the enemy sounded, she closed her senses to the outside world and melded with the tree. Within moments, if any had looked straight at her, they would have seen only another gnarled knot at the joint of the first big limb.

———————

THE TREE STARTED to groan and list. Slud had passed the midway point, and now the chops lacked the heavy *thunk* of hitting something impenetrable. The ax had made his hands and arms icy cold, but he found that he no longer noticed the pain—the bitter sting had spread throughout his body, slowing his blood and taking root in his bones. Even his breath had stopped pluming, and with every strike, crystals of frost spread from the ax blade, freezing the sap and making the wood brittle before the next whack. He'd never felt so powerful.

The grunts, yips, and clangs of fighting continued behind him as he slowly surfaced from the rhythmic trance of chopping. It was like swimming up through frozen waters and bursting from the ice. He recognized, only then, how remarkable it was that neither arrows nor blades had reached him yet.

He also recognized how much he wanted to see what the ax would do to flesh, and he spun around to find the scarred goblin circled by six wolf riders as four other pairs bled out in the snow.

The Rock Wolves had been content to ignore Slud just as he'd been ignoring them, too stupid to realize that the chopping of the tree posed the only real threat to the clan. A cluster of ten more riders had stayed by the stockade wall, more than willing to let others go up against the unceasing blades of Neither-Nor while they watched from a safe distance. Another bad choice.

Two of the riders were so brazen as to have their backs to him as they attempted to close in on Neither-Nor. Slud swung in a wide arc parallel to the ground, cleaving one and then the other through their chests; a tumble of arms, torsos, and legs flopped to the snow. The cold of the ax froze the wounds instantly, and only a couple drops of blood escaped as the bodies came undone.

Slud laughed, a deep, booming chortle at the sight. He wanted more. The others turned in horror at his approach, leaving a distracted moment for Neither-Nor to open a couple more bodies. Slud chopped through another rider and the wolf beneath to offer a fascinating glimpse of the internal workings of the halved forms. The last goblin and a couple riderless wolves retreated at a frantic clip.

Neither-Nor was left breathing heavily in the center of a ring of gore. He dropped his knives to his sides and cleared his throat. "What the fuck we doin' here?"

Slud ignored him, taking a moment to appreciate the splay of his handiwork. He spun the ax head and admired the gleam of the blade, as sharp as ever despite the bones and tree it had hacked through. But Neither-Nor had turned back toward the gate where another pack of twenty riders emerged from around the corner. More bowmen lined the wall above them, and the giant crossbow was loaded and cocked again. With the blast of a horn, all of the waiting riders leapt to a sprint toward them.

"Troll!"

Slud walked casually back to the tree and brought up the ax once more. "Have some faith, li'l fella."

"Faith is fer the foolish and desperate," Neither-Nor hissed as Slud began to chop again.

It only took two more whacks before the tree started to tilt noticeably. "Stand aside, now," said Slud as he reached up to pluck the first javelin from the slowly angling trunk.

The massive tree moved in slow motion. The creaks turned into thunderous cracks as the remaining wood at the base gave way to a jagged claw of giant splinters. Then it started to fall faster. The bowman on the wall looked up in disbelief as a few of the riders attempted to course correct their forward momentum in the deep snow. It was too late for that.

The sound of the tree coming down was deafening, drowning out the screams of all those who were caught in its path. Neither-Nor lost his footing to get a face full of snow in the mad scramble. The upper branches connected with the outer limbs of the even larger Clan tree, sending huge juts of wood and dangling cages crashing down into the houses and shops below. The felled trunk landed a second later with a furious shake of the earth as the outer stockade wall exploded beneath the weight. The riders and bowmen in its path vanished, and hundreds more were crushed within the confines of the bisected compound.

Slud was grinning as he donned the bearskin coat again. Neither-Nor picked himself up to survey the damage in a state of shock. The spared riders had stopped their approach, unsure of how to proceed after witnessing such an act. But Slud wasted no time, using the ax and a few ragged splinters of wood to hoist himself up onto the top of the trunk. He gave the prone giant a gentle pat. "Sorry, ol' girl, had to be done," he said, and then looked down at Neither-Nor. "Come on now, dey ain't gonna stand aside foreva."

Neither-Nor came, climbing up with his knives working like picks, but now his eyes regarded Slud with a wary respect that hadn't been there before. "Gimme the map, and lemme go."

Slud chuckled. "Nah, fun's just startin', 'n' I can't do it wit'out ya."

"Ya ain't gonna be happy 'til ya kill the whole world, are ya?"

Slud gave him a hard pat on the shoulder and motioned for him to follow. "We're all dead already, just too stubborn or stupid to see it yet."

SIXTEEN

Boom, Boom

MINUTES EARLIER, a big cricket had hopped up and perched on the rope tied tightly around Dingle's chest. There was something vaguely threatening in the black, bulbous eyes on the side of its little head, staring up at him like it might jump at his nose at any moment. He tried to shake it off, but he was hog-tied, gagged, and dangling from a golden hook in the feathered hex doktor's hut. The room was absurdly warm—the fire never seemed to diminish even though no new wood had been added in hours—and the undulating waves of cricket chirps were starting to drive him bonkers.

The old goblin in the corner was muttering again, but Dingle couldn't hear what he was saying beneath the crickets. He wasn't sure how long he'd been left to hang there, dripping sweat as his arms and feet went numb, but morning light streamed through the high window, and the clamor and howling of daytime had begun. He supposed it was better than bleeding out and getting pecked to death in the cage, but he wasn't sure what all the intense stares and syringes full of his blood would lead to upon the feathered goblin's return. Every time the doktor's evil eye looked at him, he shuddered and felt like he might puke into the gag.

Dingle had come too far to choke on his own vomit. He'd

met the Lord of Death and lived; his service was not finished. He needed to find a way to escape the hut, to somehow get past the stockade guards, and then to find Slud. So far, he hadn't even come close to figuring out the first part.

There was a loud cracking sound outside, and at once the cricket colony went eerily silent. Dingle could hear a series of distant pops, followed by an escalating creak, like a giant door swinging on rusty hinges . . .

All at once the world lurched. The window shattered, pots and jars flew off shelves, and a couple thousand crickets were spooked into the air simultaneously. Dingle found himself heading toward the packed-earth floor with a muffled yelp.

He turned his head at the last minute and met the ground with his shoulder as a flash of white took his vision. It returned just in time for him to see the heavy rain of crickets fall across the room. His shoulder had snapped out of its socket, and the wind was knocked out of his chest. With a high-pitched wheeze he searched for air, catching it again along with a nose full of dirt. He sneezed with another shock of pain, and a cluster of skittish crickets leapt clear of his trajectory. The floor outside the pen was now littered with them.

Through the broken window he could hear hundreds of goblins shouting, calling out for help or barking frantic orders as a series of horn blasts sounded across the compound. Dingle found the restrictive bindings around him loosened by the odd angle of his arm, and with a teeth-clenched squeal he managed to work his other hand out of the loop behind his back. The old goblin master lay on the floor across the room with his one remaining eye open wide toward him. A string of drool clung to his droopy bottom lip, but luckily a blood-stained bandage covered the hole where his evil eye had been.

Dingle's dislocated shoulder was locked and the arm hung uselessly below. He wriggled his dead hand free from the rope, the odd tingling sensation throbbing along with the eye-watering pain. He should have died at least five times in the last two days—perhaps pain was just the Lord of Death's way of reminding him of the gift of life?

He grunted and squeaked his way out of the bindings, using his good arm to yank and untie as crickets scattered from his erratic movements. Tears streamed down his cheeks by the time he was free, but he fought his way to unsteady feet and tugged the gag from his mouth. "F-f-fuck!" he screamed. The old goblin was still staring at him expectantly.

His feet and fingers felt like they were on fire as blood rushed back into them, and the throbbing in his misaligned shoulder died down beneath the warm buzz. He stumbled to the door, only to discover that it had been locked via some elaborate homemade mechanism. A wooden beam was mounted on springs and hinges, braced across the thick frame and latched into a metal cage that only opened with a key.

Dingle scanned the room for an ax or hatchet, but he doubted he'd be able to chop his way free even if he had the use of both arms. His eyes swung back to the shattered window eight feet up. Beyond, the shouting had taken on a more frenetic tone. He scrambled to the tallest bookshelf against the wall and pushed with his good arm—it didn't budge. The books were thick and old, bound with leather, fur, and unfamiliar leaves. He'd never seen so much condensed information in one place before. All that precious paper and ink, right there at his fingertips, but Death cared not for distractions.

He tossed them to the ground atop a few unlucky crickets. The haphazard pile grew, and all the while, the old warlock watched him silently from the other side of the room. The bookshelf was more than twice Dingle's height, but once empty he was able to shoulder it with his good side for a few scraped inches at a time across the dirt.

After some high-pitched grunting and more tears, he got it below the window, but climbing up with one hand seemed impossible. He heard bows releasing and the whistle of arrows outside. *It's him! Slud. He's come for me!* He grabbed the highest shelf he could reach and stepped onto the first shelf as his other arm dangled like a limp fish. His good hand skipped up to the next shelf and he stepped higher.

The hand shot up and he climbed again, amazed at how easily it all came to him. A week earlier, Dingle wouldn't have been able to do any of this. A week earlier, Dingle's primary function had been collecting wolf shit from the scout pens. Almost two hundred wolves, and except for the rare occasions when he was forced to go on the even more unpleasant scouting runs, it was his job every morning and night to gather all their crap in a big wheelbarrow and haul it over to the Dung Boys for processing.

Now I'm the minion of a wanted enemy of the clan. I tasted his potion. We're linked. He smiled as he climbed to the top shelf and peered out of the shattered window. His jaw dropped.

The sugar pine that was the twin of the Clan tree that had stood at the upper edge of the ridge for the entirety of his life and the thousand years before it had come down in Clan Center. A big branch had shattered the hut across the street, and the massive trunk stretched out of sight in both directions. Dingle hoisted himself up for a better view as the bookshelf wobbled on the uneven ground.

The egg merchant from the nightmarish world above lay

in the street amid the wreckage of his cage. The spikes had jammed through him in the fall, and a few of the bars had twisted up to pierce his back and stick out of his stomach. His legs were bent in absurd ways, and the blood flowed out of him in a fast-growing pool. Despite it, his bulging eyeballs still moved, snapping up to meet Dingle's horrified stare.

"The egg goes splat, but we still eat. For birds or wolves, we'll be their meat." The egg merchant smiled as his gaze went slack.

Dingle dry heaved as the bookshelf teetered and then settled again. This would have been his fate had the feathered-goblin not carried him down the night before. Everything was happening for a reason. He was meant to help Slud further.

That was when he saw him, the Lord of Death himself, lumbering along the top of the fallen tree in a bearskin coat with a huge ax in his hands and the scarred goblin at his heels.

His cracked little voice tried to rise over the din. "Mmmaster! It's D-D-Dingle!"

But Slud and Neither-Nor kept going, dodging arrows and ducking around branches as they headed toward the inner stockade.

"Master!" Dingle grabbed at the windowsill, cutting his finger on the jagged glass that ringed its edges. He yelped and yanked his hand back as the bookshelf tipped away from the wall. As he fell he saw Slud moving on without him, and then the full weight of the shelf came down on his already useless shoulder and the cluster of hapless crickets beneath.

This time, he managed to black out.

———

THE ALPHA WOLVES paced back and forth at the base of the throne, stopping every few passes with shifting ears as another muffled scream rose outside. The big tree had come down with such force that most of the oil lamps had fallen, and the Khan's untouched pine-ale jug had shattered on the steps. One of the roof's support beams had caught flame and was still smoldering, and some of the entrails that hung from the rafters had slopped down to the floor. The furry leg of the new Herald hadn't stopped shaking in minutes.

Arokkhan wanted answers and more ale, but he hadn't assigned a new Big Boss of the scouts to tell him what was going on, and the want of drink was a more pressing task for the old one. "Hairy Herald, fetch a fresh jug!" The furry freak shuffled off behind the throne with his lame foot scraping behind him.

Arokkhan had doubled the guards at the doors inside the hall and put two packs of twenty riders just outside. He had fifteen crossbowmen perched in murder boxes along each wall with bolts dipped in a fast-acting paralytic toxin that his Poison Boys had crafted from a particularly nasty kind of mountain spider. And the mercenaries he'd brought in from the lowland clans were spread throughout the nervous gathering of his typical lackeys. Though they were as ready a band of killers as he'd ever seen, he was starting to regret having sent his two best, Short-Fuse and Long-Pig, to the front lines.

The Herald shambled around the throne with a fresh jug of ale as one of the wolves gave a low growl. The two beasts still hadn't warmed up to the hairy bastard, snarling whenever he got too close to the Khan. Arok enjoyed watching him cringe, but at least this Herald knew how to keep his mouth shut, unlike the last screeching fool whose head was mounted outside the doors.

Unfortunately, the last Herald had been the only one in the clan who knew about the escape tunnel that Arok had built, descending from the back of the throne. He was starting to wonder if Hairy Herald here shouldn't also learn how to unlock and prep the passage in case of unforeseen complications. The Herald held the jug up toward him and lowered his shaggy face with proper respect. Arokkhan snatched the bottle, bit off the cork, and spat it rolling into the shadows. He closed his eyes as the sharp burn of the brew slid down his throat. This would be one of the only satisfying moments he got for the next twenty-four hours—the first sweet taste of his morning ale was the only thing he could truly rely on.

When he opened his eyes again, the cold hall was just as he'd left it, clustered with simpering morons and paid friends, stinking of wolves and rotten meat, and with walls too thin to block out the pitiful yelps of his people—just because a tree had reportedly fallen across a few of their houses. The Herald was still waiting at the foot of the stairs with his dark eyes on the stones. "Get outside an' silence all that fuckin' fuss!" Arok commanded. "An' someone get a good fire goin', or I'll start burnin' y'all instead!"

That really got the murmuring masses moving, and for the second time that morning he felt a glimmer of satisfaction. It sank away behind his usual disconsolate scowl when some damn fool started banging on the doors at the other end of the hall. The heavy knocks echoed about the hall: *BOOM! BOOM! BOOM!* His next swig spilled out of his mouth as he started screaming. "Kill whoeva thinks they can bang on me doors like that!"

It took four big goblins to slide the giant beam out of the lock and raise the iron jambs that sank into the floor. The doors slowly swung open with a great creak as the gathering went silent and stepped back to the shadows. The morning light cut a path between them to the fire pit in the room's center and the towering throne behind it.

Waiting outside, surrounded by the forty wolf riders, stood Short-Fuse and Long-Pig. The fat goblin was panting and rubbing his thick arms as he entered. The long, black-feathered cloak of the new Chief Doktor was hanging off his shoulders and dragging behind him. The tall mute followed, unfazed and expressionless as ever.

"The hell are ya doin' here!" bellowed the Khan.

The fat goblin huffed like a wild boar as he staggered closer, trying to catch his breath and taking his sweet time with it. He heaved out words between breaths. "Came quick as we could, boss... Compound's under attack... This Slud and Nei-ther-Nor... Here, now, comin' fer ya straightaway. Me and Pig're gonna kill 'em fer ya."

The audacity of it all was staggering, and the Khan could feel the blood instantly pounding in his temples, threatening to burst. Luckily it was early, and the booze hadn't fogged his thoughts yet; he'd always been good at thinking under pressure. He scanned the crowd that clustered around the hearth fire, and his eyes settled on a burly brute of a goblin wearing shiny armor with a wolf-skin cape draped over his shoulders. Arok was pretty sure he was the captain of the guards for the richest merchant in the clan, and the Khan had never much liked either of them.

He pointed at the big fool and smiled. "You, get ova here!"

SEVENTEEN

Hack 'n' Slash

AN ARROW SLAPPED into the branch just behind Slud's ear, but he didn't have time to see where it came from. He'd been a little surprised by the number of fight-ready goblins and wolves left inside the compound, though it was way too late for second-guessing and most of them still had no idea what was going on. Luckily, the increasingly heavy branch maze on the trunk ahead offered good cover leading up to the second stockade. Beyond that, he figured he'd figure something out.

Neither-Nor had stuck with him, cursing under his breath, "Fuck, fuck, fuck, fuck, fuck," as he cut and dodged the arrows that came his way.

Slud took a low swing mid-run and chopped through a thick branch in their path. He nudged the thirty-foot spire to the side and kept running as it crashed through a roof below with a sharp goblin cry. Now that the ax had tasted blood, the cold had settled into his thoughts as well as his hands. Despite the surroundings, he was calm and calculating. Whatever was about to happen, Slud would get in some good killing first.

Horns blew and arrows flew, but nothing hit as they slipped into the thick branches leading to the tree's fallen crown. The trunk here no longer touched the earth, suspended twenty feet above the compound and held up by the weight of the base.

Slud felt a little sway in his step as he advanced, his keen eyes picking out a spot along the inner stockade where a row of three of the sharp posts had snapped in half.

He slowed and looked over his shoulder at the pissed-off goblin. Slud almost felt sorry for him. "Oi, get ready to fight. Slud'll jump in de middle 'n' get attention. When dey ain't lookin', come down quiet 'n' work de edges real quick." Slud nodded. "Won't know what's happenin' 'fore it's over."

"Gimme the map, and I'll do it," said Neither-Nor.

Slud patted the bag slung at his back, carrying the butt end of the javelin among the other non-map paraphernalia. He motioned with his chin for the goblin to follow and picked up the pace again. With a last few swings of the ax across their path, he cleared the way of branches and bounded along the increasingly buoyant trunk before launching himself blindly through the high gap in the wall.

Slud was glad he'd leapt before looking at the number of fighters that waited below. But of the eighty-some pairs of wolf and goblin eyes loitering there, only a few turned his way before he landed among them with a wide horizontal swing. His boot clipped a goblin chin with a loud snap on the descent, and the broad ax blade passed through multiple bodies as effortlessly as if he were cutting stalks of marsh reeds. He spun and swung again, extending the ax to the full length of his reach, cleaving six more riders with barely a drop of blood in the wake of the flash-freezing blade. They hadn't even found time to scream.

It was as if the world around him was moving at half speed. The power in his grip was all-consuming. He let out a laugh, rumbling and loud, as he took a wide step and swung the ax lower; wolf heads and goblin legs flew apart like straw dolls in a hard wind. Panic set in among those that remained, wolves leaping in every direction and goblins clinging to their backs with feral shrieks. Slud's next laugh was louder than any of them, echoing off the stockade walls and shaking the timbers of the great hall between. He spun and swung again and again, sending more limbs tumbling with every pass. He didn't know if Neither-Nor would follow, and he didn't care. He'd kill them all himself if he had to. In fact, if he had his way, he'd kill every last soul on the mountain before he was through.

During his next swing he saw the scarred goblin drop between two retreating riders, and Neither-Nor's razor-edged blades were already dancing before he hit the ground. The two riders opened and gushed as Neither-Nor rolled between the wolves and came up with a slash across their snouts. Two wolf noses flopped to the snow, and the scarred goblin kept moving toward Slud.

Slud shifted a boot, and his next swing sent a rush of frigid air over Neither-Nor's head. It caught a pursuing rider midchest and exploded out of the other side with a scatter of frozen bits of blood and bone. Neither-Nor darted past him and took two more wolves down at the knees. Slud followed, removing the heads of the screaming riders a second later.

The two of them worked well together, immediately finding a rhythm. Neither-Nor darted again, moving in a quick burst that the wolves couldn't react to before his blades struck. Only Slud's ax could keep up, taking apart the riders an instant later. As the two of them tore through another group in tandem, Slud glimpsed a smirk on the goblin's rune-covered face.

A horn blast blew among a cluster of riders as they bolted away down the side of the hall, but reinforcements had already started to bang on the other side of the locked stockade doors.

Slud whacked a goblin in the back with a downward swing that also cleaved the wolf below it, but Slud's attention had already shifted to the next target. A cluster of riders dismounted in front of the gate and moved toward the heavy beam that barred it. A crossbow bolt whipped past his ear from that direction. "Watch Slud's back," he growled at Neither-Nor.

The scarred goblin spun into the space behind him with the moon blade passing through the throat of a bold wolf. His gut sticker lived up to the name an instant later as the goblin rider's intestines spilled over the dying beast's back. Slud yanked the javelin from the bag over his shoulder and cocked it as a burly goblin got his hands on the beam and started to lift. The javelin pierced his skull and came out through the bridge of his nose, pinning him to the door with his body doing the dead-man's-dance over limp legs. The rest of the would-be door openers thought better of it.

NEITHER-NOR CUT OPEN another wolf, but then he caught a crossbow bolt mid-slash. It felt like someone had punched him hard in the kidney, and he dropped to a knee with a sharp cough. He ripped the bolt out by the fletching, and already felt his skin crawling with the healing runes before the pain hit. He snarled through it and found his feet again.

A wide goblin with gold-trimmed armor was charging with an absurd war bellow. When he raised his sword, Neither-Nor darted in and opened him groin to chin, just before Slud's ax passed over to bisect the two glory-seeking goblins who followed. Without pause, they swiveled and killed more, the two of them working in such accord that it seemed like they'd been fighting together for years. Save for the troll king who'd cut him in half at the fall of the Moon Blades, Neither-Nor had never met anyone who could take him in single combat. But this troll lad with the cold ax was the most deadly thing he'd ever seen. Watching him kill was inspiring. It made the goblin's own knives spin faster.

A frigid breeze followed the ax as it hacked a path through three more goblins and a wolf, and the hulking figure behind him chuckled again. Neither-Nor could feel that laugh trembling in his bones. Despite himself, he started snickering with it as he vaulted from the back of a dying goblin and took off the head of the next rider mid-leap. Slud's ax immediately passed below with a trail of flying wolf legs.

Neither-Nor was searching for the next victim before he landed, but no others advanced. A group of almost ten riders had retreated to the gate, trying again to raise the beam. Three goblins aimed crossbows and fired. Neither-Nor jumped and cut a bolt with the curved knife before it reached Slud, and the troll slapped aside another with the flat of his ax. The third struck the troll in the meat of his chest, and a roar burst out of him that made everyone, including Neither-Nor, stop for a moment. They all stood dumbly as Slud went to one knee.

Neither-Nor's eyes went wide. *Oh, shit! Is he done?* But the troll jumped—rocketing some twenty feet into the air as the ax cocked back over his head. They all looked up, just as the hulking figure came back down on the shooter, driving him into the ground with a loud snap and a shiver of the earth. The ax chopped a big goblin and his wolf into slabs of frozen meat an instant later, and his next swing took four more goblins apart at their waists.

The rest, wolves and riders both, abandoned the door and broke toward the back of the courtyard, screaming the whole way. For a moment, it looked to Neither-Nor like the troll was going to give chase, but Slud's dark brow turned to the locked doors of the Khan's great hall instead. There were over fifty goblin and wolf bodies, dead or dying, around them. Neither-Nor had never seen or heard of anything like it—so many killed by so few in so brief a period. This was the stuff of tall tales, and somehow he had become a part of it. But the pounding continued from the other side of the stockade gate. "When they get them doors open, we're done fer," he said.

"Not if Slud kills de Khan." The troll ripped the tiny bolt out of his chest as a wet stain spread on his coat, and he swiveled back to yank the javelin from the beam just as easily. He flung aside the skewered goblin and stomped across the corpse-strewn field to jam the butt end of the javelin into the mud before the doors. "Slud'll take out de lock. Push 'em open 'n' stand aside."

Neither-Nor had seen what the troll could do with one of those javelins, and none would question his claim on the throne if the Khan was out of the way. *Fuck, this could actually work!*

Slud wound up the ax and hacked into the reinforced wood with a grunt. The whole building shook. A chunk of the door broke off, and Neither-Nor started giggling; he couldn't help himself. He could see the flicker of firelight from within, and Slud chopped again, opening the hole further. The troll changed his grip on the ax and brought it up and over at a different angle, and whatever was holding the doors shut on the other side fell away with a loud clatter. He pushed to test his efforts, but the door was still jammed shut at the bottom. This time he slid the ax across at ground level, and Neither-Nor heard the clang of iron falling away on the far side.

The troll moved the ax to his left hand as he took up the

javelin with his right. With a deep breath, Neither-Nor sheathed his blades and grabbed the doors by the trim.

"Some good deaths ya doled out, goblin," said Slud.

"You, too, troll scum," he answered.

They shared a nod, and Neither-Nor pushed the doors open.

THE HALL WAS one giant room, with thick pine trunk beams holding up the vaulted forty-foot ceiling. Torches and lamps hung from every column, and a wide fire pit burned at the room's heart, surrounded by a thick group of goblins in fancy dress who scampered back to the shadows with terrified squeals. At the far end, a big goblin sat on a tall seat of stone at the top of rough-hewn stairs.

Slud rocked back with the spear balanced above the patch of scar tissue on his shoulder and locked his eyes on the goblin chief, who stared back at him from afar. With a grunt, he released. The javelin flew hard and high, to come down dead center through the big goblin's chest. The metal tip clanged against the stone behind him, and the goblin spit blood and slumped over before tumbling down the stairs.

The hall went totally quiet. All eyes swiveled toward Slud as he stepped inside. He could feel the awe and fear spilling off of them. A cold wind whipped past to make the fire flicker and dim. The ax had taken such a hold on him that frost gathered around his footfalls as he moved across the stone floor. "Anybody else wanna die today?"

There was no answer. No one else stirred except Neither-Nor, who slipped inside and followed with his blades at the ready and his eyes scanning. The dead Khan lay on his side at the base of the throne; blood spattered his shining armor and pooled around the wolf-pelt cape bunched at his throat. It seemed like the whole room was holding its collective breath . . .

"Now!" a goblin shouted from within the crowd. At once, two lines of crossbowmen stood from concealed murder boxes along the walls and fired. They didn't have time to aim properly, but thirty bolts flew at once and Slud made for a big target. He slapped away a couple of them, but felt four more jab into his thigh, stomach, shoulder, and jaw. He gave a hard cough and found it difficult to draw breath with a bolt in his belly. The one that had lodged into the bone of his lower jaw hurt like a bastard, and already the bowmen were reloading. Slud charged with an untamed yell that shook the timbers.

As a numb tingling spread out from his fresh wounds, three tough-looking goblins moved to intercept him with swords and maces. *Have to do betta den dat!* Slud hacked through the blade and body of the first attacker, took off the arm and head of the next, and sent the third flying fifteen feet to smash into one of the boxes along the wall. But the crossbows raised and fired again. Six more bolts lodged in his body, as others sought to silence Neither-Nor's wild cursing over his shoulder.

"I'll fuckin' gut every last one of ya!" the goblin yelled, before the yelling was cut short.

Slud kept charging, breathing the pain in and out as he'd been taught. More goblins stepped out to attack from both sides as his ax flew out to meet them. One managed to stab him in the leg before Slud drove the butt end of the ax handle through his face. The others didn't even get close before he'd sent their frozen limbs to the stones.

The crowd was falling over themselves to get away, but the crossbows fired again into their midst. Goblins in fancy dress took bolts and fell all around him, but three more bolts punched home in Slud's back as well. Other unlucky targets started to jerk and froth at the mouth, but he kept going, scanning the crowd for his next kill.

He didn't see where the hatchet that buried into his chest came from, but it was a good throw and the metal bit deep. More goblins approached, emboldened by his wounds, but he hacked them down as soon as they got within reach. Another hatchet flew from the shadows to bury itself beside the first, and Slud wobbled for a step with a hard cough that sprayed red across the floor.

A fat goblin who looked like an angry toad with feathers dropped from the rafters on the other side of the fire pit. His wide, ugly head gave a nod to someone over Slud's shoulder, and a thick curving blade jammed through Slud's back and poked out of his stomach. He finally fell to his knees, the ax chipping the stone floor beside him. "Can't kill Slud. He's sent by de mountain itself."

That was when another large goblin stepped from behind the throne, flanked by a pair of big wolves. He carried nothing but a jug of ale in his hand, and his smug face looked out from between the jaws of a golden wolf pelt. He strode over the skewered goblin stand-in to retake his throne. "Only Arok, son of Grummok, is King of the Mountain!"

Someone twisted the blade from behind, and Slud could feel his innards rending. He fell forward but caught himself as blood spattered the stones below. The pain was terrible and glorious. He wanted to keep laughing, or say something threatening, but he couldn't seem to form words.

The fat goblin in feathers started laughing instead. "See, Pig, what'd I say? They all the same size on the ground."

EIGHTEEN

Butchering Heroes

NEITHER-NOR CAME TO and immediately wished he hadn't. There was no discomfort, no feeling at all, but his body didn't seem to respond to his commands, and things didn't look good upon first assessment. His head drooped over his chest with a string of bloody drool hanging between his lip and his shirt, and his eyes focused only enough to see the blurry fletching of arrows still sticking out of him in numerous spots. He'd have to rip out the bolts to begin healing, but his arms and legs were completely numb. Still, his mind continued to clear from the fog of poison.

Someone was standing before him. Neither-Nor could see the bottom of a cloak made from black feathers with a couple of dirty brown shoes sticking out beneath, but he couldn't raise his head to see more. Then a meaty fist came up fast, and his head snapped back toward a darkened ceiling.

"This one's awake too," said the goblin in the cloak.

Now Neither-Nor could see that he was dangling by his wrists before the Khan's throne with the golden-wolf-headed bastard watching from on high. Two big wolves and the fat, feathered goblin stood at the base of the steps. Beside him, Slud was also hung from chains. They'd cut off his bearskin coat to unveil a comical mess of cuts and arrows beneath, but the troll's hard eyes were still alert and locked on the Khan above.

A shaggy goblin shuffled from behind the throne with a blood-soaked book and spoke in a clear voice. "Mighty Arok Golden Wolf, Chief of the Rock Wolf Clan, King of the Mountain, and Khan of the Goblin Horde, stands over you to pass judgment."

The Khan took a swig of his jug and cleared his throat. "The great Neither-Nor . . . My men've been lookin' fer ya fer a long time. And now here ya is, trussed up like a hog fer the butcher." He gave a nod to someone behind Neither-Nor, and something hit him in the back with a weighty thud. His useless body jerked forward and spun so he could see a dead-eyed goblin with iron knuckles and the shaken collection of goblins in fancy outfits watching from the far side of the fire pit behind him.

"Arok, son of Grummok, wants ya to know that you'll feel terrible pain 'fore I lets ya die," the Khan said. "I'll stretch yer death fer days, weeks, maybe a month. Yer screams'll put me to bed every night, an' wake me up every mornin'."

Neither-Nor was surprised to find his tongue and lips respond to his thoughts. "Pain? Can't feel a fuckin' thing, ya daft prick."

The Khan's big face turned red and his bloodshot eyes moved to the crowd beyond the fire. "Ya told me they'd still feel everythin' afta the poison set in!"

As he spun, Neither-Nor could see a spindly goblin in black shuffle from the crowd with a stooped head. "Apologies, my Khan." He bowed low and raised his hands in the air. "That was the desired effect." He turned back and pointed at an even spindlier goblin among the many faces. "I assure you, my apprentice will be punished for this mistake."

The Khan just glared, until Slud's deep, rumbling voice filled the cavernous hall. "Ya ain't no King of de Mountain . . . Only de mountain's king, 'n' it don't like ya sayin' otherwise." It was as if his words were coming from all directions at once.

Veins bulged in the Khan's forehead as he struggled to maintain his cool. He swallowed hard. "Twenty years says different, troll. An' I got twenty more, an' twenty more afta that, where you got two minutes at most."

A few of the braver goblins in the host snickered in solidarity with their leader, but Slud smacked his lip against a tusk and smiled. "Borrowed time all 'round, but time's just 'bout up fer de lot o' ya . . . Play games wit' de mountain, pay de mountain's price."

As absurd as the threat was, this time no one felt much like laughing. For a long moment, only the sound of the crackling fire broke the silence of the hall. Finally, the Khan forced a chuckle himself, and soon after, the whole host followed in sycophantic mirth.

The dead-eyed goblin steadied Neither-Nor's spin as the feathered goon with the hatchets dumped out the contents of Slud's bag before the steps. That was when Neither-Nor noticed his moon blade hanging from the fat goblin's belt.

"Get yer fuckin' fingers off me blade, ya lousy shit!" he said, just before the iron knuckles slammed into his back again, this time with an audible crack along his spine. He still didn't feel any pain, but his head whipped forward and then snapped back again as his flaking cap fell to the floor at his feet. He was starting to get the sense that it was about to get a fresh coat of red.

Neither-Nor's eyes, ears, and tongue had come back

quickly, and there was now a dull ache in his back where he'd been hit. He was pretty sure he'd regret it when the feeling came back in full. He had to get them to kill him before that, and then hope they'd get sloppy with body disposal. His prospects didn't look promising as the wolves licked their muzzles and watched him swing.

The feathered goblin sifted through Slud's things on the floor with his shoe: rope, flint, a knife, and a bit of cured meat—that was all.

Neither-Nor's eyes swung over to Slud. "Where's me map, troll?"

"Slud lost dat days ago." He spat a thick glob of blood on the stones. "No worries, he finished up yer etchin' at yer ol' campsite 'fore dat."

"Ya what?" Suddenly, it was as if he and the troll were the only ones there. "Ya lost me map!"

"Yeah, but yer runes is all done."

"Ya lyin' bastard! Ya tricked me!" Neither-Nor tried to swing out and kick Slud, but of course that didn't work. "I'll gut ya like a fish fer this, I promise ya!"

The troll chuckled, but the Khan stood up, red-faced and yelling. "Silence, ya miserable curs!"

This only made Slud laugh harder; his booming chortle echoed about the hall, mocking the Khan's pretense of power. Many in the host backed away and cringed as Arok drew an absurd golden sword from his belt and stormed down toward the hanging giant. The Khan was completely unhinged, stabbing Slud repeatedly in the gut. Blood splattered the floor, and the Khan bellowed his loudest war cry, but to Neither-Nor, the most powerful goblin king looked small beside the dying troll. Arok left the blade sticking out of Slud and turned back toward the throne with a drunken stumble and heavy breathing. The laughing had finally stopped, and Slud's head hung limp over the ruin of his front.

"None can challenge Arokkhan an' live!" the Khan declared, though it sounded more like a whine.

Still, Slud's perforated chest rose and fell ponderously, and his eyes snapped open again. Now his voice was quiet and raspy, but it still echoed about the room for all to hear. "A reckonin's comin'. Slud may die, but he'll watch y'all die soon enough."

The Khan stormed to the troll's giant ax, still lying on the floor where it had fallen. He grabbed the handle and immediately dropped it with a yelp as he rubbed his palms together.

Neither-Nor couldn't help it, he started chuckling too—it was all they had left to do.

The Khan roared in frustration and took up the handle once more. Frost crawled up his fingers to the wrists. He clenched his chattering teeth as he raised the heavy ax-head and turned back to the dangling troll, but he was too drunk and the weapon was too heavy for him to get under control. The head clanged down to the floor again and chipped the stone with a fractal bloom of frost around it. The Khan let the handle drop from his grip, and he yanked out the golden sword instead as he stepped back before Slud. "I'll see ya in the pits o' Hades, troll."

"Slud'll see ya in yer nightmares first," the troll answered, just before the Khan dragged the blade across his throat and a gout of blood spilled out to the stones.

Given the opportunity, Neither-Nor would have killed Slud himself, but watching him die at the hands of this hulking imposter made him furious. He managed to gather a mouthful of blood and saliva, and spat it out in a gentle arc to land on the Khan's furry shoulder.

Arok's glassy eyes went wide, and he pointed at the fat goblin. "First his legs, then arms, then head—take 'im apart with his precious moon blade."

"What 'bout the torture?" the fat goblin asked with unmasked disappointment.

"Just chop him up, or I'll chop ya up in his place!" The Khan climbed back to his jug and chair in a huff.

The feathered goblin stepped before Neither-Nor with a wide grin and a shrug as he unhooked the curved blade from his belt. "Gonna enjoy this." He held it up and ran a finger along the edge. It had been dulled a bit by all the bodies slashed outside, but the elf metal was still plenty sharp. The fat goblin swung, and Neither-Nor saw one of his legs flop to the ground by his hat. His weight seemed off balance, but he still didn't feel a thing. Something about it seemed ridiculous, and he started laughing again.

The goblin swung again, and the other leg fell off to splat in the growing blood pool between him and the troll. How fitting that he should share his final death with the son of the nightmare figure who'd sent him to his first. The silent goblin behind him swung the gut sticker, and one of his arms was cut off cleanly, just above the shoulder. He dangled awkwardly and swung from one hand, but kept laughing the whole time.

The host of rich, worthless goblins turned their eyes and covered their ears, which only made him laugh harder. It was the most ridiculous thing he'd ever seen. The fat goblin swung again, and the moon blade cut through his second arm as his limbless torso slopped to the floor.

He bounced and rolled onto his back, his eyes pointing up

at the sight of his own dangling arms, and he kept laughing as his heart and lungs wound down.

"Finish it!" yelled the Khan.

The last thing Neither-Nor heard was his own mad cackle echoing off the vaulted ceiling. The last thing he saw was his grandfather's moon blade racing toward his own neck.

ARROWS DROPPED SILENTLY into the snow on both sides as Luther led the free wolves in a zigzag retreat up the slope. Another of his pack yelped behind him, but he didn't slow the pace to see if the freshly wounded wolf was all right. Five had fallen in battle and been left behind already. Only the gray bitch had hung with him at every step.

Twice more, the two of them had torn out of the mist along the line, killing a few goblins and sowing terror for many. Each time she'd taken a goblin with her, eating the hearts between attacks, the way Luther had shown her. But she'd had to abandon her last prize, snout deep in the goblin's guts when two snarling groups of Rock Wolves had given hard chase. Luther had been cut along his leg and side in the withdrawal. The goblin arrows and blades hadn't even touched her, though she'd killed many.

Luther's pack had been gaining ground since—none knew the climb as they did, and wolves that carried goblins couldn't keep up with those that didn't. He looked at the gray bitch again, a tireless runner with long confident strides, her haunches covered in bite scars. She remained unbroken by her years of being omega. If she was to be his queen she would need a name . . . Luther would call her

Riga, after a strange city he'd once visited in his dreams.

He glanced over his shoulder to see the wolf who'd taken the latest arrow still at the back of the pack, and he howled his approval. There were arrows sticking out of three others as well, and one of his best had the death-glaze in his eye. It had been the goblin warlock who'd arrived on wing and been left to walk who had turned the army and organized a defense. He'd blown away the mist with his dark words and led the force back toward the compound with his borrowed wolf panting hard out in front.

The dying wolf at Luther's heels had been the closest thing to a friend he'd had in the pack. A golden bolt shot from the warlock's own crossbow jutted from his side. One day, that goblin would be made to pay for these deaths; Luther would eat his heart to honor his fallen kin. But it was the night-hag who'd never shown who had sealed their fate, and what would soon be six more free fighting wolves would die as result.

Only thirteen left, not even enough to last another winter against the Rock Wolves. The Khan would send his riders in force this time, and Luther could only run for so long before hunger took hold. If he saw Agnes again, he'd snap her neck and be done with it ... Unless, somehow, the troll with the cold ax could achieve what he set out to do. Though it went against Luther's nature, something about that troll's odd vibration across the land made him believe in the possibility.

Horns sounded behind them, and Luther's ears swiveled. The Rock Wolf pursuit had turned away. He slowed, climbing up a last jut of rock to a vantage over a wide swath of snow-capped forest. The Pack followed, panting hard with tongues lolling out the sides of rictus grins. They licked their wounds, and a few whimpered in pain, but Luther kept his gaze pointed toward the distant compound and the unknown events that unfolded there. Riga stepped beside him, brushing her shoulder against his. She tentatively licked a cut across his snout, and he lowered his head to her, letting all see how she tended to him.

The last wolf with the death-glaze heaved himself up the cliff face with a ragged breath. The golden bolt had slipped between his ribs and pierced the lung below; it was time for him to stop running. Each wolf came to him as he stood there and trembled, licking his nose and smoothing his fur. Riga went last, and the other wolves backed away from her advance, paying respect to her new position. All but Luther, who kept his attention on the mountain that stretched out below—always listening, always watching for whatever would come next.

As the wounded wolf slumped to the snow to die, a loud cry rose up from the far-off compound. Hundreds of wolf voices raised in unison, maybe a thousand—the whole of the broken pack, singing their song of victory. The last troll had failed. The end of the free wolves was inevitable now.

Luther finally turned to his fallen comrade and licked his drying nose. The Wolf King bit the end of the golden arrow in his side and ripped it out in one quick tug as the wolf's eyes closed for the last time with a labored exhale. No free wolf would die with the mark of the wicked goblins still upon them. The other arrows were ripped out soon after as the brave wolves of the Pack tried to hold their whimpers at bay.

Luther returned to the ledge and tilted his answering cry to the sky, louder and clearer than that of any other wolf on the mountain. Riga joined him with her howl, and soon all the free wolves lent their sorrowful calls to the day. They sang of the fallen, and of defiance against the odds. But to Luther, it sounded like the hollow wails of ghosts, lost and wandering, who did not yet know they were dead. Still, for a moment, the howls of the free wolves drowned out the distant trumpet of their doom.

NINETEEN

Cloak and Shovel

THE GREAT HALL was spinning. Arokkhan had been drinking hard, as usual, but he'd chugged two extra jugs as they'd nailed Neither-Nor's head to the beam above the throne, and that had put him over the edge. He was shit-faced, and it was still light outside. He'd fantasized about watching the last of the Moon Blades die for years, but now that it had happened, he felt nothing. It was the troll's fault. Even in death, this Slud had robbed him of his victory. The giant, freezing ax was leaning against the throne—mocking him still. It looked powerful resting there, but the whole host had seen that it was too cold and heavy for him to wield.

The wolves were licking at the wide pool of blood before the stairs, and the Khan considered having them whipped if they didn't stop. He hadn't let the scrubbers clean the mess after the bodies had been taken away; he wanted everyone to see what was left of the great goblin outlaw and this last troll who'd dared to try for his throne. Damn wolves would ruin the effect, but he was pretty sure he would throw up on himself if he opened his mouth to give the order.

He'd had the six pieces of Neither-Nor hung across the clan compound. Short-Fuse and Long-Pig had wanted the scarred corpse so the mute cannibal could eat it, but the Khan wanted everyone inside and out to see what happened to those who rose against him. The troll, however, he wanted forgotten as soon as possible. After the tree had come down, just seeing the size of the hulking beast that had done it made Arok look vulnerable. Those in the hall who'd heard the troll speak had begun to whisper in the shadows and cast sideways glances in his direction. In just one morning Slud had commanded more fear than Arok had earned after years of working at it.

The Khan had ordered that a huge bag be stitched together, and the troll's corpse had been covered and dragged out by twenty goblins to be fed to the young wolves in the breeding pens. But the wolves wouldn't touch the meat, tucking their tails low and whimpering at the edges of the enclosure as the corpse just rested in the muck—still mocking him. The goblins had dug a big hole, then and there, and tipped the tusked monster in before covering him up to be done with. *Let him rot in the mud as the wolves piss an' shit over his miserable grave.*

But Arok couldn't stop thinking about what the troll had almost done. Nothing felt safe anymore. The doors to the great hall had been patched, and a new beam had been brought in to reinforce the lock, but the gates, bars, and army between him and his enemies seemed flimsy now. The massive tree that had been toppled across the outer stockade would take weeks to dismember and cart away. The fact that the troll and his ax had taken it down in a matter of minutes sent a shudder through the Khan. His hand went to his mouth to hold back the tide of nausea that threatened to spill forth.

Once it subsided, he eyed the murmuring host before him and waved the Herald closer. "Get rid of 'em all. Don't want 'em lookin' at me," he slurred. The Hairy Herald bowed with a whip of fur, and shuffled back down the steps and around the pool of congealed blood to where Short-Fuse waited with his newly acquired feathered cloak and curved blade.

The Herald whispered in Short-Fuse's ear, and the killer grinned with his piggy eyes swinging to the host. "Everybody's gotta fuckin' go!" he yelled, moving toward them with the moon blade in his grip. Long-Pig followed his lead with Neither-Nor's other knife held at the ready as the crowd scrambled away from their approach. All the while, the scarred goblin's severed head watched from above with slack eyes and his mouth locked in that final cackle.

Arokkhan shut his eyes against the spin, but that only made it worse. He still heard the echoes of laughter in his pounding head. There was urgent talking and movement at the other end of the hall, but the Khan kept his lids shut and breathed through his nose until the Herald's clear voice sounded from his perch on the first stair.

"My Khan, Fixelcrick, Chief Hex Doktor, has returned with the advance army."

The Khan's gaze snapped open to see the old apprentice marching toward him. At first, he didn't recognize the creepy warlock without the black feathered cloak, but then the little fucker's evil eye looked up at him, and Arok leaned over and spewed his lunch down the side of the throne.

FIXELCRICK AVERTED his gaze quickly as the Khan continued to projectile vomit over the edge of the rock. Instead, his far-seeing eye swung to his precious flying cloak, now filthy with blood, food, and char, and draped across the shoulders of the wicked goblin thug who did the Khan's most twisted bidding. He wanted it back.

Short-Fuse met his hungry gaze and sneered, his thick fingers playing with a curved blade at his belt that hadn't been there the last time Fixelcrick had seen him. The young Chief Hex Doktor looked away again, this time meeting the casual gaze of one of the Khan's two wolves as they lapped at the edges of the giant pool of congealed blood before the steps. The beast stopped licking and growled. Next, the warlock raised his eyes to the ceiling, not knowing where else to look, as the Khan finished his undignified moment with a wet rag and a boisterous clearing of his nostrils.

That was when he noticed the severed head nailed to the rafter above him—every spot of skin scarred with finely cut runes, and the neck cleanly sliced below a sharp pointy nose and red cap. Every goblin throughout the clans had heard the tales of the outlaw Moon Blade, Neither-Nor. Fixelcrick had always thought they were made-up stories that old goblins told the young to scare them into obedience. He half wondered if this was just some regular goblin who the Khan had cut and hung to make himself look more impressive. Aside from the scars and hat, he didn't look all that special, but every guard, scout and merchant in the clan was talking about what the goblin and troll had done before they met their end.

The felled tree was impossible to miss, and everyone seemed to know someone who'd either been at the battle at the doors or seen firsthand what had transpired within. The troll's giant ax was resting casually against the base of the throne beside the puddle of puke. With his far-seer, Fixelcrick could see wisps of white mist rising from the weapon. It vibrated at a tempo offset from the rest of the world.

"So . . . did ya kill me a witch?" the Khan asked, claiming his attention again.

Fixelcrick bowed low. "Banished her devils and stopped the fire, me Khan." Fixelcrick stayed down, head bowed, eyes on the stone the way his predecessor had done it. "Tried to break me the same way she done Bone Master, but I resisted, saw her plan fer the troll and goblin to attack . . . Sent Short-Fuse back with me coat to warn ya."

"Sent me? Bullshit! 'Twas my idea!" said Short-Fuse, a hatchet suddenly in his hand. "Almost had to give 'im a good whack just to get the coat off 'im."

The Khan waved for him to shut up, and an audible rumble from his newly empty stomach filled the following silence. "A troll, Neither-Nor, an' a witch—said I wanted heads. Short-Fuse brought me the other two. Where's my witch head?"

"Far away by the time we'd reached the fire. Don't know where she is, but she's hid good, and me far-seeing eye hasn't found her yet." Fixelcrick swallowed hard. "Maybe, if I had me cloak, I'd cover more ground and search her out—"

"Ya failed me, boy," the Khan interrupted. "Witch still out there, plottin' 'gainst me . . . Ya want yer coat back, bring me the witch head. 'Til then, it better serves me with him." He pointed at Short-Fuse, and the nasty goblin smiled wide with his ugly, filed teeth.

Fixelcrick's head snapped up. His eyeballs felt like they might burst. "Can't let him keep it! He'll ruin it!"

"You tellin' me what I can or can't do?" Arokkhan asked, meeting the gaze of Fixelcrick's big eye while gritting his teeth. He moved his free hand to the hilt of the battle-ready blade sheathed in a notch in the throne beside the absurdly bejeweled display sword at his hip.

The Herald's eyes bulged in warning behind long strands of hair as the second hatchet slid out of Short-Fuse's belt holster.

The tall, scary goblin with the big sword silently stepped behind Fixelcrick . . .

The hex doktor dropped his head again, this time all the way to the floor. "No, me Khan. Please forgive me. It's just, I want to serve ya best I can . . . But I'll bring ya the witch head anyway, you'll see."

"You do that, or our scarred friend up there'll get some company with mismatched eyeballs." The Khan raked his gaze across Neither-Nor's head, and spat in the general direction of his vomit. "The two o' ya could fly up there togetha. Now, get the fuck outta me hall."

Fixelcrick turned and scurried out in a hurry as Short-Fuse laughed at his back. The guards averted their eyes from his presence as they unlatched and slid aside the fresh beam at the door, but Fixelcrick couldn't help but notice the many wood splinters that still peppered the floor there.

The hinges finally creaked opened to a cold evening. The thick crowd of goblins and wolves out front still wore dazed looks from the day's events. Fixelcrick glanced back into the hall, wishing his evil eye could kill.

"Get somebody to clean up this mess, an' fetch me 'nother jug of pine ale!" demanded the Khan as the doors shut behind the hex doktor.

FOR THE FIRST NIGHT in years, the guards who manned the walls of the outer stockade did not sleep on duty. They huddled around little fires and under furs, but word of the troll's failed attempt on the Khan's life had reached every ear in the clan, and the thunderous crash of the falling tree still echoed about their heads. The returned army had set up a heavy perimeter and had been told to stay alert, but they whispered still of the dark magick they'd seen at work in the woods that morning. Something about it seemed unfinished, and the six hunks of Neither-Nor that had been hung from hooks around the compound had the opposite of the intended effect on those who had to stay up all night beside them.

Two heavy ballista teams had been stationed atop the fallen tree, and the Khan had sent a hundred riders to camp on either side of the hole it had punched through the outer stockade. A corps of goblin engineers had spent the entire afternoon attacking the trunk with axes, saws, and winches, but they still hadn't come close to doing what Slud had achieved in minutes.

Now that the work was done for the night, the compound had gone quiet. Save for the occasional yapping of the juvenile wolves, even the normally bustling and bawdy confines of Clan Center were silent. Doors and windows were shut to the cold as goblins hunched around the fires within, trying not to listen to the clatter against the windows or the bad voice that seemed to whisper in the bitter wind that whistled across the roofs. No one saw the knot of wood that moved down the trunk of the Clan tree, a vaguely humanoid shape, as if squeezed below the bark, clawing its way toward the ground headfirst.

The knot shifted and spun slowly at the massive tree's base. Jagged pine arms reached out and curled to pull free the rest. With the soft scrape of claws against the cobblestones, legs stretched out in rigid steps. What remained of Agnes articulated from the bark as her bony limbs ticked and creaked into being. Her wounds had healed, and her black eyes locked on the wolf pens across the courtyard.

She sniffed deeply of the night air and moved toward the fence that contained the wolves. The penned mutts whimpered ahead of her arrival, but she was not interested in them. She straightened beside the tall fence. Bones cracked along her spine as she rose, far taller than any goblin, to peer over the top. There was a large patch of freshly packed dirt in the center of the enclosure that none of the wolves would step across. Agnes smiled.

Footsteps approached, and she slunk back down into a bent crouch. Two shivering goblin guards moved through the courtyard on their rounds, but neither noticed the dark shadow along the fence as they passed. Once they'd moved away, Agnes turned with her ear cocked to the wind and heard the faint reverberation of someone muttering in the old giant tongue. It was her disciple, calling out to her still, begging always for the return of her stroke across his mind. She could grant him that.

———————

FIXELCRICK WAS FURIOUS. He stormed about his house, picking up unbroken vials of distilled liquids and the few jars of refined herbs that could be salvaged from the mess. A lifetime of meticulously gathered goods, scattered and smashed by the fallen tree. His unconscious goblin prisoner had been found sandwiched between his library of precious tomes and the bookcase. Escaped crickets covered everything, and the cold that whistled through the shattered window kept them quiet and unresponsive as he tried to move about without squashing more with every step.

He'd reset Dingle's absurdly angled shoulder with a hard tug, and then bound him to a chair in the cricket pen. This time the tiny goblin was gagged with a thick knot of cloth wedged in his mouth, and no disjointed or broken limbs would free him. The ever-muttering Bone Master had been returned to his cot in the corner, but he'd sat up again, with his eye locked on the open window as the nonsensical words ebbed and flowed.

The old goblin's focus didn't shift when someone rapped gently on the door, but Fixelcrick snapped around with his hand crossbow leveled. The knock came again, less gentle this time. He sidestepped to the door, trying to go quietly despite the crunch of crickets at every step. Fixelcrick put his ear to the thick wood above the gated crossbeam. Even the Khan's killers would have trouble getting through the lock he'd installed, at least long enough for Fixelcrick to escape out of the root cellar if it was Short-Fuse come to ensure he could keep his new property.

He could sense someone there, just on the other side of the door; he was almost able to see the vibration of their presence through the wood with his wide eye. Moving as slowly as he could, he swiveled the cover from the peephole and looked out. Nothing.

DINGLE WATCHED the hex doktor through squinted eyes. He'd been awake for an hour as the angry little warlock stormed and cussed his way through the cleanup of the house, and he wasn't eager to announce his consciousness after what he'd seen. The goblin had taken particular care with his remaining syringes, and one of them was newly filled, presumably with Dingle's blood, and placed gently in the little satchel he wore at his belt.

Now that someone was at the door, Dingle couldn't decide if he was better off being discovered or not. The doktor was looking through a peephole with a loaded crossbow in his hand, but Dingle noticed the tendril of dense mist that crept through the window to slip down the wall. The mist condensed, and a hunched woman in furs with long, bony limbs and pitch-black skin emerged. She looked across the room at Bone Master, who'd turned toward her and stopped his muttering. Then she looked at Dingle, with her solid black eyes boring through him. He could feel her presence in his head like an itch at the base of his skull just before his whole body went rigid.

The itch grew hot, and then it was searing. Dingle would have screamed, but he found that he couldn't move or make any noise at all. It felt like his mind had been tossed onto a bed of coals. He was certain he would die, but then she turned her attention away, and he deflated with a whimper. The warlock's head snapped around just as her claw shot out to wrap around his throat and pin him to the door. The crossbow shot off into the ceiling, and the hag smiled with a mouth full of long, needlelike teeth.

"You're the one who cast out my salamanders, yes?"

FIXELCRICK GAVE HER the evil eye, which was bulging especially large with his constricted airways, but she only smiled wider, looking like she might take a bite out of his face. His hand scrambled at the satchel and grabbed the syringe, but her other claw pinned his wrist to the door as he tried to bring it to his chest. She leaned in with her long nose hovering close, and sniffed, first him, then the syringe.

"Ah, blood magick. Clever goblin." She looked back over her shoulder at the now awake prisoner. "But where did this one get the blood?"

The tiny goblin said something unintelligible through the gag.

The witch plunged the syringe into her mouth, closing her eyes for a moment as she savored the taste of the blood. "Pure?" Her other claw constricted around Fixelcrick's throat, and she yanked him away from the door and dragged him toward the cricket pen. He tried to pry open her hand and kick his way free, but her spindly arms were as unforgiving as iron. She ripped opened the gate and tossed Fixelcrick to the terrain beside the chair before removing Dingle's gag with a sharp tug. "Where did you get it, goblin?"

"W-w-what?" Dingle sputtered as Fixelcrick coughed at his feet.

"The elixir of life, how did you come by it?" Fixelcrick tried to crawl away, but the witch's clawed talon of a foot pinned him to the ground.

"Scraped the jar b-b-by the rrriver," Dingle blurted. "I ssserve Lord Slud. I ammm his disciple!"

The witch cocked her head. "I see . . . You could be useful, yes." Her eyes shifted back to Fixelcrick, who felt like he might vomit. She had mastered the greatest alchemical feat there was. The Nectar of Amrite, Liquid Gold—it made his creation of the flying cloak look like the work of a half-wit child.

"Fixelcrick serves only you, m'lady," he gasped. "I'm a student of the Knack. Lemme be yer disciple and learn from yer great wisdom. I'll do yer bidding eternal." He ceased his feeble battle against the crush of her foot on his chest as she squeezed the breath out of him.

His vision started to blur, and his tongue rose quivering out of his mouth . . . She let up at the last second, just as he could feel his consciousness start to slip. He gasped deeply, his lungs burning. "Perhaps you too could be of use for now . . . Do you have a shovel?"

Bone Master stepped into the pen beside them and held up Fixelcrick's shovel with a bowed head.

TWENTY

Night Moves

AGNES EMERGED FROM the door with a bloody knife in one hand and two shit-shovels in the other. The three wolf breeders behind her would not rise again from their beds. The thirty juvenile wolves hunkered together at the farthest end of the pen, whimpering as they waited for her next command. Bone Master, as he'd previously called himself, was already digging in the center without pause or comment. The other two goblins glanced between the wolves and her approach, but they'd already learned to keep their tongues to themselves. She tossed the stinking shovels at their feet, and licked the knife blade clean before sliding it back into her belt. "Dig."

The tiny goblin, Dingle, was eager to comply; the young warlock, less so. He was more focused on watching her than doing what she said. Dingle's measly dirt was already flying by the time Fixelcrick had bent to retrieve the shovel. His big eye focused on Agnes, as if trying to glean her knowledge from afar. His impudence matched his ignorance.

She met his gaze with a lash across his mind that brought him to his knees in the muck—just a taste of the last Agnes's pain from when Dingle and his friends had run her through with spears and left her to char. Fixelcrick buckled over with his hands at his stomach as she approached. She leaned down with her teeth hovering beside his ear and released him from the agony. "Quickly now."

The warlock sprang to his feet and started digging beside the others in a hurry. The goblin runt who'd tasted the elixir of life struggled to outpace him, but his spindly little arms were barely long enough to get a good grip on the shovel, let alone lift the heavy muck over his shoulder.

Once the hole was dug, Agnes would drink his blood and take back what he should not have tasted. For now, she needed all the shovels she could command. Her black eyes scanned the wooden plank fence that ringed the pen, built high to block the occasional escape attempt of young mountain wolves that hadn't been broken yet. She'd been watching the courtyard for a while from above. Another patrol wouldn't be by for almost an hour.

The pen was far from the outer stockade, but Agnes could see the campfire on one of the towers from there. Luckily the night was dark and the shadows long around the Clan tree. The shops and stalls that hadn't been crushed were shut tight, and many of the torch lights had been blown out in the hard wind. The Khan had picked a spot for Slud's disposal where curious eyes could not easily see.

She whispered words to the sky, "*Ig'na'a thoch zu-ghul,*" and the wind howled across the roofs in answer. Shutters rattled and walls creaked; some of the more anxious goblins started moving beds into root cellars and bringing the goats and pigs inside for the night.

The watching wolves cringed as Agnes's eyes passed over them—small and weak compared to their free cousins. The size and instinct had been bred and beaten out of them for generations. Agnes would have made them tear each other apart then and there if not for the noise it would raise.

"Hit something," the little warlock called over his shoulder. The runt leapt into the hole and started scrabbling at the dirt with his bare hands.

Agnes approached, giving Bone Master a wave to get him out of the hole. They'd barely gotten three feet down, but there was a heavy canvas bag, stitched haphazardly and stained with blood. Dingle heaved a chunk of dirt over his shoulder and dove back for more. A couple of his stubby claws had broken off with bloody ends, but he didn't slow.

"There." Agnes pointed at the ground where Bone Master stood, and he buried his shovel again and started digging. In a few heaves he uncovered more of the bag. She pointed again, and Fixelcrick gave it his shovel, and again for Bone Master, until the whole length of the massive sack was uncovered. She didn't have to tell Dingle anything as he scurried across it to scrape away the rest.

The Khan's goblins had been in a rush to bury him; the hole wasn't deep enough and they'd rolled him in faceup. Agnes could see the shape of his giant head and outstretched boots through the bag. There was a huge stain around his neck, and the butts of arrows were still sticking up across the canvas in little blood-soaked tents.

She drew her knife again and flipped it into the earth beside the fawning little goblin. "Cut the bag over his face." She pointed. "Careful now."

Dingle moved up, mindful of the arrows as he traversed the troll's chest. He pinched the bag over the jutting tusks and sliced it with the utmost care before peeling it to the sides. The corpse had started to stink, and Dingle crinkled his nose. Slud's face and hair were painted with crusted blood, and his heavy lids were shut. The skin and lips were slack and pallid. There was an ugly slash across his throat, but it was hard to see if it had healed beneath the gore. Dingle stayed perched on his chest and bowed his little head. Fixelcrick looked at Agnes expectantly, but she kept her gaze locked on the troll lad. *Time to see if he paid attention to his old auntie's lessons.*

Dingle began to rock and mutter as the warlock waited for Agnes do something amazing. There was nothing she could do; only her long-gone daughter, Hel, had mastered the art of raising the dead, and those mindless, savage creatures would not fit her plans. The troll had to do this on his own or else stay here to fertilize the mud.

The wind whistled between buildings. The clan tree creaked; damaged branches clattered down to the stones. The cluster of wolves whimpered as the reek of decay wafted from the hole. Even if he managed to wake, the lad would never be the same as he was. Once glimpsed, death had a way of marking one of its own. Black Agnes peered at him, waiting for the slow beat of his heart . . . nothing.

She turned away with a hiss and glared up at the mountain. *The dreams lied! Another quarter century wasted!* Then she heard it, *THUMP,* slow and strong. She spun back to kneel beside the lad with her eyes held close to his face. There was a twitch in the troll's eyelids, then the gentle intake of air through his wide nostrils. Her needle teeth emerged in a grin, and she took a step back as Slud's dark eyes peeled open.

Dingle didn't even notice until the troll spoke. "Oi, get off Slud's chest," he rasped.

Dingle's face snapped up with a yelp, and tears of joy started flowing. He scrambled out of the hole and bent his forehead to the mud. "Oh, L-L-Lord of D-D-Death, I kn-kn-knew you'd come!"

"Silence," Agnes commanded.

Fixelcrick watched in awe as the troll grimaced and shifted. Slud's gaze took in his present state before rising to meet Agnes's close appraisal.

"Who're ya?" Slud stopped himself and his dark eyes narrowed. "Aunt Agnes . . . Outta de fire, aye?"

She nodded. "I've been watching, lad. You've done well, but your work's not done."

"Shoulda known." He tried to sit up, but the pain of the arrows sent him back to the dirt with a grunt.

"Need to get those arrows out for you to heal, boy," Agnes said, creeping closer to the edge. "Your auntie is gone, but I am here to help you in her stead, yes?"

His eyes held her back just beyond his reach. "Is all dis Slud's game, or yers?"

"Yours, my boy," she said with a bowed head. "All the training, all the pain, readying for this moment and the throne that's yours to take." She gave him her best smile, but he looked unconvinced. "I am but one of your pieces. Tell me what you need, and I shall see you have it, yes."

"Neider-Nor, where's he at?"

Fixelcrick stepped up to command the troll's attention. "Dead. Not comin' back this time."

He smacked his lip against a tusk. "Burned, buried, or eaten?"

"Cut in six parts. Spread 'bout the compound fer all to see," Fixelcrick answered.

Slud looked back to Agnes. "All right. First, get Slud outta dis hole . . . Gonna need a nice big sword . . . Den, ya go 'n' fetch all dem scarred pieces. Slud'll need 'im whole."

Agnes was surprised by the command the troll had gained in his gruff voice. Perhaps he'd brought back something extra from his latest ordeal after all. He stank of the grave, and she doubted the smell would ever go away, but there was also an added weight to his presence that left even her a little unnerved. *Now he's ready.*

"Ya do dat, 'n' Slud'll go get his ax 'n' end dis fuckin' clan fer good."

She hadn't been certain he'd have the strength to wield Thrym's Ax. The ancient King of the Frost Giants had never been bested until Thor's hammer had delivered his murder. None had managed to carry the frozen ax since.

There was much to do before the break of day; killing her goblin helpers could wait. She met the troll's dark gaze and nodded.

———

FIXELCRICK HAD an arm and a torso in a bag over his shoulder. The infamous Neither-Nor was not a particularly large goblin, but he was dense with lean muscle and knotted bone. The load had gotten heavy after that last arm. The warlock hadn't slept in over thirty hours, and the only thing that kept him moving was the residual effect of Dingle's blood in his system. He scurried along the felled tree through Clan Center for the third time that night, having previously swapped out the legs and the other arm. But the head still seemed like an impossibility.

Once the absurd crew had squeezed into Fixelcrick's house, the many jutting arrows had been removed from the stinking troll, and the witch had packed the wounds with a meal of herbs and alcohol that she'd scrounged from unbroken jars and piles on the floor.

Black Agnes had retrieved one of the goblin wolf breeder's bodies at the troll's suggestion, and Slud had Dingle dismember the corpse with a bone saw in the cricket pen. The tiny goblin threw up repeatedly as he worked, but he did not stop or slow, handing up the parts as they came free. Slud took the sharpest knife Fixelcrick had and set about carving little runes across the dead goblin's skin, one piece at a time. There was no pattern or reason to the symbols he etched, but the finished product came away looking surprisingly authentic once the excess mess had been wiped away.

It had been Fixelcrick's job to swap out the parts. He tried to use the loss of his beautiful coat as a reason to get out of it, but Agnes had taken another syringe of Dingle's blood and shot him up when he wasn't looking. Then she'd given him a string of strange words for controlling the spirits in the wind, and he found that he could blow out the torches and rise up to swap the limbs before the guards even bothered to look. It wasn't the same as flying freely with wings of his own, but it was enough to keep him going and remind him of what he'd lost.

The exhausted goblin fell against the door to his house and knocked slowly four times. After a moment, he could hear his key sliding into the lock of the cage on the other side, and then the heavy beam raising up from the brace on the spring and winch system he'd devised. He slipped through the opening, wedging the gathered body parts against the doorjamb before he squeezed through.

Agnes watched him with her unreadable obsidian eyes as she shut and locked the door behind him. Fixelcrick dropped the bag and stumbled to a chair while she bent to examine the contents. "No head?"

"Can't . . . I'm through. Send Dingle," he said.

Slud was sitting on the cot at the far side of the room as it bowed dramatically beneath his weight. He didn't even look up from the line of runes he was cutting across the back of the severed head braced between his knees. It looked like a toy ball in his grip, though he appraised it carefully. Bone Master stood by the fire, muttering to himself. Dingle wasn't there.

"The little one has gone to fetch a weapon," Agnes said. "This is for you to finish, yes."

"Too tired, can barely walk, let alone use the Knack effectively . . . Maybe if I had me cloak." A lance of agony shot through his mind to knock him out of the chair. *He felt a rope around his neck as he dangled from the branch of a tree. Breath would not come, and he felt like his head would explode from the pressure as arrow after arrow slammed into his body, shot by a large host of elves on horseback below.* The pressure released, and he found himself on the floor of his wrecked house again. He drew a desperate breath and clutched his throat, tears running down his face.

Agnes leaned over him with the light of the fire reflecting off her long wet teeth. "I do not ask, goblin. If you wish to learn, listen and act, or I've no need of you." She had one of his syringes in her hand, and she jammed it into her own arm and drew a tiny amount of her almost-black blood. "You like to play with blood. Try this." She grinned.

Fixelcrick climbed back to his feet and brushed a squashed cricket from his elbow before accepting the syringe. The whole house shook as the troll stood and lumbered toward them. He had to stoop to get his head below the joists, and Fixelcrick had to steel himself against the instinct to back away or drop to his knees.

"Slud punched hole t'rough de skull fer ya," the troll rasped. His voice was still a croaked whisper, but the gash across his throat had already healed to a neat line since they'd dug him up.

Fixelcrick delicately slipped the syringe into his satchel before taking the offered head. Next the troll draped a coiled rope over his shoulder. "Dat's a good knot. Just loop it 'round de chimney 'n' down ya go."

Agnes dumped Neither-Nor's newly acquired body parts onto the table beside the rest, and gave them a close sniff. She handed the bag over without looking, and Fixelcrick dropped the dummy head in.

Fixelcrick got the impression that saying no to Slud would be just as bad an idea as it was with Agnes, but he seemed reasonable enough, someone Fixelcrick could work with. "I'll do it, but when it's done, and the Khan's dead—I want me coat back."

Agnes gave no indication of having heard him, but the troll answered. "Sure t'ing."

"And I want the Elixir of Undeath too. I wanna know how it's made."

Agnes hissed and spun toward him with one of her hooked talons raised to strike, but Slud stopped her with an outstretched arm and motioned her to the door. "Done . . . Slud's buildin' a gang. If ya do dis 'n' live, ya got a spot, goblin." The troll spat into his giant palm and held it out for Fixelcrick to take.

He spat into his own palm and let his hand be enveloped in the giant's painfully firm grip. Slud held on after the shake and lowered his tusked maw close. His breath stank like a rotting corpse. "Don't get caught, boy. 'N' if ya do, keep yer mout' shut, or Slud'll etch ya live same way as dat body."

———————

TWENTY MINUTES LATER, Fixelcrick was crouched on the roof of the clan herbologist with the bloody bag at his belt and his far-seeing eye trained on the smoke hole in the roof of the great hall. The fallen tree was crawling with guards now, and this was the only other high place he could think of with a decent vantage of the inner stockade. The hex doktors had cultivated their herbs on the growing platforms across this roof for years, and it was not uncommon for them to harvest the mugwort, holly leaves, and periwinkle on a cold winter night.

He could hear the riders and wolves milling about the courtyard: coughs and foot stamps, then a snarled dispute over sleeping space among the beasts. It ended with a whip and a whimper. He'd have to fly high and get lucky for none of them to see his approach. With the flying cloak, maybe, but he'd never been good at controlling elemental spirits before the banishing of the salamanders that morning. Nothing about this was a good idea.

Fixelcrick took the syringe from the satchel and stared at the quarter vial of black liquid within. If the night-hag's memories of suffering were any indication, she'd been present among the wars of the old gods. She was maybe even one of them, hiding among the mortals for millennia, resurrected from the flames again and again. She alone knew the recipe for immortality.

Fixelcrick knew if he slipped, she'd take both his life and

spirit in an instant, but access to her knowledge was worth the risk; and despite what Bone Master had taught him, something about Slud made him want to follow. There was a vibration in the undead troll's bones that resonated deeper than the world around him. No position in any clan could compare to what they offered.

All that matters is the Knack, he reminded himself before jamming the syringe through his breastplate with a sharp exhale. He thumbed the plunger. The initial jolt knocked him back against the railing with a clatter. His body went rigid, and he fell to his side for the convulsions that followed. His face pressed into a tray of snow-covered soil as the eyes of the guards on the tree passed over. It felt like he was burning from the inside out. He tasted blood as he bit the meat of his palm to stifle a scream. This was different than the pain he'd felt through the shared memories with the hag—closer and more visceral, like he was losing control of his form and not just his mind. The witch had tricked him.

It was too much; he couldn't fight it. He gave in to the agony. The scream escaped, but no sound emerged from his stretched mouth. His blood rocketed through his veins, and he would have clawed out his own throat to release the pressure if he could have moved. Against such suffering, death would have been a gift.

Only then, as quickly as it had come, the spasm ceased and the searing heat abated into a warm throb. He could hear Black Agnes's hissed laughter inside his head. It was his laugh now, and his will was no longer his own to govern.

Fixelcrick stood and raised his palms to the sky as the words Agnes had taught him spilled out of his mouth. *"Ig'na'a thoch zu-ghul."* The stinging wind howled down the mountain and whistled through the branches of the trees. The guards who might have witnessed shut their eyes, pulled blankets around them, and hunkered low, but the cold didn't bother Fixelcrick as it had. Unseen hands took hold of his legs and arms, raising him up into the air as his gaze locked on the stubby chimney of the great hall. Without words, he willed the aerial servants forward, and they carried him across the stockade toward the pitched roof.

He glanced down at the thick host of wolves and warriors below, none of them looking up to see his passage as the bad wind whipped snow and pine needles into a frenzy. He stifled a laugh, his or Agnes's he did not know, and planted his feet on the overlapping planks of the roof as the servants of the wind released him. The night was brighter than it had ever been. The shadows held no fear, and the hidden world that lurked below the surface, which he'd spent his lifetime slaving to grasp, was now his to play with.

Surely, this was what it meant to be immortal. With the witch's blood in his veins, he could do anything. *Why waste me time retrievin' heads, when Fixelcrick can be one of the great warlocks of the age?*

A lash of torment shot through him in answer. He smacked his chin on the stone lip of the chimney before grabbing the arch of the roof to save himself from tumbling down to the courtyard. Agnes's laugh echoed in his mind.

The rope came off his shoulder as he regained his feet. He looped it around the stone vent without another moment's hesitation. The thick ceiling of dark clouds visible through the trees was getting lighter; he didn't have long. He peered through the square opening and smelled smoke; he could see little through the darkness but the orange glow of embers in the fire pit far below. He eased the rope over the edge, lowering it down slowly until its full length was through the opening.

It would have been too small for some goblins, but Fixelcrick had never had broad shoulders or been counted on for his brawn. His hands white-knuckled the rope, and he swung his legs into the smoky oblivion. With his breath held, he descended, hand under hand down the short tube of soot-black rocks until the vast hall opened up beneath him on all sides. He dangled and spun as his newly awakened eyes adjusted.

With the flames dying and the torches snuffed out, the space was vast, dark, and cold. He could hear the echoing of snores from both ends of the hall and see the shapes of goblins beneath thick layers of blankets around the fire pit directly below. He lowered himself farther, only able to hold on because of the borrowed strength in the witch's blood.

The throne was empty, but Fixelcrick could see the two wolves resting on furs piled beside the door at the rear of the hall that led to the Khan's personal quarters. Rousing them would be the end of him. Then he heard a gentle slapping sound below and smelled burning. He looked down to see the butt of the rope dragging along the coals in the fire pit. The rope was too long; the fibers were smoldering, and then a little flame burst to life.

The sound of his inhale echoed off the ceiling. He glanced at the wolves—not moving—then back to the jolly flame as it climbed the rope toward him. *This ain't possible! Could still climb back up and live!*

Agnes's psychic lash snapped across his mind, and he lost hold of the rope. His hands scrabbled desperately as his legs wrapped tightly around the cord. His fingers caught it again at the expense of a bad rope burn just before Agnes's command sounded in his thoughts: *Fetch the head or feed the wolves.*

Fixelcrick kept descending with an added swing, his far-seeing eye focused on the beam above the Khan's throne. The rope was long enough that he didn't need to work too hard to build his arc, but now the burning cherry at the tip was whipping out above the sleeping guards in one direction before swinging back toward the prone wolves in the other.

He kept swinging and reached out until his boots touched down on the flat of the rafter above the throne. With a little hop, he braced against the rope to regain his balance. Neither-Nor's head was beside him, nailed through the skull to the wood and framed on both sides by the drape of slow-dried entrails. He glanced over his shoulder at the wolves one last time, but they still hadn't stirred, though one of the sleeping goblins murmured and moved by the fire. Fixelcrick's far-seeing eye snapped around to lock on the sheen of black feathers poking up from beneath the blankets. *Me coat!*

His hand drew the knife at his belt, and his weight shifted back to the rope, but Agnes's presence reared up to stay the impulse. She loomed there in the back of his mind, reminding him that the next lash would send him tumbling to his death. He sheathed the blade and plucked the dummy head out of the bag at his hip instead.

Holding the rope in one hand and the head in the other, he crouched on the beam with a precarious sway. The replacement head was wedged into his lap as he reached down to try for a grip on Neither-Nor, but his fingers fumbled at the goblin's waxy, hairless skin. The famous red cap slipped off and fell to the coagulated pool of blood below. Fixelcrick froze, listening for the slightest rustle to send him scrambling toward the ceiling, but it didn't come.

His fingers reached down and tried again, finding a firm hold on the teeth of the goblin's top jaw. Slowly, he pulled it away from the beam with the sound of skull scraping against the iron spike that pierced it. It caught on the crown of the nail, and he had to give it a jiggle until the head popped free. The final piece of Neither-Nor went in the bag, and Fixelcrick's heart swelled with a small sense of victory. He yanked open the mouth of the dummy and gripped it the same way, but he stopped again as someone shuffled and yawned behind the throne.

No, no, no! He looked up; the sky was quickly brightening through the little square high above. Someone had stood and, by the sound of it, was getting dressed just a few feet away . . . Perhaps Fixelcrick could summon one of the salamanders from the embers, but he didn't know the words. Maybe there was enough wind in the hall for the aerial elementals to answer, but they would wake the whole room in their bluster

He remained there, helpless and frozen as the old Big-Boss-of-the-scouts-turned-Herald, Harog, scuffed by the throne directly below him. The hairy goblin yawned again as he ambled past the pool of dried blood, and took a wide path around the sleeping killers beside the fire pit. He didn't notice the fallen hat, the smoldering tip of the rope dangling above the throne, or the Chief Hex Doktor balanced awkwardly on the closest rafter. In a hurry, Fixelcrick lowered the dummy head and jammed it onto the spike through the pre-punched hole.

A hairy step from Harog later, and Fixelcrick was pushing himself up the rope with his hind legs working like one of the crickets'. He rose in a frantic rush, and the rope started to swing precariously while Agnes laughed in his mind. Just as the front doors of the great hall were opened, and the clatter of the new day awoke all within, Fixelcrick yanked the end of the burning rope over the lip of stone high above.

"*Ig'na'a thoch zu-ghul.*" Invisible hands carried him up to disappear among the shadowed branches of the clan tree.

HAROG HATED being called Hairy Herald. He'd always tried to be fair to the many goblins below him while keeping his distance from those above. The better a job he did at keeping watch and patrolling the borders, the less he had to interact with the Khan. It had been working well for years, and then that idiot goblin, Dingle, had ruined everything.

Harog waited as the exhausted guards unlocked the stockade door and slid the massive beam aside. Every wolf and goblin in the courtyard was red-eyed and shivering. A few looked like they might try to kill him out of spite as he shuffled through the creaking doors and turned toward Clan Center.

When he'd been Big Boss of the scouts, he'd never had to wake up early. He'd had his own comfortable bed to sleep in, and his own balcony for cooking meats as he looked out toward the clan tree. Technically, he supposed he still owned the house, but the Khan only let him leave the hall for brief errands, and the one time he tried to check in on his old life, Short-Fuse and Long-Pig had been sent to bring him back before long.

Harog was sure he'd be killed horribly on the first slow day the Khan found. He'd caught the wicked drunk eyeing him predatorily more times than he could count. No doubt the sadistic coward would have his killers string him up and shave him before his slow death.

His bum foot scraped through the dirty snow, and in a few steps the fur that trailed behind was soggy and black. He'd been told to fetch Fixelcrick; the Khan wanted to see him early. Arok usually liked to get the first kill in while he was eating his eggs, and Harog had overheard Short-Fuse poisoning the efforts of the new Chief Hex Doktor after he'd left the hall in a huff the day before. Harog had considered warning him, but what was the point? Without a flying coat there was no escape for any of them.

A goat and a chicken were walking down the middle of the road toward him. The chicken followed at the goat's heels and clucked in a ceaseless one-sided conversation—unlikely friends brought together after the troll's tree had shattered whatever world they'd known. They ignored Harog as he scuffed by.

Harog let the thick hair fall before his eyes. He normally trimmed it twice a day, but his scissors were at home, and there wasn't much that happened in that hall that he wanted to see. His attention went only so far as his next step, until he noticed the deep line that was scraped in the muck leading into Clan Center. He brushed the hair aside and looked ahead. A tiny goblin wearing a hat that looked like a sock was dragging a large sword on the stones of the merchants' circle. The sword was at least three times his height, and it scraped carelessly across the cobbles as the funny little goblin turned abruptly toward a house and knocked four times on the thick door.

It was the doktor's house, the one always filled with the chirping of crickets, the one that Harog was looking for. Harog recognized the goblin who awaited entry as well, though he didn't see how it was possible. It was Dingle, but Dingle was dead.

TWENTY-ONE

All Keyed Up

SLUD HAD HEARD the stories of the ancient Frost King Thrym when he was little. Aunt Agnes had told of the deeds of the Lord of the Jötnar as if she had been there herself, speaking of him with love and respect, and telling of his murder at the hands of the treacherous gods with lasting anger. Until very recently, Slud's whole life had been framed by those epic tales of old, and he'd been led to believe that he would grow to perform feats as momentous as those of the once famous heroes of a forgotten time. The reality of such actions was far less romantic than he'd imagined.

His adversaries were not bold or worthy opponents, and they had only been made his enemies by a fight that he himself had picked and lost. Just as it had been in his little world locked in the valley of the Iron Wood, life outside was defined by pain, exhaustion, and the unending test to overcome the urge to give in. Greatness, legends, and the stories of a lost age were bullshit. Life was about will and luck, and the rare moments when the two coincided—the rest was just suffering, and the fleeting illusion that the suffering abated for a few stolen minutes here and there.

Slud was a puppet at the end of Agnes's string, and the first great disappointment of his life was realizing that his efforts against the Rock Wolves were not in her honor, but at her continued command. He breathed his fresh understanding in through his nose and out through his mouth, never running away from the pain but joining with it, letting it wash over and become a part of him. He rolled his abused neck and swallowed with his newly fused throat—still buzzing and warm with that last potion's influence. Next, he arched his back and filled his lungs to capacity, relishing in the pinprick jabs that peppered his body where the crossbow bolts had been.

His eyes snapped wide as the door opened and Dingle slipped in with a sword dragging behind him. Agnes quickly slammed it shut and slid the beam into the cage before turning back to Neither-Nor's headless body. The scarred goblin's legs, arms, and torso had reconnected nicely, with the lines of runes still rearranging across his skin as the muscle and bone beneath knitted together. But Fixelcrick hadn't returned yet, and with no head there wasn't much hope for their plan.

Dingle dragged the sword across the hut toward Slud, sending crickets flying in every direction as he came. The tiny goblin presented the pilfered sword as best he could, almost knocking himself over in the process. "D-d-did Dingle do g-g-good, master?"

Slud took the blade in hand and gave it a shake. The balance was front heavy, the metal was cut-rate, and the blade was dull. "It'll do."

The little fellow smiled wide and dropped his forehead to the floor with an audible *thunk*, but his beady eyes and everyone else's attention all swung back to the door when two loud knocks came from outside. They'd agreed on four slow knocks; it had been Fixelcrick's idea . . .

"Dingle, I know you're in there! It's Harog . . . the Herald. Open up!"

Everyone froze except Slud, who stood with a grimace, sword in hand.

"Fixelcrick, I'm alone. The Khan sent me to fetch you! It's not good, but if you don't open up, Short-Fuse and Long-Pig will come back and it'll get a lot worse," Harog said.

Slud hunched and moved toward the door as the crickets leapt out of his way. Agnes gave him a nod and moved to unlock the cage and raise the brace. He shifted the sword to his other hand and flexed his fingers, sliding as close to the wall as possible. He gave Agnes a nod, and she swung the door open just as his hand shot out to grab the dangling fur of the Herald's chin.

Harog yelped as Slud pulled him inside and tossed him to the floor. Agnes slammed the door shut. Before the Herald could yell again, the dull blade had swung to his throat and pressed close. The hairy goblin's eyes went wide beneath the fur as he took in the sight of Slud leering above.

"How?" he asked.

"No point askin' dat." Slud pressed the blade under the goblin's chin, but he doubted it was even sharp enough to cut through the thick layers of fur.

"If you kill me you'll never be able to get out," the Herald said. "The Khan will send others to find me. There's more than five thousand War Boys surrounding the compound."

Slud leaned closer, and the furry goblin winced at the press of his breath. "Don't wanna get out, goblin. Wanna get in. Slud ain't done yet."

"How?" Harog asked again.

This hairy goblin was good under pressure, Slud had to give

him that. The troll nodded to the headless body of Neither-Nor on the table. "He's goin' down de chimney. Gonna open up de doors from inside."

Harog looked at the spindly, decapitated body and was glad the troll couldn't see his expression. One of his hairy legs shook. "There's no way. Too many guards and crossbows, inside and out. More than before."

Slud motioned to Agnes, who was watching with a hungry glare and a strand of drool slipping from her fangs. "Gonna have us a nice big distraction first."

Agnes stepped closer and her hooked claws opened. "Enough talk. I will drink this one. Agnes is so thirsty."

"There's another way," Harog blurted. "A better way in." He raised his hands in surrender and slowly pulled a large key on a string from beneath his shirt. "I wanna see the Khan dead too. I can get you inside without a fight . . . but we'll need to go now."

THE DAY'S LIGHT finally burned back the dark clouds that had claimed the ridge. The sky cleared through the branches as pinks and oranges gave way to an azure expanse. The cruel wind had subsided, but the goblins and wolves remained crouched and shivering beside the few fires that hadn't been snuffed out by the elements. From the thick pines upslope, Luther and Riga watched the puffs of breath rise from the towers. Even from there, looking down at the giant tree that had cut through the defenses of the mighty Rock Wolf Clan with ease, they could smell the fear of their enemies and hear the chattering of their teeth.

The Wolf King had left the Pack behind to rest and heal in

their temporary den, but Riga would not leave his side despite his snarls and snaps of warning. Eventually he'd had to give in to her persistence, and now, standing in the snow on the cold cliffs while contemplating acts of reckless hunger, he was happy for her presence.

She nuzzled him, still filthy from the battle, and brushed her erect tail across his face suggestively. He eyed her offering and felt a stirring of life within that had been dormant for too long, but turned back toward the compound before she noticed. He didn't want to give her the satisfaction of so easy a victory.

He scanned the sprawling, bisected house of his enemy, and his keen eyes stopped on a severed goblin leg that hung from a spike on the stones of the tower. Even from afar he could see the symbols cut into the skin. On the next tower he found a matching arm. The famous Neither-Nor had met his final end, but there was still no sign of the troll's fate.

Luther couldn't shake the scent of Riga's musk from his nose, but his attention darted between tiny specks moving below: a goblin guard stretching on the wall, a scrawny wolf slinking out of an open pen door, two goblins walking through the Clan Center. His eyes locked on a little goblin wearing black, not within the compound but moving along a high branch that hung over it. The goblin glanced down before stepping off the branch with his arms outstretched as the wind picked up along the ridge with an ill-omened moan. He drifted down to the stones like a seedpod, though Luther didn't see the sheen or shape of feathers.

He did spy a familiar golden crossbow beside a dirty bag at the goblin's belt. It was the same goblin who had turned the tides against the free wolves at the battle the previous morning. The same crossbow whose golden bolt had killed one of his best wolves. Luther's hunger churned in his gut.

Riga had walked in a circle and came up beside him again. This time she nipped at the shag of his mane and knocked her body into his with playful force. He growled and gave her a more substantial nip in return, but she only batted him in the face with her tail and kept walking.

Her pleasing musk hung in the air, but he forced his anger back to the surface, looking to the jutting spires of wood where the massive tree had fallen. The trunk had become a bridge, leading straight to the heart of the enemy. If Luther jumped to the top, he'd be able to run to the inner yard of the Khan's great hall in only a few seconds. He estimated at least two of the big javelin bolts and twenty or more arrows would find him in that same span, but he had the strong urge to give it a try anyway.

This time, the wing flutter of a raven distracted him from the yearning in his belly. It flapped down and landed with a hop in the bloodstained snow beside the tree, then cocked its head this way and that. Numerous bodies of goblins and wolves still littered the site, covered in frost and locked in rigor mortis. The raven pecked at one of them, claiming an eyeball.

Luther had seen this raven before, always watching from above, usually making itself known in disconcerting moments when he thought he was alone. It was not just any raven, but one of a pair of old brothers whose eyes scanned always in service of another. The bird flapped into the air with heavy beats of broad black wings and sailed up into the branches the goblin warlock had vacated. No good could come from that bird's presence on the mountain or the attention of the one who watched from afar through his gaze.

On her third pass, Riga decided to forgo the subtlety. She bit Luther hard in the haunches, and he snapped around with a snarl. She answered with a rub of her ass across his snout, which shut him up quickly. He could still smell the goblin blood mingling with her scent, and this time he couldn't resist. He mounted her from behind and bit the scruff behind her ears as he worked. She looked back and nuzzled and nipped at him as wolf-lock set in and his future son set out.

They would be connected like that for a short while, unable to pull free even if they wanted to. Luther could not easily remember feeling contentment before, a willingness to share his space with another of his kind—though he knew the hunger had only been staved off for a brief time. He rubbed his ear against the top of her head, and she let a joyous whine spill out of her open jaws.

The wind picked up again, moaning as if in answer to her cry, and Luther thought he heard words flowing with it. At first he tried to ignore it, savoring the moment with Riga, but the dark whispers continued. The words grew louder, harsher, and below, in the compound, the wolves of the clan rose up in howls all at once. Before long, goblins could be heard yelling, and then a horn blew. The words swelled, and Luther felt them pulling at his mind as Riga let out a low growl beneath him. It was the witch, Agnes—whatever had happened to the troll, it wasn't over yet.

The grumble in his belly demanded a response, and the howls below took on a more savage tone. He wanted to run down and kill whatever he could, but not Riga. He would never hurt her or the pup he knew she was carrying within. They would hunt together as a pair, and they would dine on the hearts of every goblin and traitor wolf of the clan until none were left—starting with that flying warlock and the deceitful night-hag who sought to test his will again.

TWENTY-TWO

Death March

THE MARCH DOWN the great hall had never seemed so long before. Sweat was beading on Fixelcrick's scalp, and his heartbeat was shaking his rib cage. The hex doktors had always held a place of prominence in the clan, but Harog seemed to think the combination of Short-Fuse's bad whispers and the Khan's alcohol-fueled madness might end their historical reprieve from violence.

The heavy locks of the doors banged shut, just as the howls of wolves rose up outside as if in celebration of his pending fate. Fixelcrick kept his far-seeing eye on Harog's shaggy, shuffling feet and tried to keep a step behind Bone Master, who ambled silently at his side. Maybe if things went wrong, the Khan would take it out on the old, infirm goblin instead of him, though Fixelcrick wasn't sure what his muttering spellbound master might do next.

The normal host of rich goblins and puffed-up henchmen had convened to watch the Khan eat his breakfast. As always, they hid their faces as the warlocks passed, though today their whispers behind Fixelcrick's back were charged with expectation. Fixelcrick glanced past Harog to the two pacing wolves before the throne. They seemed agitated, growling quietly as they loped back and forth before the stone steps. The effects of the witch's blood had started to slow, but he thought he heard her dark whispers from above as the wind rattled against the walls. *She's started.*

The fire had been built high, and some of the fresh logs on top were smoking heavily from the moisture of the recent snow. Perhaps that could work to conceal the scarred goblin's descent, as long as he didn't pass out from smoke inhalation halfway down and drop into the flames. Fixelcrick hazarded a look up at the nailed head on the beam above the throne. It hung at a different angle from the one he'd seen there the previous afternoon, and the color of the scars was not right. Someone had replaced the red cap that he'd knocked off just a few hours earlier. His eyes traveled higher, but he saw no sign of movement at the familiar bright square at the peak of the shadowed ceiling.

They kept marching, and Fixelcrick swept his gaze across one of the rows of crossbowmen staring back from the murder boxes along the wall. A couple didn't look away in time before the shudder from his evil eye passed through them. But the tiny triumph was interrupted when Short-Fuse blocked their path wearing the feathered cloak and a smug grin. Long-Pig waited like a statue nearby, his eyes locked on Fixelcrick, unfazed by the far-seeing eye looking back.

Harog glanced over his shoulder with a hair-covered face that showed nothing and said everything, before he left the doktors to stand at the edge of the fire. He shuffled between the killers without a glance, making a beeline toward the Herald's table behind the throne. One of the wolves growled as he passed, looking like it might lunge for his throat. He kept moving, needing to get to the dead-bolted steel door at the base of the throne for any of this insanity to work.

"Where the fuck're ya goin'?" Arok had a gold platter on his lap stacked with pig-fat fried eggs over easy. The first jug of pine ale was freshly uncorked at his feet. He opened his maw and tossed in another egg as the gathering went quiet.

Harog stopped and shuffled back like a scolded wolf. "Just fetching the ledger, my Khan." His leg was shaking again.

"Don't need it! Get back in yer place, an' announce."

Harog hesitated a moment but then bowed and scurried to the first step. He and Fixelcrick shared an uneasy glance across the flames. "Bone Master and Fixelcrick, Chiefs of the Hex Doktors," he called in a clear voice that echoed about the hall.

It was hot this close to the fire, and the sweat started to drip down Fixelcrick's cheek. His eye swiveled back to the coat—some of the feathers had been broken or bent where the fat goblin had slept on them.

"The fuck ya lookin' at?" Short-Fuse challenged with a hatchet suddenly in his hand. Fixelcrick looked away.

"So . . . where's my witch head?" asked Arokkhan.

It took Fixelcrick a moment to realize that Arok was speaking to him. "Uh . . . only been a night, me Khan. Don't know where she is. It'll take a little more time is all." He stared at his own feet to keep from looking at the ceiling. He'd never been a particularly adept liar. He could hear the vibration of Agnes's words in his head, feel the residual swell of her power coursing through his veins.

"He's lyin', like I told ya," said Short-Fuse. "Prob'ly workin' with the witch, or maybe there ain't no witch at all? I bet he called 'em fire lizards hisself, fucked up Bone Master's head so he could be Chief."

Bone Master stared at the Khan with his one little eye as he continued to mutter words in old giant under his breath. Fixelcrick couldn't quite make it out, but he was starting to understand phrases here and there.

"What say you, Bone Master? Where's the witch?" asked the Khan between eggs. A spurt of yolk spilled over his lip.

Bone Master rocked in place, continuing to spout guttural whispers. The old goblin suddenly raised his cracked voice and yelled, *"Cog-noch ig'n zu-ghul druch kul-ul-dwall!"*

Fixelcrick thought it was something like: *hearing, my compel, to self-kill, bearers of bows.* That didn't sound right, but he was surprised to find his own hand crossbow suddenly in his grip.

Bone Master raised his gnarled fingers toward the Arrow Boys on either side, and all thirty of them suddenly went slack-faced. Some of their arms began to shake; others didn't hesitate, but all pointed their crossbows under their chins.

"Shoot him!" the Khan bellowed. The crossbows all fired at once.

Bolts shattered jaws and pierced skulls as thirty goblin bowmen collapsed. The splatter hit the gathered host, who slipped easily into panic. Fixelcrick was the only one who hadn't pulled the trigger; the tip of the bolt shook a bloody groove in the wispy tuft of hair under his chin. He gasped and stumbled back as his finger twitched; the shot nicked his nose before lodging into the slope of the ceiling.

Bone Master's expression remained blank as he swung his outstretched hands toward the fire and started another string of Agnes's words. *"Ig'na'a noch zu-dracht—"*

Short-Fuse cut him off with a hatchet lobbed deep into the old goblin's chest. The other hatchet struck his face a second later, and Bone Master dropped with a last jitter in one of his legs. Fixelcrick stumbled to his ass beside his dead teacher, and

Long-Pig's sword was suddenly at his throat.

"Wait!" The Khan had dumped his eggs and was looking out from behind the platter.

The blade at Fixelcrick's throat hesitated, but Short-Fuse unhooked the moon blade from his hip and approached with his filed teeth showing. "Lemme show ya his insides, boss."

"No! Take his crossbow, but let him talk," said the Khan as he tossed the platter down the steps with a racket and grabbed the jug for the first big swig of the day. "Clan still needs a good doktor, an' it looks to me like Bone Master's the problem. Never should've trusted a fuckin' Bone Shield."

Short-Fuse kicked the hand crossbow out of Fixelcrick's grip hard enough to break his thumb before jamming his boot into Bone Master's throat and tugging his hatchets free. Fixelcrick yelped and cradled his hand, trying to decide if he should try to look meek or play it tough. There wasn't much leeway regardless, with the razor-sharpened blade still hovering above his Adam's apple.

The Khan scanned his dead and dying Arrow Boys and took another hard pull from the jug. "Bring him here."

Rough hands yanked Fixelcrick to his feet, and the curved blade jabbed into his back to move him forward. He could hear the witch's words fall across the compound like a heavy blanket—the invocation she worked was like Bone Master's compulsion for suicide, but on a much grander scale and targeting the wolves this time. He felt the potential for his own enhanced pull on the Knack waiting expectantly in his blood. Maybe he'd be able to summon the wind spirits within the hall and sail up to the relative safety of the rafters if it came down to it?

The dummy head stared down at him—not laughing, as it

should have been, but proclaiming itself an imposter for all who looked closely to see. Below, the wolves' manes bristled and their ears folded back. Fixelcrick eyed the curl of their lips and the reflection of the fire in their eyes. He tried to slow his approach, but Long-Pig's blade poked him hard enough to draw blood and propel him stumbling toward the steps.

If Harog didn't unlock that door and Neither-Nor didn't get down the rope soon, Fixelcrick would either be torn apart or cut in half in the next few minutes.

———————————

THINGS WERE GOING bad in a hurry across the Rock Wolf compound, and Neither-Nor had no idea how he'd come to be at the heart of it. He wasn't wearing shoes, and his feet were cold, standing on a steeply pitched roof beside a chimney that billowed smoke. A rope was coiled across his shoulder, and he had crap-quality replacement knives at his belt. He noticed the pitch-black night-hag behind him—her talon-tipped hands and guttural words were raised to the sky as a vicious wind wailed down from the mountain.

Snow, dust, and pine needles blew into a dervish that cut across the inner courtyard as the wolves turned on their riders below, tearing out throats and mangling limbs without warning. Goblins screamed as others rushed to open the stockade gate, not realizing that there were even more of the blood-mad wolves on the other side. The whole compound had exploded with snarls and shrieks.

Neither-Nor had come back to life only one agonizing minute earlier, wrapped in the hag's ironlike grip while floating a hundred feet in the air over the clan. He had no idea how long he'd been out, but this was a hard death to bounce back from. Every breath and gesture hurt like hell as the runes struggled to fuse muscle and bone while replenishing his blood supply from scratch. He remembered getting cut apart by the Khan's goons in the great hall with unpleasant clarity.

The great hall! That was the building he was standing on, though what he was now doing on the roof was anybody's guess. His whole life since he'd met that fucking troll had been a series of hard deaths and harsh awakenings. He glanced out to the compound in chaos, still a little blurry at the edges. The fallen tree was where he remembered it, and it was still morning, but he was beginning to think this was a different day. "What fuckin' day is it?" he asked no one in particular.

Horns blasted from the towers, and the sounds of fighting picked up on all sides. From up here, he could see over the stockade wall to Clan Center, where a Rock Wolf guard buried a spear in a wolf's chest just before three others attacked the goblin from behind. They tore him apart and started eating in a snarling frenzy. "The fuck's all this then?"

Then he saw the infernal troll lumbering down the street outside the stockade wall with a stupid sword in his hand and a tiny goblin at his heels. Even among the quickly spreading chaos, the giant was impossible to miss . . . but Neither-Nor had watched Slud die. *Maybe he really has been spat up from me nightmares?*

Slud glanced up to catch his gaze with the yawning hunger of the void behind his eyes. The troll gave a curt nod, and Neither-Nor found himself nodding back, though he wasn't sure why. If the scarred goblin thought there was a chance of hitting him from there, he probably would have started chucking his knives. Slud pointed at the chimney and then hooked his finger down, before continuing on his way to disappear behind a two-story log building with the miniature goblin scrambling after.

"The fuck does that mean?"

The night-hag stopped chanting behind him. "Down the chimney you go. He says to get those hall doors open and bleed the ones that killed you. He'll take care of the rest." She grinned at him with her hideous teeth, then thankfully turned her disturbing eyes back to the sky and started chanting again. The wolves renewed the frantic orgy of violence as goblins screamed and horns blasted from all corners.

"That fuckin' troll's the one who killed me last four times, by my count," he muttered as he scanned the chaotic courtyard and high stockade walls that surrounded him. *Nowhere to run.* He gave the witch a last glance and moved toward the chimney. The rope was pre-looped with a fine knot for the girth of the smokestack. He tossed it around with a tug and peered over the edge, seeing nothing but a face full of smoke. He reeled back with a cough that felt like bee stings across his body and almost lost his footing on the slant. "The fuck?"

The night-hag stopped halfway through an ugly-sounding word in another language. "Wet rag 'round your arm, tie it 'round your face, yes. I trimmed the rope; it may be a bit short, but I took care of the archers." She looked back to the sky and the flow of weird words resumed.

Indeed, there was a wet rag tied in a tight knot around his bicep. "Fuckin' troll." Neither-Nor took it off and tied it tightly over his nose and mouth. It was hard to breathe through the damp cloth, but better than lungs filled with unfiltered smoke. He slid toward the chimney again and lifted the rag to spit into his palms, rubbing them together before he grabbed the rope and began to lower it into the chimney. No one seemed to make a fuss about it, so he kept going until he ran out of slack.

"Dumbest fuckin' thing I ever done," he muttered as he took a deep breath, threw a leg over, and started down.

DINGLE STUDIED SLUD as he poked his head out from behind the building to watch Neither-Nor slip down the chimney. The troll immediately reversed direction, away from the stockade gate, toward a small one-story rock hut with a domed roof and no windows—not treated pine and mud brick like everything else of Rock Wolf make. Dingle had spent his whole miserable life in the compound, and he had somehow never noticed the existence of this odd hut before. The troll scanned the crudely drawn map that Harog had penciled, then he kicked the heavy door off its hinges with a loud boom and a splintering of wood and iron.

The tiny goblin chewed on his thumb with excitement. He only wished he had a nice sheaf of paper and some charcoal to record the moment in detail: the way the troll's gaze absorbed the map in an instant, and the low grunt that escaped his throat when his boot met the wood. Every gesture was worthy of a poet's pen. Dingle alone could see what the others did not; Neither-Nor, Fixelcrick, Bone Master, Harog, even Black Agnes were all just pieces in Slud's evolving game.

The hut had no light within, but the day through the doorway showed a wide stone stairwell heading down. Slud ducked and descended without hesitation, as unhindered by the darkness that waited as he was by the inevitable death that lurked somewhere beyond it.

Dingle scrambled after him with four quick steps to cover the same ground as every one of the troll's. The tunnel stretched into inky blackness, lined with rough-hewn rock on all sides. It had been engineered with a big goblin in mind, but Slud was a tight squeeze. Soon enough, Dingle couldn't see a thing, but he could hear the heavy steps of the Death Lord ahead, the scrape of his shoulders against the walls, and the stinking breath that never seemed to waver. He would follow wherever it led.

THE HUNGER OVERWHELMED LUTHER. He didn't care about anything else, ready to meet his end if only he did so with a belly full of goblin. He and Riga sprinted across the fallen tree toward the compound, only half aware that none of the defensive ballista or bows fired at their approach. The goblins' attention had shifted to the sudden attack within their walls. The giant crossbows fired down into the streets as wolves yelped and died. None of the ballista teams saw the black and gray wolves on the tree until it was too late.

Luther swallowed a barely chewed arm with rings and a bracelet still on it as Riga bit down on the sinew of a goblin throat and shook the juice out. It wasn't nearly enough for either of them. They kept moving down the line, driven faster and made more ravenous by the scene of carnage that opened on both sides.

As he ran, Luther's eyes picked out the twisted figure standing on the highest rooftop, with her hooked claws raised over her head and her vicious tongue sealing the doom of the clan. Only Luther and Riga, among all the thousands of wolves in the compound, could resist the dark words of the night-hag compelling them to madness. But Luther didn't want to resist; her magick spoke to an unfulfilled need he carried in his blood. He'd always feared the dark thing that waited within, unsure of its motives and provenance, but he'd also always been curious to see what it could do if he let it out fully. Perhaps this would be the day.

A goblin archer turned toward them with a wild shot just as Luther's jaws took him down by his shoulder and Riga bit through the wide artery in his leg. Both of them gnawed until the metallic tang was hot in their mouths and the thrashing stopped. They would have loved to bury their snouts in the body, wrest the heart free, and roll in the slop, but there was no time to savor.

The Wolf King sprang back to the run, and Riga followed. They cleared the long stretch of open trunk and tore into the branch maze. He could feel the attention of the raven upon him from high above, but there was nothing he could do about that now. Even his hunger for Agnes and the goblin warlock could wait. With the wolves of the clan at war, the Khan was vulnerable, and his was the heart that Luther and his queen needed to taste.

TWENTY-THREE

Door Jam

THE COMMOTION STARTED when Neither-Nor was ten hands down the climb. He'd cleared the stubby chimney, dangling midair in the billowing smoke as the hollers of terrified goblins were joined by the snarling of wolves, and then the choking wail of a harsh death. His eyes were clenched shut with the burn of the smoke, and the coarse rope tugged at the skin on his fingers and ankles. He heard the meaty clamor of bodies being trampled, but true to the night-hag's claims above, no arrows flew. He kept going.

Neither-Nor had snapped out of the post-death malaise once he'd started down, shocked back into the rhythm of life through adrenaline and necessity. But his breathing grew progressively more ragged behind the wet cloth, and not being able to see would soon become problematic. The heat of the fire pit rose to meet him, and he knew its light couldn't be far behind. Still, he lowered himself farther down the rope before he started to swing—leaning back and kicking his legs on the upswing before tucking them under as he swung back. After a couple lengthening arcs, he was able to clear the smoke on both sides.

He pried open his watering eyes as the blurry room began to materialize below. Luckily, he was still in the shadows, but still more than thirty feet over the hard stones and hot fire where he'd last died. There was a clamor throughout the hall, but he went through the stinging smoke again, unsure which way was which. The only things in relative focus were the two closest rafters—still a drop below him on either side. The freaky witch on the roof had trimmed the rope too short.

Neither-Nor slid down to the last handhold on the rope, and as he came through the smoke plume this time, the heat singed the bottoms of his naked feet and jarred him from the plan. His toes retracted before the landing on the rafter he was aiming for, and he swung back through the scorched air while reaching out in the opposite direction. His toes found the solidity of wood, and he came to an unsteady perch on the beam, one arm out for balance and the other stretched up with a fingertip's grip on the butt of the rope.

He froze and tried to blink his eyes clear. No one seemed to have noticed. The bandit cloth around his face was black with soot, and he could feel the runes shifting on his chest and back to make his lungs right again, but he was a lot farther from the doors than he would have liked. A cluster of goblin backs moved toward the exit, followed by one of the big wolves. The beast had a merchant in fancy robes between its jaws, and it shook its prey as manicured hands pounded on its unforgiving snout. Another goblin with shiny armor was trying to crawl away, but the crazed wolf pounced on his back with enough force to flatten the flimsy bronze plates and crush his ribs beneath. It tossed the merchant aside and snapped at another pair of retreating goblin legs.

Neither-Nor wobbled. Directly below, the other of the Khan's wolves had backed the big goblin who'd helped dismember him against the wall. The emotionless killer had a hex doktor with a big freaky eye held before him as a shield. Neither-Nor's gut sticker was at the warlock's throat, and the big goblin held a curved sword in the other hand, waiting for the wolf to make its move. Neither-Nor wobbled some more as he noticed the severed head nailed to the beam just below his feet. It was wearing his cap and was covered in fresh-cut letters. Neither-Nor could see a crude smiley face carved into the closest cheek.

"There's a fuckin' thing to see," he mumbled as he leaned over to snatch the cap while still clutching the end of the rope by his fingertips. The cap had gone brown and rigid, but he shook it out and flipped it onto his head with comforting familiarity. One way or another, it would get a fresh coat of red soon enough.

A wet cough sounded behind him, and he looked over his shoulder to where the Khan was staring up from the throne only ten feet below. As before, he had the absurd golden sword in one hand and was holding a jug to his mouth with the other.

"Not possible," the Khan said with widening eyes as ale dribbled down his chin. "Not fuckin' possible!"

The absurdly hairy goblin who had watched Neither-Nor die from the foot of the stairs noticed him as well, and immediately took off toward the back of the hall at an awkward, lurching run. Nearby, the fat goblin with the feathered cloak tossed a hatchet into the closest wolf's haunches, and when the snapping jaws turned on him, the winged thug raised his fluttering arms and shot into the air—coming to a hunched perch on the beam on the opposite side of the head from Neither-Nor.

The wolf circled and growled, its feral yellow eyes locked on the feathered goblin above as if oblivious to the hatchet lodged in its ass. It leapt into the air, and the long jaws snapped together with a loud *clack* just a few feet short of the beam before it crashed back down to the stones.

The moon blade that had been handed down to Neither-Nor from his grandfather was dangling from the fat goblin's hip. He could almost reach out and grab it, but then the toad-faced bastard noticed his precarious stance on the rafter beside him. It took a moment for him to register what he was seeing.

"Kill him!" screamed the Khan, drawing the attention of the wolf.

Neither-Nor couldn't handle the Khan, the wolf, and both killers by himself; this was his window. *Gotta get them doors open!* He sprang up and kicked the fat goblin in the face, before grabbing the rope with both hands and swinging away.

Mid-arc, he realized that he didn't have the momentum to reach the next rafter, and released at the farthest point to sail down toward the hard floor legs first. It was a long drop, but he relaxed his body on the descent and landed with bent knees before the momentum carried him into an extended roll across his shoulders. He came to his feet beside the recently dead goblins and drew his shitty knives as the near wolf turned on him.

It got a snout full of steel to send it reeling back, and Neither-Nor was sprinting toward the door a second later. He weaved through the host of panicked Rock Wolf elite, but none noticed the bandit-masked ghost among them. The furious wolf plowed into the goblins at his back, and he felt the wind of its bite brush across his neck. Neither-Nor lowered both knives as he ran, slicing goblin legs on both sides to provide easier meat. A big goblin with a big hammer turned to face him directly ahead, blocking his route, so Neither-Nor went right at him to get a feel for the stand-in blades. They danced high and low, opening the femoral artery and throat at the same time.

The knives were sharp enough for now, but they wouldn't hold the edge for long, and the handles and balance were all wrong. Still, Neither-Nor dodged the spray and kept going toward the doors, which looked much bigger without Slud standing beside them. The crossbeam was a lot more impressive from this side, too.

An unnatural gust of wind whipped across the hall, and the smoke from the fire wafted out in a choking wave. The wolf at the throne yelped for what sounded like the last time, and Neither-Nor glanced back through the chaos to see the mute goblin killer standing over it on the steps with his sword jammed through its head. The Khan, still seated above, pointed again at Neither-Nor and bellowed, "Kill him!"

Neither-Nor couldn't see the goblin with the feathered cloak and knew he wasn't a good one to lose track of. But someone outside had started pounding on the doors, and the two huge buffalo-shouldered guards ahead had their backs to him. *It's the troll!*

Neither-Nor slid up behind a guard and stuck him through the spine. The shit blade in his hand came out with the tip cracked off. Still, that guard went down, and Neither-Nor darted in toward the second. He jammed the other knife through that goblin's armpit; there was no armor there, and his aim was good, but the thick blade caught on a rib and glanced off target into a lung.

When he pulled it out, a whistle of air followed and the blade had chipped in two places. Neither guard was dead, but they wouldn't be a problem. The six-hundred-pound beam facing him at eye level would. They'd installed two new iron jambs as well. *Gimme a fuckin' break!*

He sheathed one of the blades and grabbed the closest iron rod by the curved top; it was much heavier than he'd hoped. He sheathed the second blade and lifted with both arms, able to get his shoulder under it enough to hoist the bar up to the catch on the door with a winded grunt.

Neither-Nor nudged the paralyzed guard out of the way with his foot, and got a grip on the second jamb—but lost his hold when a throwing hatchet buried itself in his back. He went to his knees and coughed as the fat goblin fluttered to a shaky landing a few paces behind him.

"Like yer knife." He grinned with filed teeth as he unclasped the moon blade from his belt.

Neither-Nor reached behind his back and with a snarl he yanked the hatchet out at a bad angle. The wound ripped further, but the runes started shifting as he found his feet again, the hatchet in one hand and a chipped knife in the other. He gave the hatchet a spin; it was well crafted and had a good feel to it. "Like yer hatchet."

The pounding grew louder at the doors, but Slud would have to fend for himself for a bit.

"Name's Short-Fuse," said the fat goblin, circling.

"Don't care," said Neither-Nor, stepping out to meet him.

"Gonna peel off yer skin this time, copy them letters fer meself." Short-Fuse feinted with the remaining hatchet, but came around with the moon blade from the other direction. Neither-Nor rolled under it and cut the air where Short-Fuse was supposed to be. The fat goblin fluttered back down a few paces away, chuckling. "Heard ya was faster than that."

"Never heard of ya at all," he answered.

Short-Fuse didn't like that. He leapt, and the wings carried him into a high arc. He raised the moon blade over his head, while flicking the hatchet underhanded at the same time. The hatchet flipped out and lodged in Neither-Nor's stomach, but as the moon blade came down, he raised his own hatchet to block it and raked the chipped blade across Short-Fuse's belly with a spray of bloody feathers.

Short-Fuse launched again and came to a perch on the rafter overhead, clutching his stomach. He thought he had a moment to regain his composure while Neither-Nor dealt with the hatchet lodged in his abdomen, but the scarred goblin was used to pain. He let his stomach muscles tear further as he wound up and chucked the other hatchet into Short-Fuse's chest.

The fat goblin pitched back and fell to the floor with a meaty thud. Neither-Nor didn't hesitate. He sprang on top of him and drove the knife up under his jaw. Short-Fuse opened his mouth to protest, but the blade sliced through his tongue, jammed through the roof of his mouth, and pierced his brain. His eyes went wide and his hand gripped Neither-Nor's shoulder, but a last twist of the hilt ended that. The moon blade clattered to the floor beside him.

Neither-Nor finally buckled over and wrenched the hatchet out of his own stomach with a gag. Blind with pain, he crawled across the floor until his hand found the hilt of his grandfather's knife. The feel of the long oaken handle in his grip was a comfort as the runes went to work, but he wouldn't have long before the next fight found him, and the troll was still waiting.

The aberrant wind blew again through the rafters with an ominous keening. The second wolf was still tearing through the frantic host. The Khan had descended the stairs, waving his pretty sword and clutching his precious jug. The other goblin killer had vanished in the shuffle. Then Neither-Nor spotted the tall mute slowly approaching down the side of the hall with his hollow eyes locked on his fallen feathered companion. "Fuck."

The banging outside had stopped, but the screams of fighting and dying had renewed there. Neither-Nor just wanted to sleep. Instead he found his feet, stumbled to the doors, and heaved up the second iron jamb from the floor. With a last glance over his shoulder, he got a better grip on the bloodstained hatchet and started chopping at the huge beam with everything he had.

AT THE FAR SIDE of the hall, Harog was also frantically trying to open a door. The heavy iron hatch at the back of the throne had apparently not been opened for years. The Khan had only entrusted him with the knowledge of its existence the day before, and Harog had immediately considered the possibility that this long-ignored symbol of Arok's paranoid delusion might be used to precipitate his demise. He'd gotten the key inside the lock, but the rust buildup had fused the cylinder within. He put more pressure on the key, scared it would break off and seal all their dooms with it, but the bolt slowly started to turn with a metallic screech.

Harog didn't know what had happened to Fixelcrick or Neither-Nor, but there was still plenty of screaming at the other end of the hall, and he hoped it would buy him enough time. The mere sight of the troll alive again, and the command he'd shown in putting this mad plan into action, was enough to make the hairy goblin want to try. Better to die quickly in an act of defiance than be tortured to death in a few days or weeks when the Khan got bored with him.

Harog braced the key with both hands, slipping his fingers close to the hole to keep it from bending as he turned. The lock protested loudly, and he was sure he would be found out, before it gave suddenly and clicked open. He blew hair from his face to show the triumphant grin beneath, so focused on the door that he didn't notice the Khan's approach behind him.

"Quick thinkin', Herald. Get it open an' grab a torch." The Khan had sheathed his big sword at his back, now clutching a little chest of precious gems in its place, while still hugging the jug of pine ale with his other hand.

Harog froze and stared at him.

"Get a fuckin' move on!" the Khan growled. "I ain't fightin' ghosts an' witches."

Harog's nervous grin was hidden beneath his fur again as he put his hands on the trapdoor's handle and his good foot against the stone. He heaved it open with a loud groan to reveal a steep rock-cut stairwell descending sharply into a lightless tunnel below.

The Khan pointed to the torch on a sconce beside the Herald's table. "Get the ledger too, an' lock it behind us."

Harog stared into the tunnel, but nothing happened. He shuffled over to the table and grabbed the ledger and torch as the Khan started down, but both of them stopped fast. The rumble of lumbering footsteps sounded from the darkness.

TWENTY-FOUR

King of the Mountain

THERE WAS LIGHT at the end of the tunnel, and the flickering definition of stairs. A heavy shadow moved at the mouth of the opening. Slud could see a boot trimmed in gold fur. The boot retracted and the shadow moved away, but Slud kept coming.

There was no way Neither-Nor would have been able to get those front doors open. Slud only hoped there'd still be someone left for him to kill after the frustrated goblin did his worst in the confined space. Slud would never tell him, but he'd actually missed the ornery little bastard's company since Agnes had dug him up.

At the base of the stairs, he hooked a hand up on the lip of the rock ceiling and stepped out. He smacked his lip against a tusk and gave the sword Dingle had found him a little spin. The wobbly blade wouldn't be able to withstand much, and the Khan of the Rock Wolf Clan stood a few paces away with fear in his eyes.

The Khan dropped a box full of gems that tumbled across the floor in a wave of sparkling color before snatching the fancy sword that had cut Slud's throat from over his shoulder with a shaky hand.

"Slud's got unfinished bidness wit' ya."

"I killed ya! I watched ya die!" the Khan shouted, backing away.

"Time to return dat honor."

The Khan banged into the Herald's table beside Harog. "Yer just a nightmare! Ya ain't real!" the Khan yelled.

"Den ya got nuttin' to worry 'bout, do ya?" Slud rolled his neck with a deep crunch.

Dingle popped up the steps beside him and started screeching. "He's the LLLord of D-D-Death!"

Slud looked down at the tiny zealot and furrowed his brow. "No more talkin', li'l fella." Dingle recoiled like he'd been slapped and snapped his mouth tight with a curt nod. Slud started toward the Khan as Harog shuffled out of the way with a big grin peeking out past his hair.

"Where's me ax?" Slud asked.

The Khan reached back to finally surrender the jug to the table. The sword was shaking in his grip, and he brought his hands together to steady it. "I'm Arok Golden Wolf, son of Grummok Green Hammer, King of the Mountain, an' Khan of the Goblin Horde! I killed more than a thousand goblins me-self!" He'd grown more comfortable with the bottle than the blade since then.

"Yer a drunk, 'n' a weaklin', 'n' Slud ain't no goblin." He swung out at the Khan in an overhead chop, but the golden sword rushed up to meet it. The steel of Slud's blade shattered at the base and clattered to the stones. He was left frowning down at the Khan with only the hilt in his fist.

It took Arok a quick moment to realize what had happened, and a glimmer of hope returned to his crazed eyes. He brought the golden sword back and thrust it toward the big target with all he had. Slud sidestepped and grabbed the Khan's wrists to pull him closer as he rammed the broken sword hilt into the big goblin's face three times. He could feel the Khan's nose and some teeth break beneath his knuckles before he tossed the hilt and grabbed the goblin by the furry lapel. Slud brought his face close, letting his stink waft over the Khan as he raised his chin to show the mean gash where his throat had been cut the day before. "Ya owe Slud a t'roat."

He ripped the golden sword from the Khan's hands and heaved him sliding across the floor past the throne. Slud gave Harog a nod and swiped the jug from the table, taking a loud gulp before following after his quarry.

"To me! To me!" Arok yelled toward the far end of the hall.

One of the wolves was savaging some well-dressed meat, and Slud caught a glimpse of Neither-Nor behind it, hacking away with a tiny hatchet at the big beam that braced the doors. The troll chuckled and looked back at the crawling Khan with another swig of the pine ale. It was much better than the stale brew he was used to.

The Khan tried to scramble to his feet, but Slud hooked a boot under him and kicked him back against a dead wolf on the throne steps. "Take yer seat, king."

Arok stumbled over the furry corpse and climbed on all fours up the steps, drawing a good combat sword from the slot cut into the stone at the top. His hands were shaking again as he turned back to face what was coming. Slud glanced down at the foolish gold and gem-encrusted blade he held, frowning as he approached. "Slud's ax, where is it?"

The Khan didn't answer as he scanned the room, searching for help that wasn't coming. Slud grabbed the dead wolf by the scruff of its neck and hurled it aside. "Can do dis clean or messy."

"To hell with ya, demon!" the Khan bellowed with a cracked voice.

"Messy 'tis." Slud cocked the bejeweled mockery of a weapon and slammed it into the Khan's parry. The silly blade went loose on the first swing against the Khan's steel, but Slud cocked back and hit it again with a little torque. The sound of the big goblin's arm snapping echoed about the hall just as the golden hilt split in half and the sword pieces fell over the edge with a clatter.

The Khan's sword slid down the stairs as he clutched his shattered arm with blood and snot dribbling over his quivering lip. "I'm King of the Mountain," he whimpered.

"Nuttin' but meat." Slud took a last swig of the jug and smashed the butt end on the stone armrest. He jammed the jagged end into the Khan's throat repeatedly as the golden pelt turned red in a rush. The Khan gurgled and tried to hold his mangled neck together, but Slud slapped his hands aside and kept stabbing.

FIXELCRICK HOVERED HIGH along the interior gable of the hall as Neither-Nor hacked futilely at the massive crossbeam below. The alpha female of the Khan's pet wolves continued to tear through the rich goblins of the recently defunct Rock Wolf Clan. Despite all the hubbub, Fixelcrick's far-seeing eye remained locked on the battered feathers wrapped around the corpse of Short-Fuse. The cloak still vibrated with the delicate interweaving of his Knack, but the golden thread had been severed in multiple places, and halved feathers lay scattered about the floor.

Once Long-Pig had abandoned him to defend the Khan at the throne, the warlock had scrambled to retrieve his crossbow—holding it now with his unbroken hand, and loaded with the last of his precious golden bolts. He'd borrowed the night-hag's words again, and the wind spirits had answered his call, or at least the call of the witch's blood in his veins. They had come down the chimney and carried him above the chaos. Their invisible grip cradled him under his arms and feet as gusts of cold rushed about the hall, buffeting the flames in the fire pit and sending smoke and loose papers spiraling about the room in rogue eddies.

Without intending it, his focus on the coat brought him sinking toward the floor, but he stopped fast as Long-Pig emerged from the shadows along the wall to stand over his fallen comrade. Someone started pounding on the outside of the great doors again, this time with enough force to bend the fresh beam inward. Neither-Nor hacked at the wood with renewed fervor as insignificant chips flew off in every direction. He didn't notice Long-Pig raising the big curving sword at his back.

"Neither-Nor!" Fixelcrick shouted as he aimed and shot. The golden bolt lodged in Long-Pig's shoulder blade, stalling the chop just long enough for Neither-Nor to spin around and rake the moon blade across the mute killer's belly. Long-Pig stepped back, as expressionless and unfazed as ever, and then charged in with a flurry of jabs and slices in response. Their two blades flew and clanged together too fast for Fixelcrick to follow as bloody nicks appeared across arms and legs on both sides.

Again the doors thundered and bowed inward, and even the alpha wolf stopped its madness to turn a curious gaze toward whatever was trying to force its way in from outside. It sniffed the air and tucked its tail low with a building growl. The beam started to crack, with long splinters peeling up from the center as Neither-Nor dove away, with the near-missed swipe of

Long-Pig's blade following after him.

Fixelcrick could no longer hear the arcane chanting of Agnes above, and the wolf snapped out of its homicidal daze with a whimper. The remnants of the goblin host turned their panicked gazes to the force that worked to break through the unbreakable doors for the second time in as many days as Neither-Nor slashed, ducked, and rolled at a dizzying pace among them. Long-Pig kept coming, always just a step behind.

But all of them, from the unflappable Long-Pig to the booming quake at the doors, stopped abruptly and turned toward the throne as a deep echoing voice filled the hall. "Oi! De Rock Wolf Clan's done!"

Slud stood atop the steps, bathed red from chin to foot, with the limp figure of mighty Arokkhan held before him. With a last tug and an audible pop, he wrenched the Khan's head from his shoulders and held it high for all to see.

The hall went completely silent. Even the wind spirits ceased their bluster as all eyes held on the towering figure.

"Ya gotta be fuckin' kiddin' me!" Neither-Nor shouted.

SLUD KICKED the Khan's body down the steps, and noticed his ax resting off to the side at the base of the rock. He met the scarred goblin's furious gaze with a nod. "Sorry, fella, had t'be done."

Long-Pig took the moment of distraction to drive his sword straight through Neither-Nor's chest, killing him instantly—just as the front doors crashed inward and the beam snapped in half amid a shower of jagged wood.

The Wolf King, and another giant gray wolf, burst into the hall, both of them peppered with arrows and cuts. Luther lunged, taking Long-Pig from his feet with a bite that cracked bones and opened arteries. The gray wolf pounced on the Khan's alpha female, biting the back of her neck with a snarling ferocity that could only be personal. Both goblin and wolf were pinned to the ground, savaged as their limbs thrashed and then stilled. The dying wolf's eyes rolled back to her killer's with what almost looked like pride, and Slud glimpsed a satisfying final grimace of pain on the mute goblin's face before Luther swallowed the head with a tear and a shake.

The last troll stepped down the stairs as Dingle and Harog moved out from behind the throne on either side. Dingle carried the ledger now, already scribbling furiously in its blank pages with a look of utter glee on his face, recording every nuance and observation he could of his master's rise. Slud handed the Khan's head to Harog and grabbed the handle of his ax with the cold comfort of the Frost King's bite taking root in his hand and over his heart once more.

Luther and his bitch finished their kills and stepped around the waning fire, licking their gore-slick chops as they eyed the Khan's body.

"Eat 'im here; let 'em all watch," said Slud.

He climbed back up the stairs to take the Khan's messy seat for himself as the black wolf approached with a growled laugh. "Mountain King."

The troll rested the cold ax on the stone by his feet, and the blood there froze solid as frost climbed up the armrest. "Told ya, wolf, Slud ain't no king. Just gonna take a seat fer a li'l while, s'all."

Luther bowed his head, pausing for a respectful moment before he tore into the Khan's chest. The gray wolf joined him as Slud raised his gaze to face the stunned goblin host. "Come closa! Somebody get dat fire burnin' bright!"

The blood-spattered gathering pressed in, and Fixelcrick

fluttered down beside Harog, wearing his feathered cloak once more. He gave Slud a deep bow, and Slud felt nothing but a tickle as the goblin's big warlock eye passed over.

"Khan's head on de spike, if ya please," Slud said, pointing to the fake Neither-Nor above. "'N' get dat sword outta Neider-Nor's chest."

Fixelcrick took the head from Harog and fluttered up to the rafter over the steps. He tossed the dummy head to the coals and jammed the Khan onto the nail in its place as Harog shuffled to where Neither-Nor had fallen.

An odd tendril of smoke drifted down in the wrong direction from the hole in the ceiling to collect above the orange glow of the fire pit. Between the distorted, shimmering heat waves, Black Agnes took shape. She stepped out from the embers with a wicked grin on her long, pointy face and clasped her clawed hands together with a gleeful laugh that sounded like a hiss. "Very good, my boy. You've learned the game well, done your auntie proud this day. Now the board sets for the next match."

"Ya ain't Slud's aunt, 'n' he didn't do it fer her neider." Slud still hadn't taken his hand from the handle of the ax. A bluish tinge spread along his skin and sank into the whites of his eyes. "Now step aside, Agnes, or we'll see if ya like de cold as much as de flame."

Agnes gave a little bow and grinned wider as she moved beside Dingle. "As you wish, my boy, but *this* one must answer for tasting the Nectar of Amrite. His blood belongs to me, yes?"

"No," Slud countered. He'd gotten fond of the idea of having a chronicler of his exploits. The tiny goblin continued to record everything that was happening around him, despite the talk of his pending death. "He stays wit' Slud. If he's tasted somet'in' he shouldn'ta, take his tongue 'n' it's square."

For a moment Agnes's grin turned to a sneer as her black eyes locked on Slud's. He gripped the ax handle tighter and smacked his lip against a tusk. She bowed again and slipped her finger blade from her belt sack. "As you wish."

Slud nodded to Dingle, and he nodded back. To his credit, he didn't even squirm as he stuck out his tongue and she sliced it off and ate it in one quick motion. The little goblin hopped up and down with wide, watering eyes before settling again. He held the ledger further out so as not to dribble his blood on the precious pages, and kept writing.

The gathered host watched with a mixture of horror and reverence as the wolves dug out the Khan's heart and shared it between them at the feet of this last troll, who they'd watched die and come back like an emissary of death itself. The hall had been bathed in blood, and all had witnessed atrocities they would never forget. But the air within was charged with expectation—the same way that Slud had always felt when listening to the legendary tales of the great heroes of old.

Neither-Nor coughed as he nudged his way between the gaping onlookers, both of his reclaimed blades back in his hands where they belonged. He ripped the filthy bandit cloth from his face and tossed it into the fire as he passed. His eyes locked on Slud above as the mosaic of runes swam across his body. He rolled his shoulders with a wince, looking like he was getting ready to charge.

"So, ya stayin' or goin', frien'?" asked Slud.

"You and me ain't done yet, troll," Neither-Nor spat.

Slud smacked his lip against a tusk. "No . . . we're just gettin' started."

EPILOGUE

MUNINN WAS LATE. Auberon, High King of the Elves, waited at the window in his study, looking out with the other raven perched on his shoulder. Once again, the day had bloomed bright and warm across the gilded halls of the ruling fae. The midmorning light streamed past him through the window, burning away the dark pockets about the room that he'd cultivated throughout the night. The heavy shadows that had gathered across his increasingly pale face were bathed again in a mask of glamour, but his back was still hunched after hours of reading.

Books and maps were piled upon the desk behind him, marked by his hand in the places where his research had uncovered the rumor of old doors between the worlds. It had become Auberon's nighttime obsession. He hadn't slept in over a century and wondered if he'd ever sleep again. The Dreaming World had begun to seem too small to sleep, and the old resentments had crept up from beneath the roots where he'd buried them long ago.

Auberon looked past the frame of rosebushes and vines, where the green hills rolled down to a stretched plain of tall grass that had been stained by a thousand battles over the millennia. Beyond, the mountain range, which had once seemed so vast, now appeared as only one dominant peak at the far fringe of the shrinking land.

He'd sent Muninn back there to observe the events that unfolded, allowing the bird to wallow in his ancient grudges, while his brother, Huginn, had again flown far off across the skies between the worlds. Despite the distance, Huginn had returned on time, as always, and delivered all the thoughts he'd collected that night.

Huginn had always been the more thoughtful of the brothers, dependable and ready with a keen observation about all he saw in his travels. He was Auberon's window to the future, while Muninn was his key to the past. Muninn, the more capricious of the birds, remembered everything he'd seen for thousands of years as if he were still there in the moment. He was often lost within himself, late, and distractible. But Auberon was beginning to grow impatient with the lessons of history.

He turned from the window, letting his eyes move across the giant sword that adorned his wall and the monstrous four-clawed hand displayed in the jar below it. The hand was withered and gray, but the black blade was as sharp as the day it had been forged in the deep caverns of the fire giants at the dawn of a forgotten age. It was almost time for that famed blade to come down from its display.

Huginn croaked at his right ear with a familiar welcoming, and the King extended his arm just as the sound of flapping approached from behind. Muninn swooped in through the window and wrapped his black feet around the King's wrist. The bird croaked a response to his brother as he hopped to his place at Auberon's left shoulder.

Immediately, the string of all that Muninn remembered seeing from that morning flowed into Auberon's mind: fallen trees and blood in the snow; wolves howling as the mightiest of the goblin clans was torn apart from within; the doom chant of a lost tongue while a hulking monster that should not have been walked with a trembling of the earth beneath his feet. A bad wind had blown across the mountain, and the name Slud was carried with it, driving, even now, down the slopes toward the lowland clans.

Auberon opened his cold blue eyes and smiled. So, a troll had lived through the culling on the mountain. This was unexpected.

Acknowledgments

As always with these things, there are many people who played a role in bringing this tale of despicably lovable antiheroes to life. I thank my early readers: Jamie Falik, Macon Blair, Peter Sharp, Ben Sharp, Marilyn Sharp, and above all, Lorna Campbell, who read it again and again with notes and encouragement every time. I thank Alex Sharp for playing goblin with me a couple Halloweens back, and being the impetus for the characters of Fixelcrick and Hairy Herald. I thank the brutal New England winter of 2014 for keeping me inside and angry; my agent, Allison Cohen, for not giving up; and the "always right" Jennifer Gunnels for seeing the wicked beauty of this warped tale and forging a home, and title, for it with the publisher of my dreams.

But the story of this book's climb to the light is unfortunately tinged with morbid serendipity that I fear deserves acknowledgment, as well. After much rejection from the publishing world, I had the fortune of getting to sit down with the late, great David G. Hartwell at a writers' conference in the summer of 2014. For forty-five minutes, he dispensed wisdom from his hallowed career in the business, and offered his willingness to read what I, and others in attendance, sent him. Months later, I heard of his untimely death. I thought that was the end of Slud's chance for a wider audience, but it was his associate editor, Jennifer Gunnels, who discovered the book while cleaning out his desk—not her cup of tea, but somehow these characters got to her.

For this, I would like to dedicate this book to David G. Hartwell and Jennifer Gunnels.

And I would also like to dedicate it to the Macensky family: Ben, Alex, Margaret, and Sam. It was at your house that the hero of this story was first summoned up by the roll of dice almost thirty years ago. You offered me the space and time to fully immerse myself in the fantastical. You introduced me to D&D, Lovecraft, Paladium, Warhammer, Python, Led Zeppelin, and Pink Floyd, to name only a few. I owe much of this story, and all the books I might ever write, to you, that house, and that era. Thank you.

Which brings me, finally, to the characters themselves. I have lived with some of them for a long time, and they've long since begun to take on a life of their own. It would not be wise for me leave them out of my most sincere, groveling thank you. To Slud, Agnes, Neither-Nor, and the whole twisted gang—I am but your humble servant. . . .